# UNSPEAKA



JENNA JORDAN

BLACK SWAN
DIGITAL

*First published in 2025*
*Concept created by Black Swan Digital. Developed by Annie Kenyon.*

# PROLOGUE

*June 12$^{th}$*

*The night before the wedding*
*Somewhere between hope and dread*

They say you always know. That somewhere deep down, some quiet organ, maybe the liver, maybe the stomach, something primitive, will throb with truth when the decision is wrong. Not the heart. The heart is far too poetic to be trusted with survival. But the gut? The gut it wise.

I suppose I've been hearing the murmurs for weeks now. Maybe longer. It's just that I've learned how to turn the volume down. You can train yourself to do that. Telling yourself it's just nerves. Just what it means to be a woman with a man and a future she's already paid the deposit on.

Tomorrow I marry him.

There. That sentence sits oddly on the page of my journal, like it belongs in someone else's handwriting. I even try to write it prettier, loop the Y in "marry" into a little swan's neck, but it still looks alien. Like someone has forged it.

Tomorrow I become his wife. I *will be a wife*. The word feels stiff and shiny, like a brand-new pair of shoes I haven't quite broken in. It doesn't feel real. Not yet. Not now. Maybe not ever. He says I worry too much. That I think myself into unhappiness. That I search too hard for darkness where there is nothing but light. And maybe that's true. I do overthink. I pick things apart until all the softness bleeds out and all I'm left with is the bone. But isn't that what women are trained to do? Dissect ourselves until we're palatable?

I want to be good. I do. I want to be *right*. A good wife is steady, and gentle, and grateful. She doesn't flinch when her husband jokes about her weight in front of company. She doesn't point out when he lies. She doesn't complain when his moods swing, or when the wine gets the better of him and he knocks something off the counter and expects her to clean it up. She makes allowances. She smiles with her teeth, even when they grind together behind the scenes.

No one wants a difficult wife.

And I've seen what happens to difficult women. My mother, mostly. Her face a cracked plate by the time I was ten. Her silence a language. Her makeup a mask. When my father raised his voice, she didn't run away. She ran inward. She folded herself into a shape that fit his fury. She told me she loved him anyway.

So maybe this is just what love is supposed to feel like. Sharp, then sweet. A pinch followed by a kiss. Maybe I just need to stop trying to be the kind of woman who gets to *choose*. Who gets to say, "This doesn't feel right," and then simply leave. That's not how it works. You don't just walk away from a man who's chosen you. Not when he's made plans. Not when you've already had the fittings and your name is etched in gold on the invitations, and your friends keep texting pictures of white dresses and cute hashtags.

People keep saying how lucky I am. How handsome he is. How stable. How serious. That I won't need to worry about anything anymore. That he'll take care of me. That he's the kind of man who gets things *done*. And isn't that what I always wanted? Safety?

Yes, he gets things done. Efficiently. Without sentiment. Like when he told me I was getting too emotional about the dog that was hit outside our building.

"You didn't even know it," he said. "Don't make a scene." He touched my chin then, firmly but not cruelly, and told me to dry my eyes. He said the world doesn't reward women who cry in public. And he was right. He's always right. Or at least, he *thinks* he is. And maybe that's enough.

Maybe certainty is a kind of love. Even if it isn't mine.

Sometimes, I watch him while he sleeps. I try to freeze him in that moment, when he's quiet and harmless and warm. I remind myself that he *can* be tender. That once, when I had a fever, he drove two hours in the rain to get me a pharmacy brand of medicine he said worked better. That once, when I lost my job, he said he didn't need a second income, just someone to come home to who believed in him.

Isn't that romantic? Isn't that enough?

I keep telling myself that love doesn't have to feel like a song. That it can be plain. That it can be practical. That not all marriages are built on some shuddering pulse of excitement. That it's okay if the butterflies are dead. That I've just grown up.

But sometimes, when he walks into the room, the air tightens. I go still. Like prey. And not in the swoony, cinematic way. In the way animals freeze right before a noise. And I ask myself, *if he wasn't mine, if I met him at a bar, would I still say yes?*

I don't know.

God, I so want to believe I'm just anxious. That I've made this into something it's not. That I'll look back in ten years and laugh at this page, all dramatic and overwritten. That I'll read these words with him asleep beside me and think, *how silly I was. How scared, for no reason at all.*

Maybe that's what this is. Cold feet. Every bride has them. But still, I packed a bag. Just a small one. Tucked behind the coats in the hallway. Just in case. It's nothing. A just-in-case bag isn't the same as a *real* plan. It's a nervous habit. It doesn't mean I won't go through with it. I will. I must.

Because he's chosen me. Because I said yes. Because tomorrow the church will be full, and the flowers are already in their buckets, and my mother is weeping with joy like this is the moment she prayed for. Because walking away now would make me look ungrateful. Hysterical. Mad.

Because I'm not brave enough to ruin everything just because a part of me still wants to run.

Tomorrow, I will smile. I will walk down that aisle. I will take his hand, and I will let the words *I do* fall from my mouth like petals.

And everything will be fine.

*Everything will be perfect.*

# 1

*Linden Court, Haverford Township, Pennsylvania, July 3rd*

The house on Linden Court looked exactly how it should. It sat primly behind a manicured lawn, its white siding gleaming beneath the July sun, framed by a row of hydrangeas trained to bloom with clinical precision. A small flag fluttered in the garden bed, a festive nod to the holiday weekend and the wind chimes on the porch gave a delicate tinkle every time the breeze flirted past the screen door. From the outside, the house was a picture. The kind of place people slowed their cars to admire.

Inside, Natalie's hands trembled as she buttered toast. She was in the kitchen, her back to the French doors, wearing a cornflower-blue robe cinched tight at the waist, her blond hair twisted into a loose knot that had already begun to droop from the morning humidity. The clock above the stove blinked 7:19. She moved in quick, practiced motions. Open bread, drop slices, push lever, like someone performing a dance she no longer remembered learning.

Thomas, nine, sat at the island, hunched over a bowl of cereal that had gone soggy. His knees were scraped raw from a fall he'd taken two days ago, and he picked at the scab absentmindedly while reading the back of the cereal box. Beside him, Eve swung her legs beneath her chair and hummed to herself, face sticky with jelly from the piece of toast she'd devoured without a napkin.

"Napkin, Eve," Natalie murmured, glancing at her daughter's mouth. "Please."

The girl pouted, then slid from her chair and padded over to the drawer. She was still in her pink pajamas, printed with galloping unicorns, her hair matted on one side from sleep.

"Mom, do I *have* to go to camp today?" Thomas didn't look up from the cereal box, voice thin and reedy.

Natalie's fingers twitched. "Yes. You missed Wednesday, remember?"

"I had a stomachache."

"You said you had a stomachache. You seemed fine once you got your iPad."

"That's not true," he muttered, not quite under his breath.

She didn't answer. Arguing only made him shut down, and then Martin would sigh when he got home and ask her why she couldn't "command more authority." As if authority was something she could pluck from the cutlery drawer.

She moved to the fridge and pulled out the eggs, the orange juice, the pre-sliced melon she'd bought even though it cost twice as much because the kids liked the way it looked in the bowl. Martin didn't believe in waste, but he believed in presentation.

Upstairs, the bathroom door slammed.

Natalie tensed.

She set the eggs down a little too hard and one cracked, yolk sliding out across the counter like a slow wound. She grabbed a paper towel, cleaned it up, tossed the mess into the trash.

Martin appeared a few minutes later. Still damp from the shower, he moved through the kitchen with clean efficiency, suit pants sharp, shirt tucked and pressed. He kissed Eve's head, then Thomas's, and made his way to the coffee pot like a man working from muscle memory.

Natalie stood straighter.

"You didn't iron this shirt properly," he said, turning to her with the cup in his hand. "Look at the left sleeve."

"I..."

"It creases at the shoulder. You can see it."

"I'll fix it."

He didn't respond, just set the cup down and took off the shirt right there in the kitchen, stripping it from his body with a practiced movement. He was lean and toned in the way men with gym memberships and time often are.

Thomas stared at the cereal. Eve watched with curious eyes.

Natalie turned and took the shirt, folding it over her arm. "I'll bring another one."

"Please do. And tonight, remember Mother is joining us."

"I know."

"She said six sharp. Don't make her wait."

Natalie nodded.

Martin sipped the coffee, bare-chested, and frowned. "This is too weak."

"I used the same amount as always."

"Well, it's not right. Did you use filtered water?"

She hesitated. "I think so."

"You think so?"

"I did."

He exhaled, one of those long, silent exhales that always

made her feel like the space in the room had collapsed. "Try again. And dinner, Mother would like roast chicken. With lemon and rosemary. Not too much garlic, it upsets her. And something light for dessert. Not cake."

"Of course."

He drained the cup, set it down, and disappeared back upstairs.

Natalie stood still for a moment, staring at the half-empty bowl of melon. She could feel the yolk sticky on her palm. She hadn't washed her hands.

"Do we *have* to eat with Grandma?" Eve asked, scrunching her nose. "She smells like old perfume and says my voice is shrill."

Natalie smiled without showing her teeth. "She's family, sweetheart."

"She said Thomas should sit up straighter or he'll grow up with a 'concave chest like a war orphan,'" Eve added cheerfully.

"That's enough."

Thomas gave a faint smirk, eyes still on his cereal.

Natalie turned back to the sink and ran her hands under cold water. The cracked egg had oozed down her wrist.

The rest of the morning passed in quiet arrangements. Lunches were packed in color-coded boxes. Eve always had extra strawberries, Thomas wanted sandwiches without crusts. Backpacks zipped, shoes tied, hair brushed and braided with little pink bands. Natalie moved like a robot through the routine, saying the right things, smiling in the right moments, adjusting collars, refilling water bottles.

Martin returned to the kitchen, now in a crisp white shirt with cufflinks that glinted like nasty little teeth.

"I left my keys," he said, not looking at her.

She moved to the hallway and grabbed them from the dish beside the door. He took them without touching her.

"Remember what I said," he added, just before stepping out. "I want the house clean. No clutter on the table. Mother doesn't need to see your writing projects all over the place again."

"Yes. I remember."

His eyes swept the room once more. Then he was gone, the front door closing behind him with a click that sounded mercifully final.

Natalie stood in the silence that followed, her breath shallow.

Upstairs, she heard the air conditioning turning on. Outside, a lawnmower buzzed faintly on a neighbor's lawn. The kids were in the hallway, wrestling with their backpacks and squabbling about who got to sit in the front seat for the drive to camp.

The house smelled of toast and anti-bacterial cleaner. The illusion was intact.

Natalie reached for her coffee, still untouched on the counter, and took a sip. Cold. She poured it out and made a fresh one.

Then she opened the junk drawer, that despite its name was orderly and dug beneath the batteries and takeaway menus and pulled out the folded slip of paper she kept hidden there. A scrap of her old manuscript. Just one paragraph she hadn't had the heart to throw out. The ink was fading, the corners smudged. She read the words quickly, as if they might vanish. A reminder of a version of herself that had once existed. Before Martin. Before Linden Court.

Before she started setting reminders in her phone not for appointments, but for what *not* to say.

A call from the porch. The kids were waiting. Natalie folded the paper and placed it back beneath the menus, smoothing her expression into something neutral. Something pleasing.

She picked up her purse, locked the door behind her, and stepped into the morning sun.

Haverford Township always looked as though it had been pressed from a mold labeled *Safe Suburbia.* Neatly spaced sycamores lined the sidewalks, their leaves a tired summer green, offering shade to rows of almost-identical colonials and split-levels with carefully weeded driveways. Lawns were uniformly trimmed, mailboxes dent-free, and the air carried the pleasant tang of fertilizer and just-cut grass. By July, the township was already draped in red, white, and blue bunting, the kind you could buy in three-packs at Home Depot, looped along porch rails like patriotic tinsel.

The residents were exactly what you'd expect: families who donated to school fundraisers and waved from their front porches, couples who took Pilates together, teens who wore Vineyard Vines and grumbled good-naturedly about curfews. Everyone owned SUVs. Everyone recycled. Everyone pretended nothing bad ever happened.

Natalie drove with both hands on the wheel and focused on the white line on the road.

Thomas and Eve were arguing again, something about who had more coins in their school lunch account. The kind of argument that fizzled as quickly as it flared, ending with one of them humming and the other sulking quietly in the back seat.

She pulled up to Carver Elementary, one of those red-brick schools built in the '60s but regularly renovated to give the illusion of progress. The morning drop-off queue was its usual chaotic blend of caffeine-fueled moms in yoga pants and retirees working the school crossing like it was a second career. Natalie offered a tight smile to the attendant as the kids hopped out. She waved too brightly and then sat frozen for a moment after the door slammed shut. She told herself to breathe.

From there, she went to Café Coco Coffee, the only place in town that hadn't been overtaken by a Starbucks franchise. It clung stubbornly to its mismatched furniture and cracked chalkboard menu, all painted brick and indie playlists that changed with the barista's mood. It was the kind of place that sold $6 lattes and felt local enough to fool you into thinking you weren't part of the machine.

She ordered a black coffee and a banana muffin she didn't want and took a window seat in the corner, where the sun streamed through the dusty glass. She set her phone on the table and checked it compulsively: no texts, no calls, no messages. Just the blinking silence of her life when Martin wasn't in it.

Natalie was halfway through pretending to eat the muffin when Misty breezed in. Misty was loud and wore leopard-print flats and oversized sunglasses, her lipstick a defiant coral. Her bag probably cost more than Natalie's monthly grocery budget. She worked part-time as a real estate agent, full-time as a gossip receptacle.

"There she is," Misty said, plopping into the seat opposite her, the perfume trailing behind her floral and loud. "Sorry I'm late. Had to drop off Cody at soccer and he forgot his shorts, so we had to go back because the coach is a maniac. You look tired."

Natalie blinked. "Do I?"

"In a cute way. Like a French art student who smokes too much. Want me to order for you? You'll never finish that muffin."

"I'm fine," Natalie murmured, wrapping the muffin in a napkin and slipping it into her bag. "I just... needed to get out of the house."

Misty raised an eyebrow. "Martin working today?"

"He's at the practice."

"Of course he is." She leaned forward, removing her sunglasses and placing them gently on the table. Her eyes were sharp, brown, and lined with perfect black wings. "You doing okay, Nat? Really?"

Natalie tried to smile. "Of course."

"Because you can tell me. You know that, right? If he's being... you know. Difficult."

Natalie stirred her coffee even though there was nothing in it. "He's just under a lot of pressure."

"Martin's *always* under a lot of pressure. The man walks around like he's curing cancer instead of prescribing allergy meds."

Natalie flinched.

"I'm sorry," Misty said, softening. "I know you don't like it when I talk about him."

"It's just... easier not to talk about it because everything seems so complicated."

"That's one word for it."

Natalie dropped her eyes to the table. The silence that followed was tangible and awkward and familiar.

They talked after that, but it was on the surface kind of talk. About summer camp fees and sunscreen brands, about Misty's mother-in-law's impending hip replacement and Eve's unicorn obsession. Natalie smiled when she was supposed to. She even laughed, lightly, when Misty made a joke about Thomas's hair looking like a Weasley twin. But the air inside her felt dense, like someone had pressed a knee on her chest. They parted just after ten, with a quick hug that left the scent of Misty's perfume on Natalie's shirt.

From there, she headed to Millford Market, the only upscale grocery store within fifteen miles that carried the specific *organic, free-range, herb-rubbed, air-chilled chicken* Martin's mother preferred. The parking lot was already teeming with carts and crossover SUVs. Inside, the air was sharp with floor sanitizer, the produce section curated like a gallery.

Natalie moved through the store with practiced speed:

collecting potatoes, rosemary, haricot verts, lemons. She held the list in her hand but barely glanced at it. She'd memorized what was expected.

The fish counter sat at the back of the store, beneath a sign that read *Today's Catch!* in cheerful letters. She waited behind a couple debating between cod and haddock, their voices muffled beneath the store music and the hum of the refrigeration unit.

When it was her turn, she stepped forward. "Half a pound of wild-caught salmon, please."

The young man behind the counter, a college student, judging by the acne and haphazard mustache, wrapped it neatly in wax paper and passed it over the glass.

And then Natalie saw him.

Across the aisle, near the olive bar. A man. Dark jacket, plain jeans, ball cap pulled low. He was standing still, hands at his sides. Watching her. Her stomach tightened. He wasn't doing anything. Just looking. Not smiling. Not moving.

She blinked, and when she looked again, he was turning away and walking down the dairy aisle with no cart, no basket, no real purpose. She stood frozen, the packet of salmon in her hand suddenly warm. Her pulse ticked at her throat. There was something about him. Something *familiar*. But she couldn't place it. He could've been anyone. A neighbor. A parent from school. Someone who'd driven past her on Linden Court or stood behind her at the DMV. He hadn't done anything. Just... watched.

"Ma'am?" the fish server asked. "You need anything else?"

Natalie shook her head and stepped away. She told herself it was nothing. A trick of the light. An anxious imagination. A weird encounter, not a dangerous one. She'd seen enough crime shows to know how women like her got themselves worked up for no reason. But as she pushed her cart past the wine display, she couldn't stop herself from glancing behind her.

The man was gone. Still, the unease clung to her. Like the perfume Misty left on her shirt, but colder. Oily. Wrong. She drove home with the groceries in the trunk, the AC on high despite the mild day. The entire time, she kept checking her mirrors. Just in case. Just in case.

# 2

*Linden Court, Haverford Township, Pennsylvania, July 3rd*

The house was still when Natalie returned from the store. She slid her keys into the bowl on the hall table, where Martin liked them kept, no jangling in her purse, no clutter on the console, and kicked off her flats beside the shoe rack. Outside, the afternoon sun had turned hot and bleached, illuminating the neighborhood into something bright and oppressively quiet.

She stood in the foyer for a moment, just listening. The air conditioning buzzed overhead, steady and artificial, and from the living room the ticking of the grandfather clock echoed like a slow, patient, finger tap.

She pulled the salmon from the grocery bag and laid it out on the counter. The rosemary went in a bowl of water to stay fresh. She lined up the potatoes like obedient children—small, golden, and uniform. Then she started to cook. There was a particular rhythm to preparing one of Martin's mother's dinners. Not the meal itself, she could make that in her sleep, but the pacing of it, like a ritual. She had to be finished before five, counters cleared and dishwasher on. Any later and Martin would frown as he stepped through the door, shirt cuffs still crisp, eyes scanning for offense.

Natalie peeled, chopped, seasoned. She seared the chicken with lemon slices tucked beneath the skin, just the way his mother liked. She avoided garlic completely. She set the table with the ivory linens and silverware and ran a damp cloth over the surfaces afterward to erase any trace of her presence.

At 3:15, the school bus exhaled outside. Thomas and Eve burst through the door in a flurry of noise and mismatched Velcro. Natalie wiped her hands on a towel and met them in the hallway.

"Hey, sweethearts," she said, bending down to kiss the tops of their heads.

Thomas brushed past her, already digging into his backpack.

"Hi, Mommy," Eve said, wrapping her arms around Natalie's waist. Her hair was tangled, her cheeks pink from the heat.

Natalie hugged her back tightly. "Good day?"

Eve nodded. "We did painting. I made a firework."

"That's wonderful, baby." She turned toward Thomas. "And you, Tom?"

He shrugged. "It was school. Can I go on my iPad?"

"After you put your shoes away and change out of your camp clothes."

"Ugh," he groaned, dropping his bag to the floor and heading upstairs, socks half off, attitude full on.

Natalie watched him disappear up the staircase, the back of his neck damp with sweat, his heavy footsteps screamed stubbornness.

Eve stayed close, chattering as Natalie chopped beans and tossed the salad. She offered to fold napkins, then grew bored and went off to draw on the patio with chalk, her tiny sneakers leaving squeaks across the tiles.

At 5:04, the front door opened. Martin's footsteps were measured, always deliberate. Natalie glanced up from the stove as he stepped into the kitchen, placing his briefcase neatly by the wall. He didn't smile. He rarely did at first. His gaze moved to the stove, to the countertops, to the salad bowl on the table.

"You started early," he said.

"I wanted to make sure everything was ready."

He walked over to the stove and lifted the lid on the green beans, steam curling toward his face. He wrinkled his nose.

"You're overcooking them."

Natalie felt her throat tighten. "I only just turned them on."

"They're already turning dull. You know how she hates mushy vegetables."

"I'll strain them now." She moved quickly, flushing with embarrassment.

He stepped back, arms crossed. "You always rush it."

"I wasn't..."

"It's fine. Just try to be mindful. Don't get distracted."

Natalie nodded, eyes on the pot. "Sorry."

He moved to the fridge, poured himself sparkling water from the bottle she'd picked up just for him, and took a sip. Then he turned back toward her.

"Mother called. She's bringing a bottle of red. I told her not to, but you know how she is."

"Of course."

Martin sat at the island, loosening his tie, his sleeves still buttoned. His gaze flicked toward the window where Eve sat cross-legged on the patio, pressing chalk hearts into the concrete.

"She looks like you, you know. When she smiles."

Natalie smiled faintly. "She's got your intelligence, though."

Martin didn't respond. An uncomfortable silence stretched between them so Natalie reached for the bowl of potatoes, her hands moving automatically. She hesitated, then decided to say it.

"There was a man," she said quietly. "At the store today."

Martin looked up. "What kind of man?"

"I don't know. Just... someone. He was watching me. Near the fish counter."

He set his glass down. "Watching you how?"

"Just... standing there. Staring."

"Did he say anything to you?"

"No."

"Follow you?"

"No, he left before I did."

"So he didn't speak. Didn't follow. Just looked at you in a public store."

Natalie paused. "Yes."

Martin raised an eyebrow. "And you thought that was important?"

"It felt off."

He sighed and leaned back in his chair, rubbing a hand over his jaw. "Natalie..."

She knew what was coming. The tone was soft but fixed, the kind that sounded like concern to outsiders and condescension to anyone who lived with it.

"You're being over-anxious again."

"I..."

"Think about it. How many people go shopping at Millford every day? A man glances your way and suddenly it's a situation?"

"It wasn't a glance. He..."

Martin shook his head. "You don't trust your own instincts anymore. You know that. You've said so yourself."

She opened her mouth to defend herself, then closed it.

His voice gentled, but the effect was more suffocating than soothing. "You're tired. You've had a long week. Hosting my mother isn't easy. Maybe you need to rest more. Take a break from the caffeine. The news. Give your nerves a chance to settle."

Natalie turned back to the stove, face burning.

"I just thought you should know," she said softly.

"And I appreciate that. But there's nothing to worry about. You've been... fragile before. Remember? It starts with small things. Imagining faces. Feeling watched. It's good you told me. That way I can help you keep perspective."

She nodded, the shame sitting heavy in her chest. Behind them, the doorbell rang. Martin stood and smoothed his shirt.

"That'll be Mother."

Natalie didn't move.

"Smile, Nat," he said over his shoulder. "Let's not start the evening on edge."

Vivienne always rang the bell twice. A short, clipped *ding-ding*, like a warning shot. As he disappeared down the hallway to answer the door, Natalie reached for the saucepan and turned down the heat. Her hands trembled slightly, and she forced herself to breathe. He always said she needed rest. That she let her imagination get the best of her. But the man had been there. Real. Staring. Unless he wasn't. Unless Martin was right. She wiped her palms on her apron, pulled a tray from the oven, and pasted on a smile she'd been perfecting for years. The one that said everything was fine. That she was fine. And everything was just as it should be.

Dinner was ready. Natalie wiped her palms on her apron and forced a breath into her lungs. She smoothed the front of her dress, a pale gray wrap chosen specifically for its neutrality, and glanced once at the dining table. Everything gleamed. The chicken rested under foil, the beans were bright green, and the potatoes glistened in olive oil. She'd even remembered to decant the wine.

Heading towards the lounge she found Vivienne waiting, prim and lacquered, holding a bottle of Bordeaux and a look of faint distaste. Her lipstick was a matte berry tone, her perfume a powdery floral that filled the room and tickling Natalie's throat when she stepped inside. The atmosphere always changed the second Vivienne entered the house, becoming cooler, laden with intent, as though her presence altered the temperature.

"Well," Vivienne said, pressing the bottle into Natalie's hands. "At least it smells like someone made an effort tonight."

"Come on through," Natalie murmured. "We're just about ready."

Martin hovered, kissing his mother once on each cheek. "You look lovely, Mother."

Vivienne beamed. "I wore the brooch you gave me. Did you notice?"

He did. He always did. He leaned in to admire the pin on her lapel, an antique swirl of pearls and gold, and made a soft sound of approval. Natalie stepped back to give them room, holding the bottle like it might shatter in her hands.

Vivienne barely glanced at her. "Is Thomas home?"

"He's in the den," Natalie said, already turning toward the kitchen. "Eve is in the garden."

"Of course." The tone she used for Eve was the one she reserved for stray animals and expired coupons.

Vivienne's heels tapped down the hall, her gait precise. Natalie could already hear her greeting Thomas in a cooing tone that made her skin crawl and in the interim, she moved swiftly, uncorking the wine and pouring two generous glasses. She set them at the table, one at Martin's place and the other beside Vivienne's. She didn't pour one for herself.

Dinner was served at six on the dot. They sat around the

long walnut table, the china Martin's grandmother had passed down gleaming under the chandelier. The dining room was too formal for daily use, and every time Natalie stepped inside it, she felt like she was trespassing in someone else's life.

Thomas sat straight and smug beside his father, feet not quite touching the floor. Eve sat to Natalie's right, her napkin clutched in both hands like a lifeline. Martin carved the chicken with surgical precision.

"Moist," Vivienne pronounced after her first bite. "A bit heavy on the lemon, perhaps, but better than last time."

Natalie smiled and said thank you, though she didn't remember the last time being bad. But memory was slippery around Vivienne.

"I told you she'd get it right if she focused," Martin said, sipping his wine.

"She just needs direction from someone more experienced." Vivienne reached for her glass, her bracelet jangling delicately. "Doesn't she, Eve?"

Eve blinked up from her plate. "Yes, ma'am?"

"You're rather quiet tonight. Did you not paint me another one of your abstract masterpieces?"

Natalie placed a hand on her daughter's leg beneath the table. A warning. A comfort.

"No, ma'am," Eve said softly.

"What a shame." Vivienne turned back to Martin. "Thomas always brings me such lovely cards. Don't you, darling?"

Thomas smirked, ducking his head. "I made one last week with a rocket ship."

"Of course you did," Vivienne said warmly. "You've always been so clever. Just like your father."

Martin reached over and ruffled Thomas's hair, then looked pointedly at Eve. "Why don't you draw something for Grandma next time? It wouldn't kill you to put in a little more effort."

Natalie saw Eve tense. "She's been putting in a lot of effort with her schoolwork and practicing her letters," she said quickly. "And her reading's improved so much this summer."

Martin didn't look at her. "That's not what I meant, she needs to have respect for her elders."

The silence that followed was sharp enough to slice meat. Natalie kept her eyes on her plate.

Vivienne chuckled lightly and patted her lips with a cloth napkin. "Well, not every child is gifted like my Martin. And that's perfectly all right but I agree, manners and kindness go a long way."

Natalie felt the words land like stones in her daughter's lap.

"Eve's seven," she said softly. "She's still discovering what she loves."

Vivienne arched one thin brow. "Of course she is. Though I do think a mother should steer her children toward... structure and social graces. It's only fair to them in the long run."

Martin nodded. "Discipline gives them confidence. Otherwise, they float through life untethered. Isn't that right, Thomas?"

Thomas nodded, chewing smugly. Eve stared at her plate, her fork untouched. Natalie wanted to reach out and hold her daughter's hand, but she didn't. She sat upright, spine rigid, willing herself to smile. To keep everything calm. The peace depended on her. It always had.

The meal dragged on. Vivienne and Martin chatted easily, exchanging stories about colleagues, real estate prices, the new receptionist at Martin's office "hopelessly slow," Vivienne snorted, "with a face like a cartoon owl". They laughed together. They sipped wine. The way they mirrored each other's tone, the way Martin glanced at her for approval, it felt choreographed, like a dance Natalie had never been taught.

She watched as Martin passed Thomas a second helping of

potatoes without asking Eve if she wanted more. Watched Vivienne ignore her granddaughter entirely except when making small, stinging observations, her posture, her hair, the way she didn't finish her green beans.

"She's always seemed so... delicate," Vivienne said once. "A little anxious, isn't she? Doesn't seem quite like the rest of us."

"She's sensitive," Natalie said, trying to sound firm. "That's not the same as anxious."

Martin gave her a look.

"You over-correct too much, Nat," he said. "Just let it go."

Natalie pressed her napkin to her mouth to keep from answering and could feel Eve's eyes on her.

After dinner, Vivienne insisted on clearing the table, though she did so with the slow martyrdom of someone waiting to be thanked. Natalie followed her into the kitchen, ready to load the dishwasher, but Vivienne waved her off with a dry smile.

"I've got it," she said. "I can manage."

Natalie hesitated. "Thank you."

Vivienne lowered her voice, just enough to be heard over the clink of plates. "You should rest. You look drawn again. Are you still on your medication?"

Natalie froze. "That's private."

"Martin mentioned you'd had another... spell last week."

Natalie felt heat rise in her chest. "I'm fine."

Vivienne glanced at her, unimpressed. "You always say that."

Natalie walked away before she could say anything she'd regret.

She found Eve in the living room, curled on the couch with her knees pulled up. Thomas was on the floor with a LEGO set, Martin hovering nearby offering unsolicited engineering advice.

Natalie sat beside her daughter and smoothed her hair. "You were very polite tonight, and I was proud of you."

Eve nodded but didn't smile.

"Dinner's always like that when *she's* about," she whispered.

Natalie swallowed hard and pressed a kiss to her temple. "Just try to ignore it, baby and remember, I'm right by your side."

And in that moment Natalie realised that surviving Martin and his mother, making sure they didn't poison Eve and Thomas, had to be her priority. They came first, always.

# 3

The house had quieted, but the walls still held onto the toxic energy of the evening. Upstairs, the bedroom buzzed with the muffled whir of the ceiling fan turning slow circles, pushing warm air in lazy currents. The windows were cracked slightly open, but the breeze did nothing. Outside, crickets chirped in syncopated rhythm. Inside, Natalie moved silently.

She folded Martin's shirt over the back of the chair and lined his loafers neatly against the wall. The dinner dishes were done, the floor mopped, the children tucked into their beds. Eve with her bunny, Thomas with his tablet hidden under the pillow. Martin had said nothing to the kids at bedtime. He rarely did. She turned to him now.

Martin stood at the dresser, stripped down to his briefs, face washed, eyes hard. He'd barely said two words since Vivienne left an hour earlier. Just poured himself another glass of wine, turned on the news, then came upstairs in silence.

"I thought the roast turned out okay," Natalie said gently. "The chicken wasn't dry."

Martin didn't look at her. He tugged at his watch strap,

setting it on the tray beside his cufflinks. "You didn't follow the technique I showed you. You always rush the basting."

"I basted it every fifteen minutes. Like the recipe said."

He turned then, eyes narrowing. "*The recipe*. Christ, Natalie. My mother's been making that chicken since before you were born. She's perfected it. You think some Pinterest recipe knows better?"

She lowered her gaze. "I'm sorry."

He let out a breath, one of those thin, tired sighs that made her feel like a child who had failed a simple task. "It's not just the chicken. The salad dressing was too acidic. And the wine, did you even decant it long enough?"

"I thought I had. I put it out an hour before."

"You need to think less. Follow instructions. You overcook everything so it turns to mush."

Natalie stood by the bed, bare feet on the carpet, fingers curled around the edge of her nightgown.

"I'll do better next time."

Martin gave her a long, unreadable look before turning back to the dresser. "Mother said the same thing. You try, but you don't follow through. You need to develop more consistency."

Natalie nodded. Martin pulled back the covers and climbed into bed. He stretched his legs out, the sheets barely covering him, chest exposed to the warm air. He watched her as she padded toward her side of the bed and lifted the covers delicately.

"You really going to wear those things to bed in this heat?" he asked, his tone somewhere between amusement and contempt.

Natalie glanced down at her pajamas, soft cotton, pale blue with tiny white flowers. The kind of modest sleepwear you'd find in a catalog. Long sleeves, full-length pants. Breathable, safe.

"I get cold at night sometimes."

"It's July, Natalie. Not February." He gave a sharp little laugh. "You dress like you're eighty."

She didn't answer. She climbed in beside him, careful not to let her thigh brush his. The sheets were too warm already.

Martin looked at her, one arm bent behind his head, eyes sweeping over her face, down to her collarbone. "You weren't always like this."

"Like what?"

He snorted. "So... prissy. You used to have some spirit."

Natalie pulled the sheet up to her chest. "I'm just tired."

"You're always tired."

She turned her face to the wall, a pulse ticking in her temple. "It was a long day."

He didn't reply.

After a moment, she heard him shift, the mattress creaking faintly under his weight. She stayed still, breathing evenly. He lay on his back, chest rising and falling, the occasional snuff of air catching in his nose as he blinked up at the ceiling.

She kept her eyes shut.

She wasn't sure how long she lay like that pretending to drift, to relax, to dissolve into sleep. She could feel his heat beside her. Hear the slow, mechanical turn of the fan overhead. But her mind was nowhere near sleep. It was back at the market. The man. She saw him again, not just his shape but the stillness of him. The way he hadn't been doing anything, not shopping, not browsing. Just watching.

Not with lust. Not with curiosity. But something she couldn't define.

And there had been something familiar in his posture, the slope of his shoulders, the way he'd disappeared so easily into the rows of dairy and canned goods. He hadn't run. He hadn't needed to. It was like he knew he'd unsettled her. Like that had been the point.

And then the way Martin dismissed her. *You're being over-anxious again.* That word. Again. She'd been told it before. After Eve was born. After the "incident" with the car that wasn't an accident. After she'd called Martin at work because she was certain someone was following her, and he told her to take one of her pills and lie down. She'd been shaky, yes. Forgetful. But not wrong.

They made her feel like she was broken. Fragile. She'd swallowed it whole. It was easier than arguing. But that man, he *had* been there. She hadn't imagined it.

Still, she hadn't told Martin the part where the man had looked *familiar.* She hadn't said how long he'd stared. Or that, for a fleeting second, she thought he'd smirked. And she certainly hadn't told him how it made her feel now, lying here in the stifling dark, her heart thudding like something trapped.

A bead of sweat slid down her spine. Martin shifted beside her. His breathing had deepened. She opened her eyes in the darkness, staring at the faint pattern of the wallpaper, the shadowed dresser across the room, the sliver of moonlight that slipped through the blinds and touched the corner of the mirror. She hadn't looked in the mirror much lately. She wasn't sure what she'd see if she did.

The man in the store had stirred something. A whisper from before, before Martin, before the children, before Linden Court. A warning that said: *remember who you used to be.* And the worst part was that she couldn't. Not really. Not anymore. She closed her eyes again and let the darkness hold her, the weight of Martin's body beside hers heavy and absolute. She didn't sleep. She just disappeared into the night.

. . .

The day was a dull, made more so by a humid smear of overcast sky that seemed to hang just above the roofline like a mood about to happen. The morning had passed in a blur of lunchboxes and mismatched socks, another minor battle with Thomas over sunscreen, and Eve's slow, distracted dressing that had tested Natalie's patience to the brittle edge. By the time both children were at school and Martin had left for the clinic, the house exhaled.

Natalie sat at the kitchen table, sipping lukewarm tea, the silence ringing in her ears. She had half a mind to take a walk, maybe even pick up her notebook, though the thought of writing felt absurd lately. Whatever she'd once had, the spark, the voice, felt as distant as a dream half-remembered.

The doorbell rang at precisely 1:02 p.m. Two quick chimes. Natalie's stomach turned to ice. She knew before she opened the door. Vivienne stood there, a sharp silhouette in her tailored slate-gray suit, her lips painted the same color as dried blood. She held a paper bag from the French bakery in one hand.

"I brought éclairs," she said by way of greeting. "Martin mentioned you've been looking run-down so maybe a sugar-rush might help."

Natalie stepped back automatically. "Come in."

Vivienne's perfume hit her like a slap, something high-end and floral, but with an undertone of powdery rot. She walked through the house with her usual critical gaze, eyes sweeping the foyer, pausing at the side table, the hall mirror, the slightly crooked family photo on the wall.

"I see the children still haven't learned to pick up after themselves," she said, nudging a discarded sock with the toe of her pump. "And those smudges on the stair rail... fingerprints, I'd guess?"

"I wipe them down every few days."

Vivienne tsked softly. “Children are like grease. They leave a mark wherever they go.”

Natalie offered a tight smile. “Can I get you some tea?”

“Decaf, please. I’ve already had two cups today. Too much caffeine and I’ll be jittery all night.” She made her way to the kitchen, heels tapping like a clock counting down.

Natalie boiled the water and retrieved the delicate china cups that Vivienne’s preferred, set with the gold trim and a hairline crack in the saucer she always noticed but never mentioned.

Vivienne sat at the table with her back perfectly straight. She opened the paper bag and slid an éclair onto a plate, then eyed Natalie as she handed over the tea.

“I won’t have one, thank you,” Natalie murmured.

Vivienne’s brow rose. “Still on your health kick?”

“No, I just don’t want another.”

“You’ve lost weight, I can tell. But not in a flattering way.” She took a delicate bite of pastry, wiping her mouth with the corner of her napkin. “Your face is a little too hollow. You must remember to eat. A mother needs energy. And you don’t want to look gaunt in front of the children. It sets a poor example for Eve, especially. What with kids these days obsessing about their looks.”

Natalie sat down slowly. “I only eat when I’m hungry.”

Vivienne gave a cool smile. “And when is that, I wonder?”

The tea caught against Natalie’s throat. She held the cup in both hands like it could anchor her to the table.

Vivienne took another bite, chewed thoughtfully, then leaned back in her chair. “I worry about you sometimes, Natalie, I really do.”

“I’m fine.”

“You say that a lot.” She tilted her head. “You’re very... quiet.

Martin needs a partner who brings balance to his life. Strength. Something sturdy."

Natalie didn't answer.

Vivienne continued. "You know, when Martin was young, Bobby and I used to say he was the most sensitive of our boys. So easy to bruise. Always trying to keep the peace between Leon and his father. But now I realise that kind of childhood makes a man strong. Teaches him to command a room."

She looked out the window with a wistful expression, as though she were conjuring some long-lost golden hour. "Martin's father, God rest him, had that quality. That steadiness. He could walk into a room and quiet it with a single look. No shouting. No drama. Just... presence."

Natalie stared into her tea. She remembered Bobby. Broad-shouldered and red-faced, with a voice like a bark and hands that moved fast when he was angry. She remembered the way Vivienne had smiled through the bruises, through the slammed doors and fractured picture frames.

But that wasn't the version of Bobby Vivienne ever spoke about.

"Bobby had his faults," Vivienne continued, smoothing her skirt. "But he was a *man*. He provided. He set the standard. Leon followed his path, of course and went into construction. I just wish he'd find a nice woman and settle down and start a family. I need more grandchildren. But I still have Martin... Martin with the vision. The brains. He was always going to do something important."

Natalie nodded faintly. She didn't trust herself to speak.

"You know," Vivienne said, fixing her with a thin smile, "Martin told me he worries about your... fragility."

Natalie blinked. "My what?"

"Your nerves. You've always been sensitive. Soft-spoken. And that's not a crime, of course. But it does make it difficult for him to lean on you. You're meant to be the foundation of the household, Natalie."

"I try my best," Natalie said, too quietly.

"Yes but trying isn't always enough. Look at how Thomas is turning out, so clever, so composed. You can see the mark of his father on him. He's developing a spine."

Vivienne took a sip of tea and then lowered her voice conspiratorially. "But Eve... well. She takes after you, doesn't she?"

Natalie's chest tightened.

"She's dreamy," Vivienne said, the word curdled with disdain. "Always in her own little world. Doesn't look people in the eye. Shy. A child like that needs structure. Boundaries. And a nudge in the right direction here and there. Martin says he's concerned about her future and the effect you have on her."

Natalie tried to keep her expression blank. "She's seven and what effect?"

"You're desire to protect and make allowances for her. If you coddle her too long, she'll never grow a shell. And in this world, you need a shell."

The air between them went still.

Natalie set her cup down gently, hands trembling just slightly. "I don't agree and anyway I think Eve is kind. And kind is rare."

Vivienne smiled without warmth. "Kindness isn't useful if it comes at the expense of strength."

There it was again. That word. Strength. As though it excused everything. As though it was the only currency that mattered.

"Shall we move to the lounge?" Vivienne asked. "We'll be more comfortable there."

Natalie's heart sank, realizing she was in for a full-on lecture, however, smiled politely before standing and leading the way. She may as well get it over with then Vivienne could report back to Martin that she'd done his bidding and put his waste of space wife in her place. Sighing, Natalie took a seat and watched as Vivienne did the same, then waited for the show to begin.

# 4

Vivienne had settled into the living room like she owned the very oxygen surrounding her. She sat in Martin's leather wingback, never the couch, never a cushion too low or too soft, her legs crossed, ankles stiff with control, and one manicured hand perched on the armrest like a delicate claw. Her teacup, the contents half-drunk, rested on the side table beside her, untouched since her last cutting remark about the wallpaper trim looking "inexplicably jaundiced."

Natalie sat across from her on the edge of the cream-colored sofa, spine straight, knees together, hands folded like a schoolgirl waiting for a scolding. The house was warm, thick with the sleepy weight of summer and a hint of beeswax polish and a housewife who knew where her duties lay.

Vivienne had been talking for twenty-two uninterrupted minutes, and Natalie was forcing her eyelids to stay open and her mouth to stay shut.

"My Martin was always gifted. Even in preschool. He could stack blocks into perfect towers before the others stopped chewing theirs," she said with a smug sip of tea. "And Leon, well, he was a fighter, of course. Headstrong. He needed his father's firm hand, but once Bobby had him straightened out, he was a golden child, too. A real leader."

Natalie nodded, tuning in just enough to survive it.

Vivienne never asked questions. She didn't converse. She delivered monologues like someone trying to talk a weak heart back into rhythm. Every sentence ended with a faint smile and an unspoken dare: *Top that.*

She launched into another anecdote about Martin building a working radio at age ten Natalie had heard this story five times already, that he'd used a kit, misread the directions, and nearly electrocuted himself, when the shrill ring of the house phone broke the rhythm.

Natalie startled. "Excuse me," she said quickly, already halfway to the kitchen.

Vivienne made a show of checking her watch. "If it's a salesman, hang up. They always call at the most inconvenient times."

Natalie grabbed the receiver. "Hello?"

"Mrs. Lane? This is Helen Murphy, head of Carver Elementary. I hope I haven't caught you at a bad time."

Natalie's heart gave a small thud. "No, no, not at all. Is everything okay?"

"Yes. The children are both fine," Mrs. Murphy said quickly. "No one's hurt."

That phrase, *no one's hurt*, only heightened the dread. Her grip on the receiver tightened. Behind her, Vivienne was clearing her throat with theatrical delicacy, still seated, still watching.

"I'm calling about Thomas," Mrs. Murphy continued. "There was an... incident during lunch today."

Natalie's stomach dropped.

"He was in the cafeteria with the other third graders. There was a bit of commotion, and it came to our attention that he, well, apparently he lifted the skirt of a girl in his class. In front of several other students."

Natalie went silent.

"Her name is Eliza Foster. She was very upset. Understandably embarrassed by it all."

"I... oh my God," Natalie breathed. "I'm so sorry."

"I know these things can sound worse than they are," Mrs. Murphy said, softening her voice. "No one was hurt, as I said. And Thomas seemed surprised that it caused such a stir. I don't think he meant any malice by it."

"Still," Natalie said, her cheeks burning, "it's completely unacceptable. I'll speak to him. Immediately. As soon as he gets home. Thank you for calling."

"Of course. I thought it best to inform you directly. We want to handle things sensitively. At this age, they don't always understand boundaries but it's a good opportunity to have a conversation about personal space and consent."

"Yes. Yes, absolutely."

"There's no need to overreact," Mrs. Murphy added quickly. "It was handled quietly, and Eliza's parents have been informed. But I thought you'd want to be aware. Boys can sometimes... well, test limits and get a bit carried away."

"Yes," Natalie said faintly. "I appreciate your call."

She hung up slowly, the air around her pulsing with the pounding of her heart.

In the lounge, Vivienne raised a brow. "Well? Should I be bracing for a tornado or a fender bender?"

Natalie walked back into the living room, trying to smooth her face into something neutral. "That was the school. About Thomas."

Vivienne's eyes sharpened. "He's not sick, is he?"

"No. There was a... situation. At lunch."

Natalie sat down again, folding her hands in her lap. "He

lifted a girl's skirt. In front of the other students and the head wants me to speak to him about it."

Vivienne blinked. Then gave a single laugh. "Why? It's just high jinx."

Natalie blinked back, caught off guard. "She was embarrassed. It upset her. I would be furious if someone did that to Eve."

"Oh, please," Vivienne scoffed. "Girls these days are encouraged to be upset about everything by those woke women's groups. Skirts are barely longer than belts now so he probably thought it was funny."

"It wasn't funny to her."

Vivienne rolled her eyes and picked up her tea. "You're not seriously buying into this. It's harmless, Natalie. Just schoolyard nonsense."

Natalie's hands curled into fists in her lap. "Mrs. Murphy said we should talk to him about boundaries. Consent."

"Consent?" Vivienne gave a brittle laugh. "He's nine. What nonsense. Next they'll be teaching him not to hug his grandmother without a signed waiver."

Natalie flinched.

Vivienne leaned forward, lowering her voice with the kind of faux concern that made Natalie feel like a hysterical patient under observation. "Don't do this, dear. Don't turn a harmless prank into a federal offense. He's a boy. A spirited one. Like his father and uncle."

Natalie felt something churn in her chest. "But that doesn't make it okay."

"Oh, come now. It's not like he pushed her down the stairs."

"Vivienne... "

"You're overreacting. Again. That poor child," she said with a sigh, "being raised under such a cloud of hand-wringing and moral panic."

Natalie stared at her. She wanted to scream. To say *this matters*. That a girl being humiliated in a lunchroom mattered. That it started small. With skirts lifted, jokes shrugged off, mothers telling boys they were just being boys. But she didn't. She nodded once, barely.

Vivienne relaxed into the chair again, smoothing her blouse. "Martin would be disgusted that the school even felt the need to report such a trivial thing. That's the real problem here, overcorrection. Making boys feel ashamed for being confident. Curious. Masculine."

Natalie's voice came out smaller than she meant it to. "It wasn't confidence. It was a violation."

Vivienne didn't respond. Just gave her that look. The one that stripped her bare. That said: *You wouldn't understand strength if it pinned you to the wall.*

The atmosphere had suddenly turned from chilled to frosty and after a few moments of awkward silence Natalie excused herself, claiming she needed to start dinner prep. Vivienne didn't offer to help. She never did and Natalie was glad.

Vivienne glanced at her watch and stood, brushing crumbs from her skirt. "Well in that case I'll leave you to your preparations. Perhaps afterwards you should take a nap. You do look rather pale, but I suppose that ridiculous phone call didn't help."

Natalie just nodded, not trusting herself to speak so stood and followed her to the door.

"Tell Martin I said hello," Vivienne said as she stepped over the threshold. "And do try to be more... present. A man needs more than silence and compliance, Natalie, so do the children."

"I'll tell him, and I'll try, especially when I speak to Thomas about his behavior today," Natalie said, feeling like she'd scored a tiny point.

Vivienne paused, then looked her in the eye.

"If you say so. I only want the best for all of you. Please try to respect that at least."

"I know," Natalie said softly. "And I do."

Vivienne gave a tight nod and turned down the walkway, heels ticking on the brick like the click of a stopwatch.

Natalie watched as Vivienne drove away then stood in the open doorway long after she was gone. The wind picked up slightly, rustling the bushes while Natalie went over Vivienne's fake concern and barbed comments. She didn't feel pale. She didn't feel fragile.

She just felt small. Shrinking by degrees in a house where she no longer belonged.

Closing the door before making her way to the kitchen, she leaned against the sink and closed her eyes. Her face was hot. Her fingers trembled. She pictured Thomas's face. Couldn't reconcile it with what she'd just heard. But there it was. And somewhere in her stomach, cold as stone, was the certainty that Martin would dismiss it too. Natalie turned the faucet on and let the water run, as if willing it to wash away the tension in her body and cleanse her mind of the thoughts swirling around inside her head.

Dinner was lemon-baked cod with steamed broccoli and wild rice. Nothing fancy. Nothing daring. Just something light and inoffensive that Natalie had learned from a women's magazine recipe section, marked *midweek crowd-pleaser* in soft cursive. She'd plated it neatly. The rice shaped into little domes with an upturned measuring cup. The fish resting like pale gold beneath curls of lemon peel. The broccoli florets still bright green and steaming.

The table was set for four and the only sound was the clink of forks and the occasional scrape of glass against the coaster. Martin hadn't spoken since they sat down. Not one word. Just that look. That flat, tight-lipped expression that was somehow louder than yelling. It was the look she'd seen as he came through the door earlier, his briefcase hitting the hall floor with just a bit too much force, his shoes thudding heavily against the hardwood.

Something had been said. She could feel it still vibrating in the air between them. Vivienne had told him. Of course she had. And Martin didn't like surprises. Especially not ones that made him look like a bad father. Not ones about his son.

Thomas looked bored. He was pushing grains of rice around the plate like it was a chore. Eve sat with her back straight, one hand neatly in her lap, her fork poised with polite precision. She wasn't eating so much as waiting and watching.

Natalie offered a brittle smile into the silence. "How was school today?"

No answer.

She tried again. "Thomas? Did you have art this afternoon?"

Thomas shrugged without looking up. "I don't remember."

Eve glanced between them, her shoulders drawn in tight. Martin stabbed a piece of broccoli and chewed, jaw stiff.

Natalie reached for her water. "Eve told me she read a whole chapter of *Charlotte's Web* without stopping."

Eve brightened, just slightly. "We're doing it in class. My teacher said I have a nice reading voice."

"That's wonderful, baby," Natalie said, trying to anchor her voice in calm.

Martin put down his fork. Not slowly. Not loudly. Just... deliberately. His plate was half full.

"This is inedible."

Natalie looked up sharply. "What, why?"

Martin gestured at the fish with two fingers like it was roadkill. "The cod is dry. The rice is mush. What *is* this? It tastes like boiled cardboard."

Eve flinched.

Natalie swallowed. "I followed the recipe. I didn't want to overcook the vegetables."

"You didn't want to use seasoning either, apparently. Jesus, Natalie."

Thomas smirked and pushed his plate forward. "Yeah, it's gross."

Natalie's hands curled under the table. "Thomas that's not true and very ungrateful, too."

Martin didn't even look at the boy. He was still focused on her. "You've been at home all day doing who knows what and now you expect me to eat this garbage? It's not fit for a dog."

Eve's fork stilled in her hand. She was still chewing, eyes downcast, trying to be invisible.

Thomas laughed. A short, sharp bark that mirrored his father's tone. "Can we just have pizza?"

Natalie didn't look at him. She stared down at the lemon wedge on her plate, already juicing a small puddle into the rice.

"I tried my best," she said quietly.

"Try harder," Martin snapped. "You have one job, Natalie. One. This household depends on you not screwing up the basics."

No one moved. The air thickened.

And then Eve, in her small, careful voice, said, "I like it."

Martin blinked, as if he hadn't noticed she was there.

Eve looked straight at her mother, a flush in her cheeks. "I think it's nice, Mommy."

Natalie looked at her and held in a sob. The tiny face, round with softness, her dark brown hair curling slightly at the ends from the humidity. Her eyes were wide and solemn. Brown. Dark and deep like coffee.

Not blue like Thomas's. Not blue like Martin's. Not pale and clear like the Lanes. Brown.

Natalie stared, almost stunned, as if seeing her child for the first time. Her little girl, the only kindness at the table. So gentle, so alert to the tension. How could she have come from the man who sat opposite her now, sneering? Be related to the man-child to her right who mimicked his father at every turn.

Natalie reached across the table and touched Eve's hand. Her fingers were warm, sticky with nerves, trembling just slightly.

"Thank you, sweetheart," she said.

Eve nodded once, fiercely proud.

Martin pushed his chair back. "I'm not eating this," he said. "I've got work to do. I'll make a sandwich later."

He left his plate where it was. Fork splayed, fish half-eaten, wasted, and walked out of the room.

Thomas followed. "Can I go on my iPad?"

Natalie didn't answer. He went anyway. The kitchen fell quiet again. Eve continued to eat, carefully cutting her broccoli into smaller pieces, chewing each one thoughtfully while Natalie sat frozen.

She felt like a chalk outline of a woman. Like someone whose presence had been erased even as she sat in the room. Martin's words still rang in her ears, *not fit for a dog*. And Thomas had echoed his tone so easily, so naturally, like it was a game they played. She looked again at her daughter. Her real, small daughter, still holding her fork. Still trying.

"Eve?" Natalie said, softly.

Eve looked up.

"I'm so proud of you."

Eve smiled then. Just a little. Natalie stood and began clearing the plates. She didn't cry. Not yet. The tears would come later. When the dishwasher went through its cycle. When the house went dark. When she was alone in bed beside a man who didn't want her and a silence she didn't know how to fill.

# 5

The upstairs hallway was cast in darkness as the house finally dipped in quiet now that the dishes were done and the lights downstairs dimmed. Natalie padded softly across the carpet, carrying the weight of dinner in her shoulders and behind her eyes. She wore a soft sweatshirt and leggings, the kind of armor she'd perfected for evenings like this, thin enough to move in, thick enough to absorb a bruise that wasn't physical.

She paused outside Thomas's room, knocking once before gently pushing the door open.

The glow from the screen hit her first. It cast the room in electric blue, flickering across piles of toys and forgotten snack wrappers. His books were stacked sideways on the shelf, half of them with the spines torn or bent from being shoved carelessly into place. A model helicopter lay sideways on his desk with a broken blade. Posters of superheroes lined the walls, men with clenched jaws and giant fists frozen mid-action, all rage and muscle and power.

Thomas sat cross-legged on the floor, clutching his gaming controller, his mouth slightly open in concentration. He didn't look up.

"Time to start getting ready for bed, sweetheart," Natalie said, her voice quiet but firm.

He didn't respond.

"Thomas," she said again, taking a step closer. "It's already past eight."

"I just need to finish this level."

"You've had screen time since you came home from school. We agreed no games after dinner."

He groaned, not dramatically but just enough to register annoyance, and kept playing.

Natalie crouched beside him, gently placing a hand on his arm. "Thomas. Now, please."

He flinched out of her reach. "Dad lets me finish."

Natalie swallowed. "Well, Daddy's not here right now. I am."

"You never let me do anything."

"I let you do plenty. But now it's bedtime."

He gave an exaggerated sigh, dropped the controller with a clatter, and stood up. He didn't look at her as he stomped across the room and into the bathroom, flipping the light on so hard the cord bounced against the wall. Natalie followed him, slowly.

Inside, he slathered toothpaste onto his brush without meeting her eye. His movements were abrupt, all elbows and irritation. He splashed water onto the counter, onto the mirror, leaving a trail of damp defiance behind him. Natalie handed him a towel. He took it without a word.

"Thank you," she said anyway, gently.

When they returned to his room, he flopped onto the bed without bothering to pull the covers back. The blue glow still pulsed from the television so Natalie crossed the room and turned it off, the screen going black with a sigh.

"Goodnight, Thomas," she said softly.

He didn't answer. She stood there a moment, watching him lie stiffly on top of the blanket, his arms folded behind his head like he was already dreaming of escape. There was something about the shape of him, hardening faster than she expected, retreating deeper into silence. Like he was learning how to shut her out before he even understood why he wanted to. She turned the light off and gently pulled the door to behind her.

Eve's room was at the end of the hall, smaller and tidier. The door was already ajar, and Natalie peeked in to find her daughter tucked neatly beneath a pink-and-white quilt, clutching her bunny tight against her chest.

The room was sparse really, just a low bookshelf, a few carefully arranged dolls on the window ledge, and a tiny desk in the corner with a jar of stubby crayons and a single coloring book. No posters. No toy bins bursting open. The space was orderly. Sweet in its own way but there was something else, like it was forgotten.

Natalie sat on the edge of the bed, smoothing a wrinkle from the quilt.

"Hi, Mommy," Eve said, her voice hushed, as if the walls could hear.

"Hi, sweetheart." Natalie leaned in to kiss her forehead. "Did you brush your teeth?"

"Yes," Eve said. "And I put my pajamas on without even being asked."

Natalie smiled. "I noticed. You're my little star."

Eve beamed, proud.

There was a pause. The air between them was soft and still.

Then Eve's voice turned cautious. "Mommy?"

"Yes, love?"

"I really liked dinner and didn't say it just to make you happy. You make lovely food, you really do."

Natalie blinked. "You did?"

Eve nodded. "Even the green bits. The rice tasted like lemon. I liked that."

Natalie exhaled gently. "Thank you, darling. That means a lot."

Eve hesitated. "Daddy was just joking. When he said it was bad."

Natalie looked down at her daughter's face which was round, innocent, brave in a way children shouldn't have to be.

"I know," she said, the lie feathering out on a breath. "Daddy was teasing. Sometimes adults say things they don't mean. But I'm glad you told me."

"Jokes shouldn't make people sad, though," Eve said.

Natalie felt something in her chest twist tight.

"No," she said softly. "They shouldn't."

She smoothed a lock of dark hair behind her daughter's ear. Eve's eyes were wide and brown, large in the fading light. She looked nothing like her father. Not even like Thomas. Natalie had never been able to explain that. She'd been told recessive genes, a fluke of biology. Still, there were moments, like now, where it struck her like a bell: how different this little girl was. Like someone had slipped a stranger's soul into the mix when she wasn't looking. A softer, kinder soul.

Natalie picked up a book from the nightstand, *The Paper Bag Princess*, and held it up. "Shall we?"

Eve nodded, tucking the bunny under her chin.

Natalie read aloud in her gentle voice, letting the rhythm of the story soothe the room. The princess burned her dress and outsmarted the dragon. Eve giggled at the right parts. Natalie read slower than usual, drawing it out, wanting to stay in the soft lull of her daughter's company just a little longer.

When the story ended, Eve yawned and nestled deeper into the pillows.

Natalie leaned down and kissed her temple. "Goodnight, my sweet girl."

"Goodnight, Mommy."

Natalie stood, pausing in the doorway to take one last look. The room glowed in warm lamplight, quiet and safe. For now. She turned off the light and pulled the door until only a sliver of golden hallway remained, then closed it softly. Back in the hallway, the air felt colder. Unfriendly. And even though the house was settling into sleep, Natalie knew it would evade her like it did most nights.

Natalie locked the bathroom door behind her with a click that sounded louder than it should have in the stillness of the house. She stood there for a beat, hand on the brass knob, forehead resting against the cool painted wood, breathing like she'd just sprinted through a storm.

Outside the door was order. Thomas in bed, headphones likely still tucked beneath the pillow. Eve, already slipping into the hush of dreams, her bunny curled against her like a heartbeat. Martin downstairs, still sulking in the glare of the television, probably nursing a second beer and a whole lot of silent contempt.

Inside the door, there was just her. The bathroom was the only room in the house with a lock that worked. The one space that belonged to her, if only temporarily. A candle she kept hidden behind the cotton swabs was burning low on the ledge, mellow vanilla. Her robe hung neatly behind the door. The tiles were cold beneath her feet. She opened the medicine cabinet and stared at the neat rows of bottles. Toothpaste, allergy meds, headache relief. Nothing for this, how she felt deep in her core.

Her reflection when she looked in the mirror startled her, gray-tinged skin, hollow cheeks, hair scraped back too tightly, the whites of her eyes fogged with fatigue. Like a woman dissolving at the edges.

Natalie sank to the closed toilet lid and pulled open the drawer under the sink. Behind an old box of tampons and facial wipes, she found the small floral notebook, a small pencil secured with an elastic band. She hadn't written in it since last fall. She ran her fingers over the cover, then peeled it open to the last blank page. And she wrote –

*July 10th*

*I am afraid I am coming apart again. I don't know where else to put this but here. In a notebook hidden in a drawer beneath expired medicine and amongst things for when I bleed. I feel like I'm bleeding out right now but not in a physical way that a box of tampons can help with.*

*I'm not going to say it out loud. Not to Martin. Not to anyone. Otherwise, they'll think I'm weak. I told him again what happened at school. About Thomas. I chose my words carefully, like I always do, like someone approaching an open flame. I told him what the head teacher said, that Thomas lifted a little girl's skirt. That the girl was upset. That Mrs. Murphy just wanted us to talk to him about boundaries.*

*He laughed. Then he got angry. He called the school 'a cesspool of soft, stupid women.'*

*He said Thomas was just being a boy. A curious boy. A strong one. "Not some feminized porcelain doll raised to apologize for having testosterone," he said. His words. Not mine.*

*When I said I thought it was serious, that Thomas needed to understand that what he did was wrong he looked at me like I'd insulted him personally. "He's expressing himself," Martin said. "And you're going to make him soft."*

*And then, the real blow: "You'd side with a stranger's brat over your own son?"*

*That's when I stopped talking. I said I understood. I agreed. Like I always do. Because it's easier than pushing back. Because if I push, he'll push harder. But I didn't understand. I still don't. And Thomas...*

*He's changing. I can see it. He's learning how to be cruel. Learning how to mimic the tone Martin uses with me. Learning what earns him praise. I'm watching it happen in real time, and I can't stop it.*

*And then there's this fog in my head. A pressure behind my eyes like something dammed up and waiting to burst. I'm not crying. I don't cry anymore, not if I can help it. But it's there, like the aftertaste of something rotten.*

*I thought I was better. I thought the worst had passed after Eve. After the diagnosis. "Postpartum depression," they said, like it was something that could be measured, scheduled, medicated away. I took the pills. I did the therapy. I smiled through appointments with people who said I just needed to sleep more, exercise more, keep a journal. Like this one. This stupid, private, pointless journal.*

*But the fog is back. And tonight, I felt something else. A pain. Not emotional. Physical. A sharp cramp in my lower right side. Not the first time, either. It's been coming and going for days now. But tonight, it doubled me over. Like a knife between the ribs. I pretended to stretch. To adjust my waistband. To yawn. But I wanted to scream.*

*I don't want to tell Martin. He'd take me to the practice and pass me off to one of his colleagues with that smug, quiet pity. "She's always been delicate," he'd say. "She gets in her own head and there's probably nothing wrong with her." And they'd nod and smile and chalk it all up to hormones and a lack of fresh air or something equally ridiculous.*

*I don't want him in that part of me anymore. So tomorrow, I'm calling my old doctor. Dr. Keene. She's not on our insurance, but I don't care. She saw me before. She knew when I was lying. She saw through the performance. I'll make something up. Tell Martin I'm picking up groceries or seeing Misty.*

*I must know what this pain is. If it's just stress, fine. If it's something worse, at least I'll know. But something in me is whispering that it's a sign. A flare. A warning. I feel like my body is trying to tell me something. And I'm afraid I've forgotten how to listen.*

. . .

Natalie stopped writing. The words had started to blur. Not from tears, they never helped anyway, but from exhaustion that seeps into your marrow and settles like rot. She closed the journal, slid it back under the sink, and flushed the toilet to mask the sound of the drawer scraping closed. A practiced move. She rinsed her face under cold water, not bothering to dry it, and stared at herself in the mirror again. Still there. Still her. But which version she wasn't sure.

From downstairs, she could hear the faint roar of the baseball game. The announcer's voice rose and fell like waves. Natalie opened the bathroom door and walked softly to the bedroom. She changed into her cotton pajamas, the ones Martin mocked and slid into bed without turning on the light.

She listened. To the fan. To the footsteps downstairs. She didn't know what would happen tomorrow. But she knew she had to find out. Before she disappeared completely under a sea of pain and uncertainty.

# 6

The house was still quiet when Natalie slipped into the kitchen, the air just beginning to warm in the late morning rays. Sunlight filtered through the blinds in pale yellow strips, landing across the tile floor like bars. The children were at school. Martin was long gone. He'd left early without a word, just the low thud of the front door and the fading sound of his car pulling away.

Natalie clutched her mug with both hands, the coffee inside untouched and cooling fast. Her stomach turned as she stared at the phone on the counter, her finger hovering just above the call button. The digits were already typed in. She'd sat down to make the call at 9:12. It was now 10:07.

She drew in a breath and pressed *Call*.

Three rings. Then a woman's voice answered. "Dr. Keene's office, this is Carla."

Natalie cleared her throat. "Hi, um... yes. I'd like to make an appointment."

"Of course, hon. Is this your first time with us?"

"No. I saw Dr. Keene a few years ago. After I had my daughter." Natalie's voice dropped slightly, as if the word *daughter* were something to be hidden.

"Oh, okay. Name, please?"

"Natalie Lane."

"Okay, Natalie. What are we seeing you for today?"

Natalie hesitated. Her eyes darted toward the hallway, as though Martin might suddenly appear, even though she knew he was at the clinic. She swallowed. "It's... I've been feeling off. Not quite myself."

Carla waited a beat. "Can you be more specific?"

"Just... some discomfort. Physically. And mentally. It's hard to explain."

Another pause. The kind of pause that made you wonder if the person on the other end was writing *hypochondriac* in your file.

"We can get you in tomorrow afternoon. Two fifteen. Would that work?"

"Yes. Perfect. Thank you."

She hung up and let the phone fall face-down on the counter. She pressed her palms flat against the marble and stayed there for a long moment, breathing when a knock at the door startled her. It was Misty. Of course. She was already letting herself in, her oversized tote slung over one shoulder and her dark curls piled high on her head in a messy bun. She wore aviators, ripped jeans, and a loose green blouse that looked expensive but probably wasn't. Misty always had that magic of looking like she belonged on the cover of a coffee table book, even when she hadn't showered.

"I brought pastries," she said, holding up a brown paper bag. "I figure you're not eating again."

Natalie managed a smile. "You figured right."

They sat in the kitchen, the coffee reheated, the pastries placed delicately on mismatched plates. Natalie tore at a croissant without really tasting it.

Misty sipped her drink and watched her. "You look like you didn't sleep."

"I didn't."

"Let me guess. Martin being his usual charming self?"

Natalie didn't answer right away.

"I made a doctor's appointment," she said instead.

Misty blinked. "For what?"

"I don't know. Just... something's not right. I've been getting these cramps. And I can't focus. I feel like I'm... drifting most of the time."

Misty leaned forward. "Good. That's good. That you're doing something. You don't have to be a martyr, Nat."

Natalie offered a ghost of a smile. "You're the only one who says that."

"That's because I'm the only one who hasn't been scared off by Mr. Lane and his death glare. Don't think I haven't noticed. You know, the disappearing friend act. First it was Lauren. Then Kate. Then that couple from down the street, remember, the ones with the fire pit and the golden retriever. Poof. Gone."

"They weren't comfortable around..."

"Martin. Yeah. I know."

Natalie stared into her coffee. "He doesn't like people in our space. He says it disrupts the children's routine, and he likes his home to himself."

Misty snorted. "He just doesn't like people seeing how he speaks to you, or the children."

Natalie's shoulders stiffened, but she didn't deny it.

Misty sat back. "You know, when you first married him, I thought, *wow, she's really landed herself a catch.* You were glowing. Like straight out of a bridal magazine."

Natalie smiled faintly. "He was... charming. At first."

"He *swept* you up," Misty said, eyes sharp. "That was the word you used. 'He swept me off my feet.'"

Natalie nodded. "And then he brought me to Philadelphia."

"To be near *her.*" Misty's lip curled. "Vi the Viper."

"And now I haven't seen my mother in three years."

Misty's expression softened. "You could invite them, you know. Even for a weekend."

"She's too sick to travel. And my father hates flying. They'll never come east."

"But *you* could go west."

Natalie gave a helpless shrug. "Martin says it's too disruptive for the kids to travel during term. And summer's always full of activities and expensive. Besides, I don't think I'd know how to be there anymore, it's as if they are strangers."

Misty studied her. "That's so sad, Nat, but I'm sure you'd remember how you used to be around them and I'm sure they'd love to see you. You just need to take a chance."

Natalie said nothing. Her fingers pulled at the flaky edge of her pastry, reducing it to dust.

Misty leaned in. "Can I ask you something? And please don't shut down."

Natalie nodded.

"What's going on with Thomas?"

Natalie looked up, startled.

"You've said a few things lately. About him being cold. About Martin favoring him."

Natalie hesitated. "Yes that's true and something happened at school. Yesterday."

Misty said nothing, letting her fill the silence.

"He... lifted a girl's skirt. In front of the cafeteria."

Misty blinked. "Are you kidding me?"

"No. The school called. The girl was upset. The headteacher just asked that we talk to him about boundaries."

"What did Martin say?"

Natalie pressed her lips together. "That it was nothing. That boys are curious. That I was blowing it out of proportion."

Misty's expression darkened. "Jesus."

"I tried to tell him it mattered. That we should say something. But he turned it around. Said I was weak. That I was going to make Thomas the same."

"You *have* to nip that in the bud, Nat. Seriously. That kind of behavior doesn't just vanish on its own. It escalates. He's copying what he sees. That's not just a boy being curious, that's a boy testing how far he can go."

Natalie swallowed. "I know. I just... I feel like I'm losing my grip on him. Like he's already decided who he wants to be. And it's not someone I know, well, unless you count Martin."

Misty reached across the table and touched her hand. "Then remind him. Who *you* are and what your values and morals are. Who *he* could be if he chooses the right path."

Natalie looked at her, eyes glassy. "What if it's too late?"

"It's not. I'm sure of it but you have to act soon otherwise incidents like that will keep happening."

They sat in silence for a moment. The clock ticked in the hallway. Outside, the wind nudged the hydrangeas in the flower beds. Natalie felt the old familiar swell of dread in her stomach. But also, something else. A tiny flicker. A spark. Like maybe, not today, not yet, but maybe she wasn't entirely gone. And maybe, just maybe, Misty had been right all along.

The surgery waiting room was meant to suggest calm and cleanliness. The walls were a cool eggshell blue, the chairs minimalist gray, and a potted fig stood in the corner, spindly yet proud. Natalie stepped inside and hovered just past the automatic doors. For a second, she felt like turning back. Her palms were damp. Her skin felt too tight. But the pain that had been pressing against her lower abdomen all morning gave a subtle, mean twist, just enough to remind her why she was here.

The young woman behind the reception desk didn't look up at first. She was scrolling on her phone with one manicured hand and slowly chewing gum with the other, her jaw moving in a rhythmic, vacant loop. Her nails were long and pointed, lacquered in a baby pink that caught the fluorescent light. She wore a cropped blazer and shiny gold hoops, and her ponytail was curled into glossy perfection.

Natalie took a step forward, feeling every inch of her oatmeal knit cardigan and the sensible ballet flats she'd owned since Eve was born.

"Hi," she said softly. "I'm Natalie Lane. I have an appointment with Dr. Feldman. Two fifteen."

The receptionist's lashes fluttered as she glanced at the computer screen. "Insurance?"

"Oh. Um. I'm paying cash."

That made the girl glance up, just for a moment. "Okay," she said, and handed over a clipboard with a single form. "Just fill this out. Dr. Feldman's running about ten minutes behind."

Natalie nodded and took the clipboard to the nearest chair. She sat gingerly, tucking her bag beneath her feet. Her pen hovered over the form for a moment before she began writing in her careful, slanted hand. She kept her head down. She didn't want anyone to recognize her. Didn't want word to travel.

She was supposed to go to *Martin's* practice. He was her doctor. His colleagues were her doctors. This was the arrangement, the rule, the unwritten law of her marriage. But she couldn't face it. Not this time. Not with the whisper of something wrong curling tighter in her belly each day. She needed someone who didn't know her husband. Someone who wouldn't try to translate her symptoms into his language.

Across from her, a woman in a camel trench coat was flipping through a *People* magazine, her wedding ring catching the light. A child beside her picked at a Band-Aid on his finger.

Everything in the room felt too bright. Too clinical. Natalie shifted in her seat, the cushion squeaking beneath her.

"Natalie Lane?" a voice called, warm and clear.

She looked up. A petite woman in navy scrubs and thick tortoiseshell glasses smiled at her from the hallway. "Dr. Feldman's ready for you."

Natalie stood quickly and followed her through the hallway, her pulse tapping fast in her neck. The office was small but inviting. Pale wood shelves lined with medical books. A framed print of a hummingbird. A glass of water already poured on the desk.

Dr. Kay Feldman rose from her seat and offered her hand. "Natalie, it's good to see you. Please, sit."

Natalie sank into the chair opposite her and clasped her hands tightly in her lap. Dr. Feldman had kind eyes. She looked to be in her mid-fifties, with cropped gray-blonde hair and a patient, open face. She wore a simple gold chain and no makeup, just a soft balm on her lips and a kind of no-nonsense gentleness that reminded Natalie vaguely of a favorite teacher she'd once had.

"So," Dr. Feldman said, folding her hands, "what brings you in today?"

Natalie exhaled. "I'm... not sure, really. I've been feeling off."

"Off how?"

Natalie hesitated. "I've had some pain. In my lower abdomen. Comes and goes. Sharp, sometimes. Like a cramp."

Dr. Feldman nodded, listening. "How long has that been happening?"

"About a week. Maybe longer. I've been ignoring it."

"Anything else?"

Natalie looked down. "Fatigue. Trouble sleeping. Brain fog. And... I've had depression in the past. After my daughter was born. I'm worried it's... coming back."

Dr. Feldman tilted her head. "Have you had any changes in appetite?"

"Yes. Less hungry. Some nausea in the mornings. Not always, but enough to notice."

"Bloating?"

"A little."

"Missed a period?"

Natalie paused. "I—I think so."

Dr. Feldman nodded again, slowly. "Okay. We'll start with a few basic tests—bloodwork, urinalysis, maybe a pelvic ultrasound depending on what we find. Nothing too invasive right now. Just information gathering."

Natalie nodded, fingers curled tight into the fabric of her cardigan.

"I'll also run a standard pregnancy test," the doctor added gently.

Natalie looked up sharply.

Dr. Feldman offered a calm smile. "Just to rule things out."

Natalie's throat felt dry. "Of course."

But her stomach sank like a stone. They finished the intake questions, and Natalie allowed the nurse to draw her blood. She booked a follow-up for the next week and collected her things with shaking fingers.

"Take care of yourself, Natalie," Dr. Feldman said softly as she walked her to the reception. "You're doing the right thing getting checked out."

Natalie smiled and nodded and thanked her. But when she stepped into the sunlight outside the clinic, she felt no relief. Just that gnawing, clawing unease in the pit of her stomach. The one that had started days ago and had only grown louder. She climbed into her car and turned the ignition. The radio came on low, some upbeat pop song with lyrics she didn't recognize.

She took the back roads home, avoiding the highways. She

didn't want to move fast. Didn't want to arrive just yet. At the intersection near Old Mill Road, she pulled up to a stop sign. Another car came to a halt beside hers, a shiny navy sedan with a familiar driver. Dr. Marcus Ellery. One of Martin's colleagues. A smug, good-looking man with perfect teeth and a habit of laughing a little too loudly at Martin's jokes at parties. He spotted her immediately and gave a broad, cheerful wave.

Natalie's stomach turned to ice. She hesitated, then forced a polite wave back, her fingers trembling. His smile lingered, but the light changed, and he turned away, disappearing down the road. Natalie sat still for a moment longer, her heart in her throat. He'd seen her. He wouldn't think anything of it, just Natalie Lane, Martin's quiet little wife, out running errands. But still, the knot in her gut pulled tighter. And then the thought came.

What if she was pregnant? She gripped the steering wheel, knuckles white. *No. No, no, no.*

It couldn't be. She and Martin barely touched each other. It had been months. Maybe longer. But sometimes when he was in a certain mood, when she couldn't say no without consequences, it still happened, and she hated it.

Natalie pressed her forehead to the steering wheel. *Please,* she thought. *Please don't let this be that.* She didn't pray anymore but just then, in that moment, she did and in the silence that followed, there was no answer. Just the sound of her own breath and the slow, steady beat of dread.

# 7

The kitchen was quiet which Natalie relished as she stood by the sink, her coffee untouched in front of her, the rim stained with the faintest pink of her lip balm. The morning sunlight streamed through the blinds, illuminating the marble countertops, sterile and perfect like everything Martin approved of.

When the phone rang Natalie flinched. Her hand hesitated just above the receiver. For a moment, she was sure it was Martin checking in, tracking her movements like he sometimes did under the guise of small talk. But then the caller ID flashed:

DR. K. FELDMAN, OFFICE

Her stomach dropped. Her mouth went dry.

She picked up. "Hello?"

"Hi, is this Natalie Lane?" a young, bright voice asked. It was the same gum-chewing receptionist from before, Carla.

"Yes, speaking."

"Hi there. I'm just calling with some results from your recent tests. Dr. Feldman would like to speak with you directly. Can I put you through?"

Natalie felt her pulse in her throat. "Yes, of course."

There was a soft click, then the rustle of a line being connected.

"Natalie?" Dr. Feldman's voice came on—calm, warm, grounding.

"Yes. Hi." Her voice sounded thinner than she meant it to.

"I wanted to speak to you directly. Some of your results have come back and... I need to share something that may be a little surprising."

Natalie gripped the edge of the counter. "Okay."

"There's no easy way to say this, so I'll be direct. Your tests came back positive for *Trichomoniasis*. It's a sexually transmitted infection."

Natalie blinked. "How? I don't understand."

"It's fairly common. It can sometimes be asymptomatic in men, which means it's often passed unknowingly. But it is almost exclusively transmitted through sexual contact."

Natalie felt the floor tilt beneath her. She stared at the kitchen tiles. One of them had a small hairline crack. She'd never noticed it before.

"I haven't... I haven't been with anyone else," she said. Her voice sounded detached, like it belonged to someone else. "There must be a mistake. Maybe the samples got mixed up."

Dr. Feldman's tone remained steady. "We ran the panel twice. I know this is distressing, and I want to make sure you're safe and well moving forward. I've already sent a prescription to your preferred pharmacy as marked on the form you filled in. It's a simple course of antibiotics, very treatable."

Natalie barely heard her.

"You may also want to get an HIV test," Dr. Feldman continued, gently. "As a precaution."

Natalie's mouth opened, but no sound came out. The room

blurred slightly, as though she were underwater or in fog. Martin's voice echoed somewhere in her brain. *You get in your own head. You overthink. You're not strong enough to handle real things.*

"I just..." Natalie finally said, "I really think there's been a mistake."

"I understand," Dr. Feldman said with empathy. "It's a lot to process. If you need to speak again or come in for a follow-up, just call. You're not alone in this."

Natalie managed a soft "thank you" before hanging up.

The phone sat in her palm for a few seconds before she placed it face-down on the counter like it had burned her. The kitchen seemed suddenly alien, every surface too clean, too bright. Her breath caught in her chest. *He gave this to me.*

It wasn't possible. It couldn't be. Martin, her husband. Her *doctor*. The man who monitored everything from her sleep to her vitamins. Who timed her cycles like clockwork. Who made her feel insane when she questioned anything. *He* had given this to her. Her stomach roiled. Without thinking, she moved. She walked up the stairs, quiet as a breath, her footsteps hushed against the thick carpet. At the top landing, she paused, listening for movement. The house was empty. Still. But her heartbeat thundered in her ears.

She moved to the bedroom. Martin's side of the closet was precise. His pressed suits, folded sweaters, rows of neatly aligned shoes irritated her more than usual. She opened one drawer, then another. Belts. Ties. Receipts from dry cleaning. Nothing unusual. She opened the small drawer on his bedside table. Inside: a watch he didn't wear, a box of earplugs, a half-used bottle of melatonin, a nail clipper. Natalie closed it gently, her hands trembling.

She turned next to the home office. This was *his* space. She rarely went inside. Even dusting was done with a sort of reverence, like crossing a threshold she wasn't meant to. The door creaked faintly as she pushed it open.

Inside, the air was cooler, the blinds drawn. His desk was spotless. No papers, just his laptop, a mouse, and a coaster that bore no rings. The drawers were locked. All except one.

She opened it carefully. Stationery. A file folder labeled "Household." Another labeled "Clinic." And beneath them, tucked under an old business card, was a small black USB stick.

Natalie stared at it. She picked it up, just for a second, noting how light it was in her hand, ordinary. Her reflection bent in its glossy surface. Then she quickly put it back exactly as she'd found it. Too dangerous. Too soon. She needed time. She needed a plan. She closed the drawer softly and adjusted the coaster. One inch to the left. Exactly where it had been. Her hands trembled as she turned to leave. And then the front door slammed. Natalie froze. Her heart seized. For a second, the only sound was her own breath, ragged and shallow. Then footsteps. Heavy. Male.

She stepped into the hallway, pulling the office door closed behind her with careful precision. Her pulse hammered in her ears. Downstairs, keys jangled. A voice, familiar, humming something tuneless. Martin was home. Natalie ran her hands through her hair and smoothed her cardigan, wiping the fear from her face. She pulled her features into something resembling calm and descended the stairs slowly, quietly rehearsing a lie on her lips. She had to. Because now, she knew something was wrong. Not just with her body. With *him.*

The bell above the pharmacy door gave a cheerful chime that felt entirely out of place. Natalie stepped inside, the dry chill of the air-conditioning licking across her skin, raising goosebumps beneath the sleeves of her cardigan. She pulled them tighter around her, although the cardigan did nothing to hide the sudden tremble in her hands.

The pharmacy was small but bright with rows of neatly labeled shelves. There were racks of vitamin gummies for children, display stands full of seasonal lip balm, and the inevitable aisle of greeting cards with awful puns printed in swirling gold script.

The counter at the back stretched across the width of the store like a border checkpoint and Natalie hesitated before approaching. She'd picked this pharmacy carefully, far enough from Martin's practice not to overlap with patients, but still local enough to avoid suspicion if anyone *did* find out she'd filled a prescription.

Behind the counter stood a woman in her sixties, with short, tightly curled gray hair and mauve glasses perched halfway down her nose. She wore a navy smock embroidered with *Tyla*, and as soon as she looked up, her entire face lit up.

"Natalie Lane! Well, would you look at you. It's been a hot minute since I saw you last!"

Natalie's smile came automatically, brittle and stretched. "Hi, Tyla, I didn't know you worked here."

Tyla leaned on the counter, hands folded. "I do indeed. Fancied a change and this is nearer to home. I've been here a few weeks and just about settling in, now, how's that husband of yours? Still running half the county's healthcare from his office chair?"

Natalie's cheeks twitched. "Yes. He's... keeping busy."

"And the kids? Thomas and little Eve, right? Must be, what, nine and seven now?"

"Exactly," Natalie said, voice soft, almost a whisper.

"You always made such sweet babies. I swear, that Thomas had the bluest eyes I'd ever seen when he was born. You know, I still remember how he screamed his little lungs out when he got his first vaccinations? Nearly broke my heart!"

Natalie nodded, her face warming. "Yes. He's still loud."

Tyla chuckled and turned to her screen. "So, what are we picking up today, honey?"

Natalie leaned forward, her voice low. "I believe my doctor called in a prescription for me?"

Tyla nodded and began tapping the keyboard with long, practiced fingers. "Yep, I've got it right here. One sec."

She turned to the shelves behind her, humming under her breath. Natalie, swallowed and prayed again that Tyla didn't notice the prescription hadn't come from Martin's surgery, then nervously glanced over her shoulder at the door. It hadn't opened again. Yet.

Tyla returned with a small white bag and set it down on the counter. She didn't pass it over immediately, though. Instead, she smiled again, her tone turning conspiratorial.

"I'm surprised to see you here, Martin always sends folks to that big chain pharmacy over on Waverly, but I say there's no substitute for a friendly face so thank you for the custom."

Natalie's stomach knotted. "Right. Yes, I like it here."

Tyla tapped the screen again. "You're all set. Just waiting for the label to finish printing."

Natalie nodded, feeling sweat begin to bloom beneath her hairline. Then the bell chimed.

The air in the pharmacy shifted, just slightly. Natalie didn't turn. She didn't have to. She recognized the voice.

"Hi, Tyla! I've got a pickup for Lorraine Ford."

Natalie stood frozen, eyes trained on the counter. Her heart thudded. She heard the soft shuffle of boots, leather heels on linoleum. Lorraine was just a few feet behind her now. Natalie could feel the burn of her gaze settling between her shoulder blades.

Tyla, bless her, was still oblivious. "Lorraine! Oh, honey, you're in for the migraine meds again? Did you try that magnesium trick I showed you?"

"Hasn't helped," Lorraine said, voice clipped.

Natalie risked a glance to the side. Lorraine Ford stood with her arms crossed, sunglasses pushed up into her sleek blonde hair, her lipstick a perfect brick-red slash across her mouth. She looked polished. Sculpted. Furious. Their eyes met for half a second. Lorraine looked away as though Natalie was a dirty stain.

Tyla didn't notice. "Lorraine, you know Natalie Lane, don't you? Your kids go to Carver Elementary?"

"Oh, I *know* her and her son," Lorraine said, still not looking Natalie's way.

Natalie's throat dried out like paper. Tyla's cheer faltered slightly, sensing tension at last. She turned back to the screen.

"Ah, here we go." She printed the label, stuck it carefully onto the prescription bag, and finally handed it over to Natalie.

"There you are, sweetie," she said.

But as she passed it across the counter, her eyes flicked briefly to the label. She raised one neatly plucked eyebrow, just for a split second, before replacing it with her usual customer service smile.

Natalie flushed scarlet and reached for the bag, muttering a quick "Thank you," and turned to leave.

Lorraine didn't move aside to let her pass. She simply stared at the rack of cough syrups, jaw tight. Natalie squeezed past her, the prescription bag crackling in her hand. As she pushed the door open, the bell chimed again. Behind her, Tyla and Lorraine were chatting about the weather, about how *hot this week's been,* and *how there's always something going around this time of year.* Neither of them said goodbye.

The door swung shut behind her, the glass smudging her

reflection. She crossed the lot quickly, like someone escaping a crime scene. Inside the car, Natalie sat with her hands on the steering wheel, staring ahead. Her face burned. Her pulse was a hammer in her throat. She didn't know whether to cry or scream or vomit. She didn't do any of those things. She started the engine and drove home.

# 8

The navy dress lay on the bed like a portent. Silk. Long-sleeved. High-necked. Hem just below the knee. A pearl clasp at the throat that Natalie's fingers struggled to close. She hadn't chosen it.

Martin had laid it out for her before he left for the clinic that morning, smoothing it carefully on the bedspread. "Wear this," he'd said. "It's elegant. Modest." His smile had held the soft menace she was accustomed to.

Now she stood in the bedroom's full-length mirror, hands twisting at the waist of the dress, watching the way it clung to her frame in all the wrong places. The color drained the warmth from her skin. She looked like someone being dressed for a memorial service. Or a trial.

In the en suite, she heard the sharp hiss of aftershave and water running. Martin emerged a few minutes later, adjusting his cuffs. He wore a tailored charcoal suit with an indigo tie and a glint of silver at his wrist. He paused behind her, scenting the air between them like a dog.

"I told you to wear the pearl studs, not the gold ones."

Natalie flinched and reached for the nightstand.

He fastened his cuff with a snap. "Don't dawdle. I don't want to be late."

She changed the earrings silently. He watched her in the mirror, his eyes cold and assessing. The cologne he'd used was new and unfamiliar. Something musky and expensive.

"You're wearing a new scent."

He didn't respond, just grabbed his blazer and wallet from the dresser while downstairs, the taxi honked. A single, impatient beep. Natalie slid on her low heels, the black ones with the scuffed toe she hadn't had time to polish. Her stomach turned yet she hadn't eaten all day which was a bonus and hopefully meant she wouldn't throw up.

After saying goodbye to the kids and the sitter who looked bored and was already playing on her phone, Natalie hurried to the metallic red sedan with sun-faded upholstery. The A/C was on too high, freezing the sweat that had just begun to form under Natalie's arms. She slid into the backseat of the cab, Martin too close beside her, thigh pressed against hers. The driver was a middle-aged Latino man with a kind face, deep lines at the corners of his eyes, and a soft country radio station playing low.

"Radley Hotel, Center City," Martin said crisply.

The man nodded. "You got it."

They pulled away from the curb. The sky was a bruised navy blue, the edges of dusk curling in. The car moved through the familiar streets of Haverford before bleeding into the wider arteries of Philadelphia. Natalie stared out the window at rows of brownstones, their porches lit like stages. The glass vibrated with the rhythm of the tires.

Martin adjusted his tie, then reached over and placed a hand on her knee. It wasn't affectionate, it was controlling. Possessive. A hand that meant *be good.*

"I want no silly scenes tonight," he said, voice low enough

the driver wouldn't hear. "This isn't the time for one of your moods or migraines."

Natalie nodded.

"Smile. Laugh at the right moments. Don't drink anything stronger than club soda. Understand?"

"Yes."

His grip tightened briefly. "These are *my* people tonight. The mayor will be there. Judge Holloway. The donors who keep the lights on at the clinic. Don't embarrass me."

She didn't answer. She didn't need to. The driver met her eyes in the rearview mirror. For a moment, he looked directly at her. Not at her husband. Not at the expensive dress. At *her*.

And what Natalie saw reflected back wasn't judgment or interest. It was pity. Her stomach hollowed and she looked away from his judgement or was it kindness?.

The Radley Hotel stood like a monument to wealth, all polished marble and gold-leaf signage. Doormen in pressed navy uniforms opened the car doors with synchronized bows. Martin stepped out first and adjusted his suit jacket. Natalie followed, blinking against the glare of chandeliers pouring light from the lobby and onto the sidewalk.

The taxi driver lingered as Martin paid. Natalie caught his eye again and this time gave him a tiny, grateful nod. He returned it before driving off.

Inside, the lobby buzzed with voices and the sharp clink of cutlery against crystal. A white banner reading *Hope for All: Annual Fundraiser for Philadelphia's Homeless* arched over the entrance to the ballroom. Natalie felt the irony like a slap.

Martin was already in full stride, greeting people by name, his voice modulated to its professional register, laced with warmth but authoritative. He shook hands, accepted compliments, and laughed a fraction louder than necessary.

Natalie followed a step behind, smiling on cue. She didn't

recognize many faces, just the vague outlines of people she'd seen at other events like this, like at the symphony fundraiser, the medical board gala, the holiday party at the art museum. Always the same smiles, the same topics, the same barely contained hunger for status.

A waiter appeared with a tray of champagne flutes. Martin took one and Natalie reached for a glass of sparkling water. She sipped it slowly and stood close to the wall, letting the crush of gowns and suits move around her. The ballroom reeked of perfume and salon products sprayed over carefully coiffed hair.

Martin was deep in conversation with a city councilman and she could see him gesturing slightly with the hand that held his drink, his expression earnest. He had a way of making people feel like he saw right through to the heart of them, even when he wasn't really listening or interested in anything they had to say, or them.

A woman beside Natalie complimented her dress. Natalie murmured thanks but knew she was lying while the persistent voice in her head got louder. *Don't embarrass him. Don't be yourself. Don't let anything show.*

She could feel it under her skin now, the truth. A dirty word folded inside her: *infection.* She shouldn't even be here. She should be at home, under a blanket, trying to make sense of the new world of betrayal that she'd stepped into.

Instead, she was a prop at a charity gala. Draped in hideous silk like a straitjacket. A photographer wandered by and snapped a picture of her and Martin together. His arm snaked around her waist at the last second, fingers squeezing just a little too tight. The flash lit up her face and she imagined the result would look like a photo from an autopsy.

Later, she found herself standing at a table near the dessert trays. The noise had risen to a roar. Martin was across the room again, now with the mayor. Natalie kept her eyes on him even as a woman in pearls tried to engage her in conversation about elementary school reform. It was all too much and her ears rang. She felt the pressure building in her chest, like the breath she was holding might never fully release. Another waiter passed with a tray of mini cheesecakes. Natalie took one just to have something to do with her hands at the same time as she caught Martin's eye across the ballroom. He smiled. But it didn't reach his eyes.

The evening dragged on and on while the ballroom still shimmered with chandeliers and polished glass. A string quartet played something syrupy near the dais, the notes swirling with the laughter of well-dressed donors and the clinking of champagne flutes. Natalie followed behind Martin, one careful step after the other, her heels whispering against the gleaming marble floor. When he held her hand she wanted to pull away from the performative squeeze of his fingers around hers, like she was a prized possession to be displayed. His palm was slightly damp, his grip too firm. At home, he rarely touched her yet here, in the eye of the crowd, he acted like a man in love. His smile was rehearsed, and his touch, strategic.

Natalie's mouth smiled too. Her lips curved mechanically, without meaning.

A woman in a sapphire gown passed them and murmured to Martin, "Looking well, Dr. Lane."

He nodded, not breaking stride. "Thank you. My wife keeps me on my toes."

Natalie gave a soft, obligatory laugh. She felt like she might choke on the lie. They approached a pair of colleagues clustered near the silent auction table, where glossy photos of struggling families and outreach vans were arranged between bouquets of lilies and sponsorship plaques.

"Martin!" said a tall man with salt-and-pepper hair and a

gold watch too big for his wrist. "Glad you made it. You remember my wife, Karen."

Martin gave the man a confident clap on the shoulder and turned to Natalie. "Edward Moorcroft, head of cardiology. And this is Dr. Sara Bloomsbury, new research lead."

Sara, a woman in her early forties with a razor-cut bob and cool green eyes, extended her hand toward Natalie. "Lovely to meet you. Martin speaks of you often."

Natalie shook her hand, fingers cold. "All good things, I hope."

"Oh, of course," Sara said, voice warm. But her eyes flitted to Martin, then back to Natalie, assessing. Not cruel, just curious, like a woman used to cataloguing people in layers.

Martin kept his hand on the small of Natalie's back. Not quite possessive, but enough to say *mine.*

"And how's the clinic?" Edward asked.

Martin launched into one of his polished spiels about new outreach initiatives and funding hurdles. Natalie nodded at the right moments, her face aching with the strain of pleasantness.

A waitress appeared beside them, balancing a tray of champagne flutes. Her hair was twisted in a neat bun, her eyes glazed with the fatigue of too many passes through a crowded room. She extended the tray toward Natalie. Natalie hesitated. She could already feel Martin shift beside her. But the eyes were on her. The performance demanded more. She reached out and took a flute.

Martin's jaw tightened almost imperceptibly. His hand dropped from her back. He didn't say a word, but the air between them lowered a few degrees.

Natalie felt it in her throat.

She turned to the waitress, her smile tight. "Thank you."

The waitress nodded and vanished into the crowd. Sara

noticed the moment too. Her eyes flicked between them again, quicker this time, harder.

Natalie brought the flute to her chest, cradling it without drinking. The bubbles rose like tiny gasps. She turned back to Martin, made sure his eyes were on her, and delicately placed the glass on a nearby table, untouched.

"I need to freshen up," she said softly.

Martin didn't reply. Natalie turned away, walking slowly at first, then quicker as she crossed the ballroom. The music trailed behind her, violins weeping gently into the chatter of politicians and socialites. She pushed through the tall swinging door marked *Ladies* and was swallowed into the hush of marble and cool tiles.

The bathroom was lit with soft, warm bulbs that made everything appear gentler than it was. The stalls gleamed. The granite sinks sparkled. A woman at the mirror dabbed powder across her jawbone before slipping out, heels echoing as she left. Natalie stepped into the nearest stall and sat down, the cool porcelain pressing into the back of her thighs. She let out a breath that seemed to shake through her ribs. Her hands went to her temples, fingers pressing lightly. She shut her eyes.

Something wasn't right. Not just tonight. Not just the champagne or the look Martin had given her, part punishment, part warning, part performance. She was tired. But it wasn't the kind of tired a good night's sleep could fix. There was a fraying at the edge of her thoughts, like static under her skin. Was it the medication?

Dr. Feldman had warned her it might cause dizziness. Confusion. Nausea. Still, Natalie couldn't shake the gnawing fear that it was something deeper routed. The way she'd forgotten her car keys last Tuesday. The strange moment at the grocery store when she'd blinked and found herself in the detergent aisle with no memory of walking there. The dream she kept having, her standing on a balcony, and someone screaming from far below. *Jump.*

She hadn't told anyone. Of course she hadn't. Martin would use it against her. He'd remind her of those years. The fog after Eve. The visits to the therapist. The white pills she'd swallowed without question.

*You're not strong enough, this was a mistake, another baby,* he'd said once, in the kitchen. She remembered the way his mouth had twisted around the word *strong*, like it was a joke she wasn't in on.

Natalie's breath came faster now. She pressed her hands flat against her knees and forced herself to think. Focus. She wasn't crazy. She was scared. There was a difference. She stood and left the stall as she straightened her dress and wiped her palms on her thighs. At the basins she reached into her small clutch for her lip balm and applied it with trembling fingers. She dabbed under her eyes with a tissue and a quick check in the mirror revealed her face was flushed, a little drawn, but still arranged.

Still passable. Still his dutiful wife.

She rehearsed the smile. Not too wide. Not too stiff. The kind of smile that said *I'm fine, thank you,* and didn't invite questions. With a deep breath, she left the safety of the bathroom where the music met her like a wave.

She threaded her way back through the ballroom, passing tables of well-heeled donors, clinking glasses, women in sequins tossing their heads back in laughter. Martin was where she'd left him, now flanked by two more colleagues. When he saw her, his mouth curved into the smile he used in press photos as Natalie took her place beside him. She smiled, too. And no one, not even the keenest eyes in the room could see the cracks spiderwebbing beneath her skin.

# 9

Vivienne sat at the head of the table as though it were her rightful throne. Her spine never touched the back of the chair. Her perfectly lacquered nails tapped lightly against the water glass, a rhythmic tick that grated in Natalie's ears like a metronome. The roast lamb Martin had insisted on was going cold.

Thomas sat beside his grandmother, flushed with pride, his elbows on the table despite Natalie's gentle nudge to his side. He was talking animatedly about the day's soccer game, his words punctuated with exaggerated gestures and occasional glances to Vivienne, who gave him her undivided attention as though he were delivering a speech on the Senate floor.

"That's my boy," she said, leaning over to brush his hair from his forehead. "So confident. Just like his father was at that age. You remember your soccer games, Martin?"

Martin, seated across from her, gave a self-satisfied smile and sliced the lamb. "I do."

Natalie watched the exchange in silence, her fork untouched beside her plate. The warmth from the oven and the scent of rosemary hung thick in the room. Eve, small and quiet in her floral dress, sat across from Thomas, swinging her legs beneath the table. Her hair had fallen into her eyes again, but no one reached to tuck it back. She hadn't spoken in twenty minutes and Vivienne hadn't acknowledged her once.

"You must have inherited your speed on the field from your Uncle Leon," Vivienne continued, her gaze fixed on Thomas. "He could outrun any boy in his grade. Still does his morning jogs along the riverbank, rain or shine. That man has discipline."

Natalie forced a smile. "We've not seen Leon in a while and he's always fun and kind to the children."

Vivienne's eyes didn't flick to her. "Kindness is lovely, don't get me wrong, and I'm glad Leon possesses that quality but it's strength that matters in this world. Backbone. Fortitude. Something you and your brother were both born with, Martin."

Martin nodded like a modest prince accepting the praise. Natalie, however, swallowed the bitterness creeping up her throat. She picked up her knife and began cutting into the meat, though her appetite had long since vanished.

"Do you ever see much of Leon these days?" she asked gently, eyes moving from her plate to those of her mother-in-law.

Vivienne's face twitched.

"He works too much for socializing," Martin answered instead. "He's busy building things and that takes up his time. I don't think he even has a girlfriend."

"He's particular, that's why" Vivienne added quickly. "Not like some people who marry the first girl who bats her lashes."

Natalie looked down, cheeks burning. Her fingers gripped her cutlery tighter than they should. She remembered how she and Martin met, at a friend's party just after college. She was still dreaming about grad school, half-employed and scribbling short stories in a journal she kept in her purse. He was already in his residency, pressed shirt, clipped vowels, a wall of certainty she mistook for charm.

He'd told her she was beautiful in a room full of much more beautiful women. That she had "depth," the way someone might describe a vintage wine. He sent her flowers, told her about the house he wanted, the children they'd raise. She'd been twenty-four and uncertain, her parents a state away and her job about to disappear. He made everything feel simple. Until it wasn't.

Vivienne never liked her. Not from the start. She'd shown up to their engagement dinner in a black dress and funereal silence, and by the second glass of wine, had asked Natalie point-blank if she planned to get a job anytime soon. When Natalie stumbled over an answer, Vivienne had smiled like a spider drawing in silk.

"I'll be honest with you," she'd said. "I always imagined Martin would marry someone a bit more ambitious."

Now, years later, she still never let Natalie forget it.

"I've been telling Martin he should think about enrolling Thomas in St. Andrews," Vivienne was saying. "That school does wonders for boys with leadership potential. And he's certainly got that. Don't you, sweetheart?"

Thomas beamed. Eve reached for her fork, eyes downcast.

Natalie watched her daughter's shoulders hunch inward, a quiet withdrawal.

"Eve did very well on her spelling test this week," she said, too quickly, as though pulling the words from a well. "Twenty out of twenty."

Vivienne's lips barely twitched. "That's nice, dear."

And then the conversation inevitably moved on so Natalie reached under the table, closed her hand gently around Eve's, and gave it a soft squeeze. The girl looked up at her, her dark brown eyes glossy and solemn. So different from the icy blue of

Martin's. Of Vivienne's. Of Thomas's. Eve squeezed back, then turned back to her plate.

Vivienne, oblivious or uninterested, was now recounting some story about Leon winning a county math prize in eighth grade. Her voice took on a dreamy reverence when she spoke of him, as if his achievements somehow mended the hole Bobby Lane had left when he'd collapsed on the kitchen floor one spring afternoon, hand clutching his chest, Vivienne's name still forming on his tongue as the blood slipped away. Or so she said.

"I've been meaning to get some photos framed of Bobby," she said now, passing the gravy boat to Martin. "He hated getting his picture taken, but I found one from our honeymoon. He looked so strong. So proud."

Natalie's knife slipped, clinking against the edge of her plate. She caught Martin's eye. It was unreadable while Vivienne poured herself a second glass of wine, her rings catching the light like small weapons.

"You know," she went on, "he once lifted a tractor off a neighbor's dog. Crushed its hind legs. The vet said it was hopeless, but Bobby wouldn't hear it. And that dog lived another six years. That's the kind of determination and wisdom I admire."

Natalie cleared her throat. "He certainly left an impression."

Vivienne finally turned her eyes toward her.

"He left a legacy. A family of strong accomplished men to carry the mantle and he taught his sons all he knew. Which is more than most men do these days, present company excepted of course."

Martin laughed and Natalie felt her hand curl into a fist on her lap. She wanted to scream. She wanted to pick up the gravy boat and throw it through the French doors. But instead, she reached for the breadbasket and passed it to her son.

"Would you like another roll, Thomas?"

"No," he said, wrinkling his nose. "They're dry."

Martin chuckled and took one anyway.

The moment passed and once again the clink of cutlery and the rustle of napkins filled the room. Another evening. Another display. Another grueling ordeal. Natalie glanced across the table again. Eve was still eating quietly, slowly, the only one who hadn't insulted the meal. Her plate nearly clean. Natalie caught her eye again. That same quiet look, half-curious, half-resigned. And Natalie wondered, not for the first time, how this child who was so soft and open could have come from a family like this. How she had survived in the shadow of Vivienne's icy praise and Martin's expectations. Maybe she wouldn't. Unless Natalie did something.

She smiled at her daughter. A real smile this time and under the tablecloth, she squeezed her hand again, a little tighter and as though spotting the moment between mother and daughter, Thomas kicked Eve under the table. Not a hard kick, just a jab but enough to make her yelp and drop her fork, which clattered too loud on the plate.

"Jesus, Eve," he muttered. "Do you have to be so clumsy?"

"Thomas," Natalie said sharply, barely above a whisper.

Vivienne didn't look up from her wine glass. Martin continued carving meat like it was any other Tuesday.

"She kicked me first," Thomas said, not missing a beat, not even looking at his sister. "She's always trying to get attention."

Eve's face flushed crimson. She reached for her fork again with trembling fingers, eyes downcast, trying not to cry. Her bottom lip trembled, and her shoulders curled inward like a folding flower.

"She didn't kick you," Natalie said, more firmly this time, turning to her son. "Don't lie."

Thomas shrugged, unapologetic. "She did."

"That's enough," Martin cut in, his voice clean and final. "Eat."

That was it. End of discussion. Natalie stared at him across the table. Martin didn't meet her gaze. He was spooning green beans onto his plate like a man with a hundred more important things on his mind. Thomas resumed eating, smug in his silence. Eve, silent as a mouse, picked at her vegetables without raising her head again.

Vivienne reached over and patted Thomas's arm. "He's just got spirit. You can't punish a boy for being assertive and taking the lead. Martin was exactly the same at that age, stubborn as anything but unafraid. The world respects that."

Natalie bit the inside of her cheek until she tasted copper. She wanted to say it. She wanted to scream it. He's nine. He's mean and cruel and you're ignoring and excusing and letting him become just like his vile father and your vile dead husband. But her mouth refused to open. Her voice had learned to stay buried, tucked behind her teeth like a frightened thing.

She glanced at Eve again, who now looked less like a little girl and more like someone trying to disappear. Natalie reached under the table, slid her fingers across, but Eve didn't reach back this time. Her small hands stayed folded in her lap.

Martin cleared his throat. "I've been thinking," he began, placing his fork down, fingers tented. "Our anniversary is coming up. Ten years."

Natalie's stomach tightened.

"Maybe we should go to the lake house. A few days. Just the two of us."

The lake house. The place he'd inherited after Bobby died, all dark timber and worn rugs and taxidermy eyes watching from the walls. They went every summer and Natalie hated it.

"I think that's a wonderful idea," Vivienne said before

Natalie could respond. "You two need time away from everyday things."

Natalie smiled politely, her mind racing. "Yes, that could be nice."

Martin turned to his mother. "Would you be all right watching the kids?"

Vivienne gave a dismissive wave. "Of course. I practically raised Thomas anyway."

Natalie's throat caught. "I'm not sure..." she began.

Martin interrupted. "It's settled, then. A weekend. Two nights at least. We'll leave Friday morning and be back early Sunday evening."

Natalie blinked. "I thought maybe we'd take the children. They enjoy the lake."

"I don't think you should this time," Vivienne said coolly. "You and Martin need to reconnect. Like a date night."

Natalie looked at Eve again, who hadn't spoken since the jab. Who sat still, as if her silence might make her invisible.

"Yes," Martin added, nodding toward his mother. "It's important to prioritize the marriage. We need to celebrate. Ten years. That's a milestone."

Natalie offered another brittle smile. She didn't remember the last time they celebrated anything. Their last anniversary had been spent in silence after she forgot to buy champagne. The one before that, Martin had taken a late-night emergency call, one she later suspected hadn't come from the clinic at all. She hadn't asked. And she wasn't asking now.

Instead, she nodded. "That sounds...lovely."

Thomas scoffed. "You always say that. 'Lovely.' It's such a stupid girly word."

"Don't speak to me like that Thomas, please remember I'm your mother and due some respect," she said, sharper than she meant to.

He shrugged. "I didn't say anything bad."

Martin narrowed his eyes. "Thomas, enough."

But his tone lacked heat. There was no reprimand, just a perfunctory flick of disapproval. A performance.

Vivienne laughed softly. "He's just being playful. He's definitely got your sense of humor, Martin."

Natalie said nothing. She could feel herself blinking slower, as if time was thickening around her. Her limbs were heavy, her breath shallow. Her skin felt too tight. The lake house. Just the two of them. Her mind drifted to the USB drive she hadn't dared plug into the laptop. The pain in her stomach that hadn't returned, yet. The prescription bottle in the back of her drawer.

She turned back to her plate and forced herself to eat.

Across the table, Eve picked up a piece of bread and took a small bite. Natalie tried again to reach her foot forward, a silent nudge of affection. But Eve had curled into herself completely. She'd retreated. Like Natalie had. A long time ago.

"More wine, Natalie?" Vivienne asked with an arched brow, already reaching for the bottle.

"No, thank you," Natalie said quickly. "I've had enough."

Vivienne poured herself another glass, eyes cool and unreadable.

"Suit yourself."

Natalie sat back in her chair, her hands folded neatly in her lap. She could see the reflection of the chandelier in the wineglass. Distorted, elegant, dangerous. In a few weeks' time, she'd be alone in the woods with her husband. A weekend away. Ten years of marriage. Time to "reconnect." She smiled again, teeth clenched behind closed lips. It was already too late to say no and even if she did, would anybody hear her?

# 10

*Lake Wallenpaupack, Pennsylvania – July 4th, 2019*

The water shimmered, the sun was riding low on the horizon. It had been a long, bright day. Completely cloudless, the sky too blue to feel real and the type people put in photo frames. The kind of day you're meant to remember fondly.

Natalie stood on the wraparound porch of the lake house, her arms crossed loosely over her chest. The faint scent of charcoal and singed meat still hung in the air. Her ears rang with the echo of laughter, of distant firecrackers popping like champagne corks.

The children were tumbling down the small hill that sloped from the backyard to the lake. Thomas had grass stains on both knees and a smear of ketchup down his shirt, but he was beaming, arms flung wide like he could catch the wind. Eve was close behind him, her pigtails flapping like little flags as she squealed. Leon jogged after them with a goofy grin and a sparkler still lit in one hand.

"Go easy, Eve!" Leon called, his voice easy and warm. "Don't let your brother knock you into the lake again!"

Natalie smiled. The real kind, not the kind she wore at home. It surprised her how easy it felt here. That day had been a good one. Or that's how she used to remember it.

Martin had insisted they leave the city early, to avoid traffic. Natalie had spent the morning packing snacks, swimwear, sunblock, coloring books, a first-aid kit she hoped she wouldn't need. The lake house had been Bobby's, and now it was Martin's, but it never really felt like hers.

It was all heavy wood and darker rooms. Stag heads mounted above the fireplace, outdated furniture that smelled of damp. But the outside, the lake, the trees, the rocky little beach where the kids hunted frogs, that part she could love.

Mercifully, Bobby and Vivienne were at home, but Leon had joined them that summer. He'd driven in as a surprise, just him and his overnight bag and that big lopsided grin that reminded her there were still men who didn't measure their worth by silence and control. He was eight years younger than Martin, born when Vivienne thought she couldn't get pregnant again. An builder, smart but gentle, never married, never hard-edged like his brother.

He brought fireworks in his trunk and marshmallows for the kids. He played board games and didn't let Thomas cheat but didn't make him feel bad about trying, either. He showed Eve how to tie a bowline knot with pink rope. He called Natalie "Nat," and she didn't mind.

They'd all eaten burgers from the grill that evening, Leon in an apron that read *Kiss the Cook* in tomato-red letters, the kids wearing glow stick necklaces, laughing with mustard on their chins.

Martin had been in a good mood, or his version of one. Detached, but not cruel. He let Leon handle most of the entertainment. Natalie remembered how Martin kept refilling his glass with bourbon and lime, not saying much but watching. Always watching.

She remembered smiling too much, the way she always did when Leon was around. It made Martin tense sometimes, but she couldn't help it. Leon made her relax. That night, they all walked down to the dock to watch the fireworks. The children lay back on a plaid blanket, mouths wide in awe as explosions bloomed in the sky. Reds, purples, oranges like bursting suns.

Leon sat cross-legged with a beer in one hand, Eve curled into his side. Thomas kicked at the dock planks with his heels, counting under his breath.

Natalie stood a little apart, the wood warm under her bare feet. She'd felt dizzy earlier, a strange lightness behind her eyes. She'd blamed the sun, or the stress of travel, or maybe the two ciders she'd allowed herself with dinner. She hadn't told anyone. She rarely did.

But now, years later, as she stood in her kitchen with the memory blooming hot behind her eyes, she remembered something new. She'd woken the next morning in bed, no recollection of how she got there or who tucked the children in, and with a bruise on her hip the size of a plum. She couldn't explain it.

There'd been another on her shoulder. Faint but tender to the touch. And the morning after that, one under her knee. She asked Martin, half-joking, if she'd fallen or bumped into something during the night.

"You do toss like a tornado," he'd said, smirking over his coffee. "You probably tripped over your own feet going to the bathroom."

But she'd never gotten up that night. She was sure of it. Or thought she was. The memories were cloudy. Like she'd dipped her mind in lake water and shaken it dry. And now, when she tried to piece it all together, the seams didn't line up.

She remembered Martin's glass always full. His voice lower, slower that weekend. She remembered that when she'd lain down on the dock beside him later, her body had felt heavy, and her head fuzzy. She remembered the stars shifting above her, smearing into strange patterns.

She remembered Leon looking concerned.

"You okay, Nat?"

She'd nodded. Told him she was just tired. But something was wrong. Now, in retrospect, something was deeply wrong. Natalie rubbed her wrist absently, standing by the stove in the present, miles and years away from that lake house night. Her skin still knew things she hadn't admitted out loud.

She went back to the window. Outside, the swing in the backyard creaked in the breeze. It was almost dusk now. In a few weeks, she'd be back at that lake house. Alone with Martin. Just the two of them.

The memory of the bruise on her shoulder bloomed again. She could almost feel it now.

Her hand slipped down to her hip. Nothing there. Not yet. But her body remembered how her most private places had ached. And this time, there would be no Leon. No children. No witnesses. Just water, trees, and her husband. Natalie closed her eyes and tried to breathe.

The fireworks had been beautiful that night. But something had exploded inside her too. And it had never quite stopped smoldering just like the memory of the day Bobby Lane died.

*Family Home, Haverford Township – November 2022*

It had been a bleak, sunless afternoon and the house had felt dim, like someone had turned down the brightness on the world. Maybe it had been a sign. Natalie had just finished folding laundry, a basket of warm clothes balanced on her hip, when the phone rang.

She recognized the sound of Vivienne's voice immediately, sharp and deliberate, every word clipped as though emotions were beneath her. Natalie stood in the kitchen doorway, basket at her feet, as Martin took the call in the hallway, one hand braced against the wall, his body going rigid.

She couldn't hear Vivienne's exact words, just the tone. Controlled. Cool. Efficient. When Martin lowered the phone, he looked like something vital inside him had snapped. His face turned ghostly pale, his lips slack, eyes too wide.

"What is it?" Natalie asked, stepping forward.

Martin's mouth moved before sound came. "My dad. He's dead."

Natalie blinked. "What?"

"Heart attack," he said, voice dull and robotic. "He collapsed at home. Mom found him."

She moved to place a hand on his arm, but he brushed past her, walking straight into the living room like he'd forgotten where he was. He stood in front of the fireplace, fists clenched at his sides, his breath shallow and ragged.

"She said he was on the kitchen floor," Martin said to the air. "Said he'd been trying to open a jar of pickles."

Natalie almost laughed out of sheer discomfort and nerves. But Martin wasn't joking. His mouth trembled, and then his whole body did the same, and then he dropped to the couch like a man shot where he remained, inert. Worried by Martin's reaction Natalie had called his mother and asked if she could call over, saying Martin needed her and then they could grieve together. And still Vivienne didn't come.

No suitcase. No plans. No sudden arrival at their door in tears. She didn't ask to stay. Didn't even suggest they come to her.

Instead, she texted later that evening with details about the will and arrangements, saying there'd be a closed-casket funeral the following Thursday and that Bobby had always preferred things simple. Martin didn't question it. But Natalie did.

There was something off about all of it. The tone, the distance, the lack of any visible grief from a woman who still couldn't mention Bobby's name without attaching a glowing adjective. Even Martin's breakdown seemed... strained, like he'd rehearsed what it should look like. Rage, sobbing, isolation and he cycled through them like a script.

He barely spoke to her for three days, shuffling around the house like a ghost, snapping at the children, silent at meals. Natalie remembered trying to comfort him, stroking his back in bed as he curled away from her, his shoulders hitching with silent sobs that never quite sounded real.

She hated herself for doubting. But she did. Because Natalie had never liked Bobby Lane and was surprised anyone else did. He was a small-framed man, physically unremarkable, just over five foot seven, slim to the point of frail in his last years but he had a presence that filled any room he entered. He'd always reminded Natalie of a chess master: calculating, smug, patient in that way that made your skin crawl. She couldn't recall an occasion where he'd raised his voice, but he never had to.

She remembered the first time she met him, the way his eyes had traveled over her with clinical detachment, not hungry exactly, but dissecting. The way he smiled like he already knew something about her that she didn't. And he always stood too close. At Christmas dinners, he'd lean in when she passed him a plate, brushing her hand longer than necessary. When she nursed Eve as a baby, he always managed to walk into the room at the wrong moment, his eyes landing on her chest before drifting away like a bird pretending not to see a crumb.

Martin didn't notice. Or maybe he did and didn't want to.

Vivienne never intervened either. She would hum through meals, refill Bobby's wine glass before her own, laugh at his dry, barbed jokes.

Once, when Natalie had asked her tentatively if Bobby was ever harsh when no one else was around, Vivienne had just smiled and said, "You learn to adjust to strong men. It's a gift, not a burden."

After Bobby died, Natalie didn't shed a tear. And she hated herself for that too. She tried to picture him in that kitchen, hunched over a jar, lips twisting into one of his smirks, then collapsing with a thud. She imagined him lying there, tiny and powerless, staring at the ceiling with glassy eyes. And a guilty thrill shot through her. She told herself it was relief.

Because after he was gone, she didn't have to pretend anymore. Didn't have to navigate the strange dance of evasion, the tightening in her chest every time he visited, the way she kept Eve within arm's reach whenever he was in the room.

There was a moment a flicker of a second when she looked at her daughter's face after the funeral and thought, *she feels it too.* The relief. Because even though Eve had never said anything, she had clung tighter to Natalie whenever Bobby was around. She'd stiffened in his arms when he'd kissed the crown of her head. She'd gone mute the few times he offered to babysit alone. And now, months after his passing, she laughed louder. Slept deeper.

"Do you think the children will miss him?" Natalie had asked Martin once, gesturing toward Eve and Thomas.

"*She's* too young to understand, but I think Thomas will," he said.

But Natalie wasn't so sure because Thomas behaved like he didn't care, either.

That day, after the news came, Martin had spent hours pacing the house. He pulled down old photo albums. Opened a bottle of wine he would usually reserve for guests. By the time evening fell, he'd gone through half of it.

Natalie found him in the den, cross-legged on the floor, holding a faded photo of Bobby standing in front of a fishing boat, one hand shielding his eyes from the sun.

"He taught me everything, he was the best man I've ever known," Martin mumbled.

She sat beside him.

"He wasn't perfect, though, none of us are," she said gently.

Martin turned to her then, something wild in his eyes. "Don't say that. Don't ever say that about him."

Natalie didn't speak again. Later that night, when the children were in bed, Martin touched her for the first time in days. It wasn't tender. It wasn't affectionate or seeking comfort. It was something else, possessive and punishing, a silent war against grief and her thoughtless words. She let him, body stiff as driftwood, staring at the ceiling, mouth pressed shut. Afterward, he rolled over and slept like the dead while Natalie had gone to the bathroom and looked at herself in the mirror for a long time. She didn't like the woman who stared back.

Now, months later, she still thought about the call. About Vivienne's eerie calm. About the details that didn't sit right: no autopsy, no visitation, no family gathering apart from the funeral. Just the sudden closing of a door on someone's life.

# 11

Natalie's suitcase sat half-packed on the bed, a confused mess of rolled cardigans and damp-palmed indecision. Every time she zipped it up, she found herself unzipping it again, as if forgetting something might somehow buy her more time. There was a knot in her stomach that hadn't loosened since morning.

In the hallway, Martin whistled as he brought down a duffel bag, his mood unnervingly buoyant. She could hear the weight of his boots on the stairs, the familiar creak of the third step that was always worse in humidity. Outside, the car doors thudded open and shut in a rhythm that felt final. Like punctuation marks on a sentence that she hadn't finished writing yet.

He was excited. Of course he was. Natalie wasn't. Three hours north. Lake Wallenpaupack. A weekend alone. Ten years of marriage, ten years of whittled silence and inching dread tied up with a bow of celebration.

Downstairs, Vivienne's voice drifted up, syrupy sweet and full of self-importance. "Thomas, darling, come here and let me look at you. Honestly, how do you grow every week?"

Natalie exhaled through her teeth and forced herself to fold another pair of socks.

Eve was in the corner of the bedroom, sitting cross-legged on the braided rug with her threadbare bear in one hand and a picture book open on her lap. She hadn't spoken much all morning. Her small body seemed to shrink deeper into itself with each hour, like she already knew something was wrong but didn't have the words to explain it.

Natalie watched her daughter quietly from the bed. Eve was still in her pajamas, little rabbits on her leggings, a pale-yellow top that hung off her slight shoulders. She looked up occasionally with that too-old gaze, like she was checking the mood of the room.

"Sweetie," Natalie said gently, kneeling beside her. "Mummy and Daddy will only be gone for two nights. Just two. You'll be good for Grandma, won't you?"

Eve nodded, silent, clutching the bear to her chest. Natalie leaned in, kissed her temple, and smelled strawberry shampoo and something less pleasant beneath it, anxiety.

"She'll be fine," Martin called from the hallway, his voice cutting through the moment like a blade. "Vivienne raised two boys, for Christ's sake. She can handle a weekend with our two."

Natalie stood, smoothing the front of her jeans. "I wasn't saying she couldn't."

"You didn't have to."

He passed through the room with a garment bag slung over one shoulder, his cologne trailing after him. The newer scent. Not one she remembered him owning until recently.

Natalie's hands flexed at her sides, agitation and nerves making her stall. Downstairs, Vivienne laughed loudly at something Thomas said. The sound made Natalie's stomach tighten further. Vivienne always laughed at Thomas's jokes, no matter how inappropriate or dull. She encouraged his brashness, told him he had the confidence of a man already.

Natalie feared what kind of man he might become under that kind of praise.

The last of her things, the slim notebook, her toothbrush, travel-sized face cream, went into her bag. She zipped it up slowly, trying not to look at Eve, because it was too hard to walk away from her when she looked that small and defenseless, but she managed it, just.

In the foyer, Vivienne stood in a pale blue sweater set, lipstick perfect, hair shellacked into its usual bouffant. She greeted Natalie with a chilly nod that passed for politeness.

"You'll remember Eve's allergy meds?" Natalie asked, her voice clipped.

Vivienne raised a brow. "Of course I will. I'm not senile."

"She needs them with dinner, not just lunch."

"I know how to care for a child, Natalie. I did it without Google and organic snacks or your advice."

Natalie bit the inside of her cheek and said nothing. Vivienne reached out and adjusted Thomas's collar like he was a museum artifact. Thomas rolled his eyes and swatted her hand, but she only chuckled and swatted back with affection.

"I swear, you get more handsome every day," she said, cupping his chin briefly.

Natalie moved toward the door, suitcase bumping awkwardly along behind her. Outside Martin already stood beside the SUV, loading the last of the bags into the trunk. The sun glinted off the chrome edges, bright and too bold. The air was thick with sticky heat that settled on your skin and didn't move.

He smiled when he saw her, that smile he reserved for the public but it didn't reach his eyes.

"You ready?" he asked.

Natalie glanced back at the house. Eve stood just inside the front door, still clutching her bear, watching. Not crying, not waving. Just watching. Thomas had already disappeared, probably to his video games or backyard target practice with sticks and a fence post.

"Yeah," she said finally. "Ready."

Martin opened the passenger door for her with exaggerated chivalry and played to the audience. She slid in, the leather hot against her thighs. He walked around the car, climbed in, and cranked the AC.

"God, I love summer," he said, backing down the drive. "Country music, the lake, cold beers at sunset. Don't you?"

Natalie didn't answer. She knew what came next. Always the same. The gravel crunching under tires, the turn onto the long road north, and the sound of twanging guitars and drawling voices on his curated playlist. She used to pretend to like it, used to sway her head slightly, mouth the words to please him. Now she didn't bother.

The music started, predictably upbeat. He tapped the steering wheel, whistling along. The rumble of the engine settled into the rhythm of escape or was it entrapment? Natalie shifted in her seat, adjusting the seatbelt across her chest. The tightness in her gut hadn't gone away. If anything, it had grown, spreading to her spine and deep within her lungs. Something about this trip felt different. Not because it was their tenth anniversary. Not even because it was just the two of them. But because for the first time she realized that now they were alone she had no control over the next 72 hours. None.

Back at the house, Vivienne would be tucking Eve in, likely skipping bedtime stories, insisting they weren't necessary. Thomas would be spoiled and praised. Eve would get ignored, corrected, folded down like linen and pressed into silence. Natalie's hand hovered near the window switch. She almost rolled it down. Almost let the wind slap her across the face, shake her out of this daze. But she didn't. Instead, she folded her hands in her lap and watched the rows of houses blur past, the familiar fading into the unknown.

Beside her, Martin turned up the volume. The music grew louder, dumber.

"Hey," he said, grinning. "Try to smile a little, huh? It's our anniversary."

Natalie nodded. Smiled. And felt the knot in her stomach tighten like a noose.

The drive was exactly what Natalie had expected. Three solid hours of braying country music, punctuated only by Martin's occasional humming and the slap of his hand on the steering wheel. He didn't speak much, but he didn't need to. The music filled the silence, soaked up the air between them, left no space for small talk. Natalie stared out the window as trees grew thicker, the scenery bleeding from suburban developments to something more feral. The last hour was just forest and the occasional flicker of a deer disappearing into the brush.

By the time they reached the cabin, dusk was creeping up around the lake. The sky was a bruised lavender, the moon already hanging low like a watchful eye. Natalie felt it before she saw it, the familiarity of the place wrapping around her ribs like a cold hand. She hadn't been back since before Bobby died. Since before she started keeping secrets from herself.

The cabin stood crooked at the edge of the water, surrounded by a mess of pine and birch, its dark wooden slats already disappearing into the blue hush of night. Martin pulled the SUV into the gravel patch beside the porch and cut the engine. Silence swooped in with unnerving swiftness.

Natalie unbuckled slowly, her body stiff from the drive. Her ears rang with the echo of twanging guitars. She hated that music. Had always hated it. But she'd smiled through it for years, mouthing along to the choruses like a good wife.

Martin popped the trunk and slung his bag over one

shoulder. "Just like I remember it," he said, stretching. "Smells like pine and testosterone."

Natalie said nothing. To her, the cabin always smelled like mildew and dust and something faintly animal. Inside, her memories were confirmed as the air was stale and cool, tinged with the unmistakable scent of a place left closed too long. Natalie stepped into the living room, her shoes creaking on the floorboards. The old plaid sofa sat under its dust cover like a mummy. The fireplace was black with soot. A row of old VHS tapes still lined the bookshelf beside it, and the TV looked like it belonged in a soap opera from the early 2000s.

Martin dropped their bags in the corner and moved to the wall, flicking the light switch. Nothing. He tried again. Still nothing.

"Breaker must be off," he muttered and headed toward the back door.

Natalie stood in the darkening room, arms wrapped around herself. The quiet here wasn't like the quiet at home. This was deeper, heavier. Even the trees outside seemed to be holding their breath.

After a few minutes, Martin returned, brushing his hands on his jeans. "Well," he said cheerfully, "we've got ourselves a visitor. Little bastard chewed clean through the fuse box. I saw the wires. Shredded."

Natalie blinked at him. "So we don't have power?"

"For now? No." He shrugged. "No lights. No fridge. But I'll head into town, grab some torches and candles. Make it romantic." He winked.

Romantic. She almost laughed. But something about the forced sweetness in his voice made her stomach clench. He hadn't been sweet in a long time. Not like this. Not since the early years, when he still brushed her hair behind her ears and let her choose the restaurant. Back then, his attention had felt like sunlight. Now it felt like surveillance.

"I'll be twenty minutes," he said, already heading for the door. "The town's not far. You stay here, get cozy. I'll bring back wine too."

Natalie opened her mouth to protest, but he was already stepping into the twilight. The car engine sputtered to life. Its red taillights cast long, thin beams across the front yard before disappearing into the trees. And just like that, she was alone and the silence dropped like a curtain.

Natalie stood in the doorway, watching the spot where the SUV had vanished. The lake was visible beyond the trees, a wide smear of silver under the moon. The surface barely moved. Not even a ripple. The air was thick with moisture and mosquitoes. She could hear them, the soft drone just above her ear, a sound you couldn't slap away. The woods made no sound at all. No birds. No wind. Just the brittle tension of waiting.

Natalie stepped off the porch barefoot and crossed the yard to the dock. It groaned beneath her weight as she walked to the edge. The water lapped gently below. She could see her reflection in the surface, distorted, pale, eyes large.

Her stomach twisted. This wasn't just dread. It was memory. Her body knew this place, and not kindly. But what did it know and why was it remembering now? She sat down slowly, tucking her knees to her chest. She was sure that when Martin had looked at her in the car, it was like he was proud of her. As though she was a well-trained pet performing her trick. The smile, the clothes he'd chosen, the silence. She'd worn all of it obediently.

And now he was playing the part of attentive husband, fetching torches, bringing wine. Acting like he still loved her, when what he loved was the illusion of her. Natalie looked up at the cabin. The windows were dark, like greedy open mouths.

She thought of Eve. Small, solemn-eyed Eve with her battered bear and her quiet strength. She thought of how Vivienne had hovered around Thomas all morning, ignoring Eve unless she needed her to do something. Natalie hated herself for leaving them. She should have refused. She should have said *no.* But Martin didn't accept *no.* He never had.

Something cracked in the woods, brittle and clear. A branch? An animal? Her heart jolted.

She stood quickly, arms prickling, and hurried back toward the porch. The stairs creaked under her feet. The door stuck a little in the frame as she shoved it open. The stale air rushed to meet her again.

Inside, after feeling her way around the room she found a candle in the drawer by the sink, a box of matches shoved behind some loose batteries. She lit it with shaking fingers. The flame flickered high, throwing jagged shadows across the walls. Everything looked warped and unfamiliar.

She sank into the old armchair, pulling a scratchy throw over her lap, wafting the smell of damp and mothballs. Her ears strained for the sound of tires on gravel. But there was nothing.

No Martin. Not yet. She reached into her bag and pulled out her notebook. The one she never let him see. Turning her body towards the window so the moonlight rested on the page, she paused, her pencil hovering above the paper, hand trembling.

*August 3rd.*

*Here we are again. I can feel the lake watching and I'm spooked. I don't know why I'm so afraid, but I am. My skin, my senses, know something my mind won't say out loud.*

She paused. Wrote again.

*He's being kind. Too kind. Like someone mimicking human behavior and I don't recognize this man. And I don't think I want to.*

The wind shifted. The candle flame danced. Outside, through the window the trees stood motionless, tall and waiting. The lake lay still and silver.

Natalie closed her notebook and whispered to the quiet, "Please let this just be a normal weekend."

But even as the words left her mouth, something deep inside knew better.

# 12

The sound of tires crunching on gravel snapped Natalie out of her trance. She'd been staring at the candle so long she'd begun to hallucinate movement in the flame. Shadows in the shape of fingers. The tick of the old wall clock behind her had become unbearable, a metronome of dread.

Martin returned like a man arriving home from battle, cheerful and loaded with supplies, slamming the SUV door with theatrical flair.

He entered the cabin with a breath of outside air and a box of groceries in his arms, the yellow light from the porch briefly haloing him in something almost divine. For a second, Natalie saw him as he must have wanted her to – provider, husband, protector. It felt fake, like a performance he'd been rehearsing on the drive.

"Power's still going to be out," he said, setting the bags on the counter. "But I got candles, matches, battery lanterns. And food. A feast, actually. You hungry?"

Natalie smiled thinly and nodded. Her throat felt too dry to speak.

He unpacked with unusual efficiency. Within minutes, the

table was set with paper napkins, mismatched plates, and a twinkling line of votives along the windowsill. He grilled steaks in a skillet over the gas range, humming along to a song she didn't recognize. His face glowed with candlelight, strangely youthful in the gloam. Like the version of Martin she'd once fallen for.

He poured them each a glass of red wine, the dark liquid sloshing richly in the glasses. He held his up toward her, waiting.

"To ten years," he said. "Still standing."

She raised hers, hesitated, clinked. Still standing, she thought, but with a hairline fracture no one could see. The wine was heavy on her tongue. Not quite the vintage he used to buy her, but familiar enough to set her on edge. She set the glass down after a sip and nudged her plate closer.

Martin carved his steak with surgical precision. He made small talk, light and harmless, about the weather, traffic, some ridiculous lawsuit one of his colleagues had to fend off.

Then, predictably, the conversation pivoted and as though invoking the memory of a saint, Bobby's name entered the room.

"You know, my father loved this place," he said, slicing through a baked potato. "He'd come here alone sometimes, just to think. Said the lake cleared his mind."

Natalie chewed slowly, the meat like rubber in her mouth. She nodded, waiting.

Martin grinned. "He was the most disciplined man I ever met. Firm, but fair. He could walk into a room and make you sit up straighter just by breathing."

*And make women hold their breath until he left,* Natalie thought. She didn't remember Bobby as awe-inspiring. She remembered the way his eyes lingered too long on her legs when she crossed them. The way his voice hardened when he didn't get his way. He had a habit of gripping her shoulder too tightly, always under the guise of reassurance. She'd hated him. Still did, even in death.

Martin continued. "He taught me that men don't need to explain themselves. That if you want something, you take it. That's how he built his practice. How he raised us. Hell, Leon would've been a wreck without him."

Natalie glanced up. "Leon turned out okay."

Martin snorted. "Because Dad whipped him into shape. You don't remember how soft he used to be. Always crying, always clinging to Mom."

She flinched slightly. She remembered a boy who used to sneak crackers to the dog under the table and who once helped Eve fix the zipper on her coat without telling anyone. A boy who had grown into a man who smiled without baring teeth.

The second he'd swallowed the last mouthful of his steak, Martin stood abruptly and cleared his plate before she could offer. He disappeared into the kitchen and returned with another bottle of her favorite wine. The label made her chest tighten.

"You found that in town?"

He smiled, pouring her a generous glass. "Special occasion. You deserve it."

Natalie took the glass slowly, her hand trembling. She felt like a marionette. The strings were pulled and she danced. She sipped once, then set the glass down. Her stomach twisted with guilt at leaving her children and disgust at herself for being so weak. The warmth of the wine threatened to curdle in her throat.

Martin raised his own glass. "This... This is nice, isn't it? Just us. No kids. No nagging."

He said it like a joke. A wink. But the word *nagging* landed like a slap. Natalie offered a faint smile and focused on her fork. She barely touched the salad he had assembled, though he'd stacked it artfully, drizzled something vinaigrette-like across the top. He even lit a candle in a jar with a label that read *Cedar Spice.* It stank of fake nostalgia.

The light flickered against the window behind him and he looked strangely golden in the dark.

"You used to love this place," he said, his tone softening. "Remember the Fourth? Leon grilled, and the kids stayed up to watch the fireworks."

She nodded. "I remember."

What she remembered more was the blackout that followed. The bruises she couldn't place. The ache in her limbs when she woke up with no memory of falling asleep and now the nagging doubt that the same thing had happened before.

Martin lifted his glass to drink again then went to fetch dessert. When he wasn't looking, Natalie slid her wineglass to the edge of the table and poured the wine into the wooden salad bowl. Then she stood up, took her plate and glass to the kitchen, Martin smiling as they passed.

Once she was alone, she turned the tap quietly and poured the wine down the sink. The burgundy liquid spiraled into the drain, vanishing with a hollow glug before she tipped the soggy red salad into the trash can and scraped the rest of her food on top. Her hands shook as she rinsed the glass and refilled it with water.

When she returned to the table, Martin returned to talking about his father. His fingers traced the rim of his wineglass, face dreamy with tales of sailing and fishing, hunting and skinning, campfires and legacy. Natalie sat and nodded at the right times, her smile practiced. She felt like she was watching herself from across the room and rated her performance as amateur.

She thought of the STI diagnosis. The shame of it. She wondered who the other woman had been. Or even how many. She wondered if he ever looked at them the way he used to look at her. And if they believed they were special. If they, too, were now sitting in dark rooms with flickering candles and a man playing make-believe. Or taking pills to fight an infection that they didn't deserve.

Natalie pressed her hands into her lap and prayed that the night would end without incident. But something in the way Martin smiled, too charming, too calm, made her feel like the night hadn't really started yet. And while Martin waxed lyrical, his voice slowly fading like a backing track to a boring movie, a memory began to surface, of a weekend at the cabin that for some reason she'd buried deep, but it was still there, waiting to be remembered.

*Inside the Cabin by the Lake – April 2021*

The cabin reeked of firewood that had long since turned musty. It was April, but Lake Wallenpaupack still held the breath of winter in its ripples, and the trees around the property clung to their dead brown leaves like tawdry secrets. It was the first time the family had reunited since the pandemic had slithered in and made strangers of everyone.

Vivienne stood by the door like a statue wrapped in powder-blue wool, her face entirely obscured by a KN95 mask, a second scarf wrapped over that. She wore gloves too, latex ones, and Natalie could hear them crinkle every time she adjusted her glasses or waved a hand in the air.

"I won't sit indoors," she'd said upon arrival, as if daring someone to challenge her. "I won't risk exposure."

Natalie hadn't even tried to argue even though she wondered why she'd even bothered to come. No one did. Not even Martin.

Outside, Thomas and Eve tumbled on the patchy grass, voices shrill with excitement, limbs coated in mud. They were too young to understand social distancing or the intensity of a grandmother's paranoia. And Natalie had been glad for it. Let them be kids, she thought. Let someone have a normal afternoon.

Inside, the atmosphere felt anything but normal. Vivienne perched stiffly in a deck chair on the porch that she'd demanded be brought closer so she wouldn't have to "contaminate" herself on the sofa. She kept her coat on. When she spoke, it was through the fabric of two layers and into the empty air, as though she were dictating to actors on a stage.

"Leon," she said, snapping her fingers without turning her head. "You're too close."

Leon, who was already standing six feet away, backed up another two. "Right," he said mildly. "Of course."

Leon's eyes met Natalie's and offered a sheepish, conspiratorial smile. He was the only person who ever seemed to read the room like she did. Unlike Martin, Leon was tall and wide across the chest, with thick, capable-looking hands and a softness to his movements that reminded Natalie of childhood blankets and overripe peaches. He had the kind of demeanor that made you feel like he'd always be able to carry the heavier box, patch the leaky ceiling, know how to fix the jammed back door. But there was a gentleness there, too, a quiet that didn't scream for attention.

Vivienne hardly acknowledged him. At one point, when he offered to get her a cup of tea, she waved him off like he was a waiter at the wrong table, saying she'd brought a Thermos and would drink from that. Meanwhile, Bobby had stationed himself near the fire though it wasn't lit, and complained about the draft like it personally offended him.

"What kind of idiot designed this place?" he said to no one. "Crosswinds all over. Should've had this whole wall knocked down and done it properly myself years ago."

Vivienne didn't react. She rarely did when Bobby barked.

Her silence wasn't submissive; it was strategic. Like she'd transcended reacting to men like Bobby and had instead chosen to haunt them with her presence alone.

But that didn't stop Bobby from sneering. "You hear me, woman?" he added, without looking at her.

"I hear you," she replied, as though she were being summoned from some place far beneath the surface.

Martin chuckled quietly and shook his head, as if his father was just a lovable grump. He handed Natalie a mug of coffee. "You've got to admit, he's not wrong. This place needs a lot of work."

Natalie took the mug but didn't drink. Her fingers hugged it for warmth only. "It's fine just the way it is and it's not like we come here often to warrant the expense."

Martin smirked. "That's because you don't know anything about much, especially property."

Behind him, Bobby laughed, delighted. "That's my boy. Say it like it is."

Leon sat down in the chair across from her, stretching his long legs out in front of him. "I like it here, the simplicity of it," he said quietly. "Reminds me of summer when we were kids. Fishing with Pop. Sneaking sips from his hip flask."

"You were nine," Martin said. "He let you drink?"

Leon smiled. "Let me? No, I don't think so. But I knew where he kept it."

Vivienne made a sound, something between a scoff and a sigh. "That's probably why you're soft in the middle now, full of liquor."

Leon didn't rise to it. He never did. Just patted his stomach and said, "All the better for carrying this family's river of guilt."

Natalie looked at him then, really looked. There was something guarded in his eyes, something that tugged at the edge of memory. She'd seen him on the porch once, a year earlier, holding Eve on his lap while she cried about a nightmare. Vivienne had walked past and said nothing. Didn't even look at them.

She doted on Martin, yes. On Bobby, obviously. But Leon? It was like he was a distant cousin who'd been accidentally invited to the reunion. Natalie had once asked Martin about it. Why Vivienne barely seemed to register Leon's existence. Martin had shrugged.

"Leon was always Mom's disappointment," he said. "Too sensitive. Too soft. She thinks Dad babied him even though as far as I remember he treated us the same, taught us both the same tricks."

"What tricks?" Natalie had asked.

Martin had given her a look, the kind that meant the topic was over.

Now, in the cabin, that strange triangle, Martin, Bobby, Leon, reassembled itself like clockwork. Martin and Bobby traded jokes, inside references, and comments about *the business.* Leon watched them like someone watching a game he'd never learned the rules for or cared to learn, like he was happy just being part of it with no desire to lead.

And Natalie? She stood in the kitchen, listening, her back to them as she sliced tomatoes for a salad no one would eat. Vivienne's voice rose now and then but always directed at Martin, always clipped and urgent.

It had been Leon who finally wandered out to play tag with the kids. Natalie had watched through the window as he chased them across the patchy grass, his laughter real, his legs pumping in slow, exaggerated arcs to let them win.

"Daddy doesn't run like that," Eve had giggled.

"Daddy doesn't run at all," Thomas had said.

Martin hadn't heard. Or maybe he had and chose not to respond. Vivienne eventually drifted further afield, her coat still buttoned, gloves still on. She stood stiff as a scarecrow near the porch steps and watched her family like they were specimens.

When Natalie brought her a chair, Vivienne didn't even acknowledge her kindness and said simply said, "I'll stand."

Dinner had been much of the same, the children at least ate heartily, and the men weren't shy when it came to drinking beer and wine, unlike Natalie who refused both much to the annoyance of Martin who called her a bore, seconded by Bobby. Leon abstained from the name calling, at least while Vivienne pursed her lips and went to bed early.

That night, Natalie had lain on top of the duvet with the window cracked open, the sound of the lake lapping gently against the dock. Martin had already fallen asleep, snoring lightly. But she had lain there staring into the dark, her thoughts circling like birds over something dying and preventing her brain from resting until eventually her eyes began to close.

The next morning, when Natalie woke it was as if she'd come round from a surgery or drank far too much wine. Martin batted away her observations saying it was a result of the mountain air and the long drive. But when she went to take a shower the bruise on her thigh was real and so was the tenderness she felt inside, even though she had no idea why. Just like always.

## 13

The remainder of dinner had been a quiet affair. Too quiet. The empty plates sat in front of them, her apple pie barely touched, all that remained of his were crumbs. Martin's wine glass was drained to the dregs, while hers remained mostly full, like a dark, garnet-colored omen.

She reached for it with shaking fingers and took a sip, then another, suddenly feeling the need for Dutch courage, watching to make sure Martin's eyes stayed on his phone.

He was scrolling. A slow, idle flick of the thumb. Something with a smirk tugging at the corner of his mouth, like he was laughing at someone who didn't know they were the joke.

"I'll clear this," Natalie said softly, pushing back her chair.

Martin didn't look up. "You don't have to."

But she did. Of course she did. She collected the plates, stacking them with mechanical precision. Her wine glass came last. She held it delicately, letting the liquid swirl slightly then she turned and walked into the kitchen.

The sink was deep and stainless steel, and the water was already hot when she ran it, letting the steam ghost up to meet her face. She poured the wine slowly, carefully. Let it bleed into the drain like a secret. The dark swirl vanished without a trace as she filled the basin with soap, watching the foam mount like sea surf.

Behind her, Martin chuckled. She turned to glance at him, but he didn't look up. Whatever was on his phone was more interesting than her. Good, she thought. She scrubbed the plates, one after another, methodical, like penance. Her hands sank into the suds, the water growing hotter. The sponge squeaked against ceramic. The candles on the counter flickered weakly, casting faint glows along the wall, warping the room's corners into strange shapes.

Then, something shifted. A strange warmth crept up the back of her neck. Her knees softened. The sponge slipped from her fingers and floated uselessly on the suds. She gripped the edge of the sink. The room tilted, just a little. Like a painting knocked off kilter. Her breath came shorter.

"Martin?" she called, her voice thinner than she meant. She blinked hard. "Martin, something's wrong."

The fork she held in her free hand slid down the sink's edge and vanished beneath the foam.

Martin stood and crossed the room. "You okay?"

Natalie turned toward him. The floor felt like it was moving under her feet. She tried to answer, but her words slurred together, sticky and wrong. Her lips didn't want to form the shapes.

"I... feel..." Her knees buckled.

Martin caught her. He eased her down onto the sofa like she was a doll. She heard her own breathing, shallow and fast and felt the strange fluttering of her heart against her ribs, like a bird panicking in a cage when it sees a prowling cat.

Martin knelt beside her. His hand stroked her hair, slow and soothing.

"You're okay," he said, voice low and gentle. "You've just overdone it. You're tired, that's all."

Her eyes struggled to stay open.

The ceiling blurred. His voice became echoey, like it came from inside a deep cave.

"Sshhh," he whispered. "Just close your eyes. Sleep. You'll feel better in the morning. I promise." He kissed her forehead.

She tried to speak, to say *No, something's not right*, but her lips barely moved as the room darkened at the edges and her limbs stopped obeying her.

The last thing she saw before the world went dark was Martin's face above hers, smiling too softly. And then –

Nothing. Blackness. She was not asleep. She was not awake. She was somewhere in the middle, trapped in a place where nothing made sense and everything felt wrong. The walls around her rippled like oil-slicked water, glossy and distorted. They bowed inward, then melted, dissolving into liquid shadows that slithered down to the floor, pooling in strange, throbbing shapes. The wood-paneled ceiling stretched above her head like a canopy of skin. It pulsed. It breathed.

She couldn't move. She couldn't scream. Her limbs were heavy, her bones soaked in wet cement. Her mouth hung open, but no sound came. Even her tongue felt detached, flabby and useless, like a slug on a sidewalk.

Faces swam into view. Strange, male faces. All of them grinning. All of them warped. Their eyes gleamed like glass marbles. Their mouths moved too fast, teeth clicking, tongues darting. None of them spoke words, just gibberish. Static noise. Like a broken radio turned all the way up.

Cameras flashed bright, searing bursts of light. Again. Again. Again. The light stabbed at her skull. She flinched with each pulse, but her body stayed still. Frozen. Her mind screamed *stop* but her body didn't listen. Couldn't.

A low moan slid from somewhere in the room. Hers? Someone else's? Then the heat started. A sudden, blistering rush. Her skin prickled. Her forehead burned. She felt scorched from the inside out. Her clothes, were they still on? She couldn't feel them. Her thighs ached, pulsing with pain. A soreness settled in her groin like a bruise blooming beneath the flesh. She felt peeled open.

Something was wrong. Something *bad* had happened. Martin's face surfaced above her like a photo rising in darkroom fluid. Clear at first. Then blurred. Then warped into a grin too wide, too white. His teeth looked like a row of piano keys, perfect and awful. He laughed.

Pointed.

"You know you want this really," he said. "You've always wanted it like this."

She whimpered. Or tried to. The sound was no louder than a thought. His eyes gleamed in the half-light. They didn't look like his anymore. They looked empty. Slick with cruelty. Like Bobby's. Like Bobby used to look at her when she wasn't supposed to notice.

Martin reached for her face. His fingers were made of smoke. They slid right through her skin and into her head. Natalie tried to move, but the weight of her own limbs was unbearable. Her body wasn't her own. It was someone else's, a puppet left in the attic, limbs dangling, joints unhinged, being flung this way and that.

She smelled something sour. Burning. Like hair singed too close to a flame. She tried to scream again. Nothing. The faces were back. The strangers. Grinning, leering. Whispers in a language she didn't understand danced through the air. It wasn't English. Or maybe it was. Just all wrong. Chopped up. Played backward.

She felt exposed. Naked. Every inch of her tingled with

awareness, as if unseen hands had been on her, poking, pressing, tearing. She wanted to claw her own skin off. The crawling started then. Tiny legs. Thousands of them. Across her stomach. Up her thighs. Under her arms. She couldn't see them, but she felt them. Insects. Or something worse.

She began to sob silently. *Please let me wake up.* She blinked hard, her eyes darting wildly in the dark dream and then she saw her reflection.

A mirror? A window? She wasn't sure. Her own face stared back. Swollen. Ashen. Wrong. Her lips were cracked. Her eyes were red-rimmed, pupils blown wide. Her skin was slick with sweat. She looked... dead.

Am I dead?

She didn't know anymore. She felt like a ghost tethered to a body she no longer recognized. In the reflection, something moved behind her. A shadow. A figure. Was it Martin again?

No. It was something else. It loomed. Long arms. No face. It didn't walk. It slithered upright. She tried to scream again, and this time, somewhere in the depths of her psyche, she *heard* it, a broken sound, a warbled screech that came from deep inside her and echoed off the edges of this nightmare.

But nothing changed. The thing behind her leaned down. She felt the air shift around her. Cold and sharp. Like standing in front of an open freezer. It whispered her name. Not aloud. In her mind. Like it lived there. *Na-ta-lie.* Syllables stretched like rubber bands about to snap.

*He knows my name.*

She didn't know who *he* was. She didn't want to. Her body convulsed inside the dream. Her legs kicked once, twice. Her stomach turned over, bile rising in her throat. She gasped and the shadows collapsed inward.

The heat returned in a rush. She was burning again. Sweat poured down her neck. Her breath came in gasps. She could hear Martin somewhere far away, calling her name. Soothing. Patient. Patronizing. *Be a good girl, Natalie, don't make a fuss.* Like he was patting the head of a stray dog.

The darkness rippled and she floated upward and downward at the same time. Her body became numb. Her thoughts stopped making sense. Just before everything went black again, she felt a single tear slide from the corner of her eye. Even that didn't feel like hers.

# 14

Natalie woke to stillness so unnatural it scraped at her skin. A flickering glow painted the walls in orange and shadow. The air was suffocating, scented with something too sweet, like burnt sugar, overripe fruit, and something else... something familiar yet alien, feral and musty, and then a whiff of blood beneath it. She blinked, eyes crusted at the corners, lashes sticky. Her vision swam.

It took a moment before her brain registered the sensation. Her wrists were bound. Not tightly. But deliberately. Leather, buckled, one strap around each wrist and ankle, shackled to the corners of the bed. She tested the restraints instinctively. They gave only an inch.

She was naked. The sheets beneath her were damp with sweat and other fluids that smelled bad, clinging to her back and thighs. Her hair was soaked, plastered to her scalp. She tasted salt and something bitter in her mouth and on her lips. She knew what it was but wouldn't admit it, couldn't. Her stomach rolled and the room spun.

Candles were burning on every surface, the dresser, windowsill, side tables. They flickered with soft menace, casting shapes that twitched with each breath of stale cabin air.

Something hummed. A small mechanical whirr. She turned her head slowly even though her neck felt like it belonged to someone else.

A camera. It sat on the tripod, steady, silent. Its red recording light blinking at her in a steady, metronomic pulse. She froze.

The sound was so loud in the stillness... blink... blink... blink, just like a heartbeat. No, not a heartbeat. A countdown. Natalie stared at it. Her own face reflected in the lens. Pale. Wide-eyed. Animal.

The chains rattled as she twisted her body, desperate to pull the covers up, to hide herself, but there were no covers. Just the clammy dirty sheet, stuck to her like a second skin. Her head throbbed with brutal insistence. A migraine blooming behind her eyes. She couldn't tell how long she'd been out. Minutes? Hours? A whole night? She couldn't remember. Not clearly.

She remembered wine. Martin laughing. A kiss on her forehead. She remembered the wooziness starting in her legs. And then – Flashes. Faces. Cameras. Crawling skin. A scream that never came.

"Martin?" she croaked.

Her voice barely carried. It was a croak, dry and weak. Her throat burned. She waited but heard nothing. The cabin was silent.

"Martin?" louder now. The sound trembled out of her.

Still nothing. No footsteps. No familiar creak of the floorboards. Just the blinking of the red light. Like a watcher. Like a warning. Natalie's heart began to hammer, uneven and fast. It hurt her ribs with every pulse. Her body was working against itself, panic rising and dragging her back under the waves of nausea. She felt bile climb her throat.

Her eyes darted around the room, catching every flicker,

every cruel gleam. The walls were theirs she was sure, yes, the walls of their bedroom. Knotty pine, varnished to a sickly gloss. The same curtains she'd chosen, now drawn tight. The dresser where she used to keep sun lotion and crossword puzzles. The lamp with the chipped base from the trip to Cape May.

This was their room. But it felt different now. It was too hot. Too quiet. Too staged. A theater. A set. A trap. And she was the performance.

Natalie turned her face into the damp sheet and gagged. Nothing came up because her stomach was too empty but the spasms racked her body, each one lighting up her nerves in pain.

She lay still for a long moment, breathing ragged. Think. Think. The camera wasn't there before. She would have noticed it. The red light. Blinking. She followed its rhythm and found herself counting. One, two, three... Was someone watching? Was he watching?

She tried to speak again, softer now. "Martin, please. This isn't funny."

Her voice cracked. The sound of it frightened her. She sounded like a girl. A girl locked in a basement. A girl they'd write newspaper stories about after they found her bones. She struggled again. The shackles groaned. Her left ankle ached where the leather dug in. Why?

Why would he? She stopped the thought. She already knew. She knew the answer, but her brain wasn't ready to hear it yet.

It was easier to pretend. Easier to believe this was a dream. A hallucination. That she'd woken too soon, still caught in the fever dream of that psychedelic hellscape from earlier.

She closed her eyes tight. Opened them again. Still the same room. Still the flickering candlelight. Still the blinking red dot.

She turned her head and sobbed once, hard and sharp. It echoed off the walls and sounded foreign in the room that used to be hers. It rattled something inside her. The smell. She tried to place it again. It was... cloying. Like incense and chemicals. The scent of something being covered up. Chloroform? She didn't know what chloroform smelled like, but that thought entered her mind unbidden and stayed there. Had she been drugged by her own husband, a doctor who had access to medicines?

She lay still and stared at the camera. Blink. Blink. Blink. She didn't know how long she stared before she realized she was waiting for someone to walk in. That throughout the hellish night there had been many visitors to this room and at any moment another might enter. With a final tug of her restraints Natalie gave in and tried to prepare for what came next but all she could think of was her children, willing, praying, hoping and believing that they were safe.

The moonlight slipped through the slats of the blinds in Thomas's room, striping the walls in pale silver and soft shadow. His bedroom was a boyish mess of video game controllers on the floor, a heap of LEGO spilling from an overturned box, books stacked haphazardly on a chair that no one ever sat in.

Vivienne sat on the edge of the bed like a statue in mourning. Her spine rigid, her hair set and sprayed into a dark halo, not a strand out of place. Her silhouette looked almost regal under the sliver of moonlight, a queen in exile. She hummed low as her fingers moved gently through Thomas's hair, slow strokes like someone brushing a beloved pet.

Thomas lay curled on his side, eyes heavy but still awake, soaking in the sound of her voice. The lullaby she sang was ancient, toneless, a low murmur passed down from some place so old even Vivienne herself may not remember its origin. There were no real words, just hums and soft mouth shapes, like incantations hidden in a melody.

"There we are," Vivienne said softly. "My clever boy. My strong, clever boy."

She leaned down and kissed the top of his head, where the hair still stuck up in tufts despite her smoothing. "You remind me of your grandfather. And your daddy, of course. Spitting image. You have that same look about you."

Thomas blinked up at her, his face glazed with that strange mixture of adoration and sleep.

She smiled at him, not warmly, more predatory. Vivienne's smiles never were kind and full of love and more like fierce pride.

"You're going to be special, Thomas. Do you know that?"

He nodded vaguely, not fully understanding.

"A very important man one day. Powerful. Respected. Maybe even feared. Not in a bad way, no. That's the way it's always been with the men in our family. Your grandfather had it. Your daddy has it. And one day, you'll have it too."

Thomas shifted beneath the covers. "Have what, Granny?"

She paused, as if weighing her next words. Then she leaned in closer, her lips almost brushing his ear. "A gift."

He squinted up at her. "Like a birthday gift?"

Vivienne chuckled low in her throat, shaking her head. "No, darling. Not a toy. Not something you can unwrap. It's something inside you. Something that grows. A birthright. That's a very grown-up word, I know. But it means it's something passed down. Only to the boys. Only to those who are strong enough. And you, Thomas, you are."

He turned toward her slightly, his expression uncertain. "Like magic?"

She gave him an approving look. "Not like what you see on the television. Not spells or rabbits in hats. Real magic is about power. Control. Understanding the way the world works better than anyone else. You'll see it one day. You'll see the patterns.

The weaknesses. You'll know what to say to people to make them do what you want. And they won't even realize it."

She stroked his cheek with the back of her hand. "You're already learning. Your teacher told me you stood up for yourself last week. You showed a girl who was boss, didn't you?"

Thomas squirmed, suddenly unsure whether he should be proud.

Vivienne didn't give him the chance to hesitate.

"You were asserting yourself. Boys have instincts, Thomas. Don't ever let small-minded women tell you your instincts are wrong. Your grandfather was the same. He always saw through people. Could look right into someone and know their truth. Your father too. Brilliant. That's what makes him a leader. And that's what you'll be."

She pulled the blanket up to his chest and tucked it tightly beneath his chin.

"And when you're old enough, you'll be given the gift properly. The real inheritance. The legacy. But you mustn't tell anyone I told you. Not your sister. Not even your mother."

"Why not?"

"Because it isn't for them. They wouldn't understand. Some women don't deserve that kind of knowledge. It's too much for them. But me and you..."

She paused and placed her hand over his heart.

"We're different."

Thomas stared at the ceiling now, his eyes wide and unblinking. The fan spun lazily overhead. His fingers curled slightly at his side.

Vivienne lowered her voice again, the whisper of something ceremonial.

"There are rituals. Traditions. Things you'll learn in time. But it starts with knowing who you are. You're a Lane. That means something. Never forget that. And never forget that I'm the one who guided everyone towards greatness. Another woman, not like me, birthed your grandad but I made him see who he could be. And then I carried his sons who were destined for better things, just like you."

A beat of silence stretched between them. Vivienne sat still for a moment longer, watching him with that fixed, satisfied look.

"You should get your rest, darling. Big boys need sleep. Big things are coming and no matter what happens I will be here to care for you and guide you."

She stood slowly, smoothing the front of her skirt, then glanced around the room with mild distaste at the chaos, the scattered toys, the crumpled clothes in the corner. Her mouth thinned, but she said nothing. Instead, she moved to the doorway, pausing there for a final look.

Thomas hadn't moved. His eyes were still open. Still watching the ceiling.

"Sleep well, my beautiful boy," she said, voice lilting with sugar. "Tomorrow is going to be another beautiful day."

And then she was gone, her footsteps quiet and precise as she retreated down the hall, the soft creak of the floorboards vanishing with her.

## 15

The candles had burned low. The wax bled over the nightstand in trails. Natalie lay still. Sweat clung to her skin in a thin, fevered sheen. Her wrists were raw where the metal had bitten into them, tethering her to the bedframe. She had screamed until her throat grew hoarse. Then she'd whispered. Then she'd simply stopped.

The smell in the room, cloying, familiar, was the only thing that anchored her to reality. It reminded her of something masculine. Aftershave and smoke and rust and sex. Her mind twisted around it, trying to avoid it but it sat in her lungs and heart and brain like lead. Then the door creaked open. She didn't lift her head. She just observed.

The man stepped inside with the casual arrogance of someone who had a right to be there. He paused halfway into the room, his silhouette sharp against the candlelit gloom. When their eyes met, something shifted in his expression. Not fear. Not guilt. Just a brief, passing irritation.

"Well," he said, clicking his tongue, "that's a surprise."

Natalie blinked slowly. Her breath hitched in her chest. Recognition stirred like a cold worm in her gut. She knew him.

The man from the fish counter. The one who'd watched her too long, too intently, with eyes that knew things. She hadn't imagined it. She hadn't imagined any of it.

"You were supposed to be under," he muttered. His voice was flat, unbothered. "Someone didn't give you enough."

He stepped further into the room, his boots creaking on the old wooden floorboards. Natalie tried to shrink away, but the chains clanked in response, a cruel reminder that escape wasn't on offer.

He studied her like a scientist might examine a specimen. Detached, clinical.

"Martin didn't say you were going to be awake this time," he murmured. "Then again, he's full of shit, isn't he?"

She didn't answer. Couldn't. He walked around the bed slowly, deliberately. The camera sat there on the tripod like another figure in the room, its red light winking like an eye. He reached for it, twisting it free from the stand, cradling it in his hand. He flicked a few settings, then turned the lens toward her. Zoomed. The digital hum of the device filled the silence.

"Shame," he muttered. "You look sexier when you're still."

Natalie squeezed her eyes shut. "Don't," she whispered.

He mimicked her in a high, mocking tone. "Don't," he said, a sneer curling his lip. "I've seen it all before, sweetheart so don't be shy."

He circled the bed again. The camera whirred in his grip, focusing and adjusting.

"You know I definitely preferred last time," he said, crouching slightly to tilt the lens. "When you didn't talk. When your eyes were shut."

Her stomach turned.

He clicked his tongue again, disappointed. "Wasn't supposed to be like this. I don't like it when they're... aware. That's not the arrangement and I'll be having words with Martin."

The arrangement. The words stung Natalie's ears, foul and impossible. He moved toward the tripod again, returning the camera to its perch. Secured it. Adjusted the angle.

"I'll let him know," he said as he stepped back toward the door. "Tell him next time he'd better do it right and I want my money back."

Her voice broke free. "Martin!" she screamed.

The man paused, hand on the doorknob. "He's not coming. They've all gone into town for breakfast, get their strength back, if you know what I mean."

She screamed again, louder this time, the sound tearing up her throat. "Martin!"

The man opened the door, looking back one last time with something close to boredom in his eyes. Then he was gone. The latch clicked into place behind him. Natalie lay trembling. Every inch of her was screaming. Her skin felt like it had been peeled back. Her brain burned. But it was the humiliation that bloomed worst of all. That Martin, her husband, had known. Had arranged it all, and taken money.

The camera blinked at her, still watching. Still recording. She turned her head into the pillow and screamed once more. This time, no words. Just sound. Pain and terror in its rawest form. No one answered and outside, somewhere in the black forest ringing the lake, a wolf cried out in the night.

Natalie tugged again at the restraints. The metal tore at her wrists with a grinding bite. There was no give. No secret softness in the bindings, no trick hinge. Only steel and leather and the pulsing ache of her skin splitting open.

She whimpered, her breath coming fast. *Get out. Get out. Get out.* She twisted again. Her body arched and writhed, slick with sweat. The sheet beneath her was damp and sticking to her back. Her thighs were shaking. Her arms screamed from the tension, muscles taut, wrists screaming. Her scream rose with it.

It wasn't even a word, just a feral sound, jagged and raw. It filled the cabin and bounced off the wood-paneled walls. It made the candles quiver. And still, no one came. She was alone in the cage of her own flesh.

Natalie sobbed. Her voice was hoarse, her throat raw. The bile had been sitting in the base of her throat for what felt like hours. The pounding in her head came in waves now, like a migraine turning into thunder. And then, the poison Martin had fed her came up. There was no warning. No time to prepare. She turned her head instinctively as her stomach convulsed and she vomited. A thin, burning stream that splattered across the bedsheets, dripping to the floor in thick, acidic strings. It smelled like wine and chemicals. It reeked of something foreign and rotten.

The puddle sat there next to her like a second presence. She tried to edge away from it, to shift her hips and legs, but her range of motion was tight and shrinking. The liquid inched closer. Soon, it was pressed to her side. Soaking her hair. Sliding over her skin. A warm, noxious trail.

She gagged again but there was nothing left to bring up. The taste in her mouth was a bitter artificial coating. Natalie blinked back tears, staring at the ceiling. She called his name again.

"Martin." Her voice cracked, barely more than a breath. "Please."

There was no response. The camera blinked red. Always blinking.

"Please," she begged the air. "Please, just tell me why."

No one answered. She lay there in the darkness, the stink of vomit surrounding her like a shroud. The cold air pricked her skin. Her teeth began to chatter. Her mind drifted, too tired to be frightened, her body too sore to keep fighting.

She thought of her mother. A woman who used to sing hymns while cleaning the windows, who baked banana bread every Saturday morning, who wore the same threadbare cardigan for years because it was her "lucky one." Her mother would have torn the house down to find her.

She thought of her father's quiet laugh. The way he used to sneak candy into her coat pocket before school. Her mind snagged on her children next. Thomas. His sharp little jaw, the way he chewed his lip when he concentrated. His swagger, his bursts of cruel humor. And Eve. Her gentle girl. The softness in her voice. Her wide eyes always watching.

*Are they okay? Why did I leave them with her?* She pictured Vivienne's hand on Eve's shoulder. The same hand that had nudged Natalie once at the stove, hard enough to bruise, when she'd spoken back. Natalie's body tensed again with helpless panic.

She thought of the lake just outside. The silence of it. How it had always felt slightly haunted, even on bright days. She used to walk down to the waterline barefoot, just to feel the coolness between her toes, to remind herself she still existed. Now it might as well be a thousand miles away and she too felt like she was fading. Like her bones were hollowing out.

Natalie's body went limp and this time, she didn't have the energy to fight it. The sweat, the blood, the bile, the restraints, they were just facts now. She catalogued them like someone watching a story happen to someone else.

The candles sputtered. The room tilted. Then darkness. Natalie passed out with the taste of chemicals on her tongue, her body curled in vomit and bodily fluids. The last thought that moved through her mind, like a whispered curse, was – *I don't want to die here. Not like this. Not for him.*

# 16

*Lander, Wyoming – The Reservation, Spring, 2000*

The wind in Wyoming had a personality. It didn't just pass through, it spoke. It carried scents of sagebrush and sweetgrass, and sometimes, if the season was right, the faint metallic tang of thawing earth and animal musk. Natalie used to sit on the porch of her grandfather's home, a squat, timber-wrapped structure near the Wind River Reservation, and try to understand what the wind was telling her.

She was ten years old that spring. Her knees were always scraped, her hands always dirty. Her voice, back then, was louder than it would ever be again. She ran wild across the land behind her family's house, which backed into the reservation's borders. Her mother called her "a little stray," but her grandfather just smiled and called her *Little Coyote*.

High Bear wasn't tall. He stood solid and sun-darkened, his body shaped by decades of hunting, skin lined from weather and wisdom. His hair was iron-gray and pulled back in a low braid. He wore flannel even in the spring, and his moccasins made no sound on the dry earth. His face was the kind of face you could stare at for hours and still not know the half of what it had seen.

"You walk quiet, but the land hears you," he told her that day, his voice low and rumbling like distant thunder. They were seated cross-legged in a clearing behind his house, the air rich with the scent of pine sap and the last breath of winter. "Even your silence has a sound."

Natalie nodded, not fully understanding, but memorizing the words like scripture. She wanted so badly to be good at this. She wanted to belong.

He handed her a small pouch of tobacco and nodded toward the fire pit. "Make your offering. Thank the spirits for the sky, for the deer, for the morning."

She pinched a bit between her fingers, her palms trembling with the weight of the ritual. She whispered the words he taught her, even if they stumbled on her tongue.

"I give thanks for the wind," she said softly, "and for Grandfather, and for the dream I had last night."

He smiled then. "You dream like a woman with old blood. That is good. Listen to your dreams."

Natalie loved him more than anyone in her world. Her own father was a quiet, practical man who worked in town and left his spirituality on the kitchen table next to his newspaper. Her mother was kind but hurried. Her siblings squabbled and stared at Game Boys and rolled their eyes when she said she was going to visit High Bear.

But when she was with him, the world felt different.

He told her stories of the buffalo hunts, when he was just a boy himself, running barefoot beside the elders, watching the great creatures thunder across the plains before the world changed. He told her about the spirits in the trees, the ones you could only see in the shimmer of firelight or just before dawn.

"People think the old ways are gone," he said, stirring the embers of their fire. "But they are only sleeping. Like the bear in winter. You forget to call them, and they get quieter. But they never die."

He showed her how to watch the birds, how to read the sky. He showed her the ceremony of the sweat lodge, and though she was too young to join fully, he let her sit nearby and listen. She remembered the rhythmic chanting, the hiss of water on stone, the steam curling like spirits into the open night.

One afternoon, he told her about the Sun Dance.

"Pain can be prayer," he said, solemn. "When the boys become men, they give part of their flesh to the Creator. It's not about hurt. It's about sacrifice. You give what matters."

She didn't flinch. Not even when he told her about the hooks through the chest, the tethering to the sacred pole. Her young eyes were steady.

"You are not a boy," he added, gently. "But you are strong. One day, you'll have your own way to show your strength."

She believed him. On her last night of that spring visit, Natalie sat beside him on the porch, her bare feet tucked up beneath her, her head leaning into his side. He smoked from a pipe, the scent of burning sage curling around them.

"Do you ever get scared?" she asked.

He exhaled slowly. "Fear is not the enemy. Forgetting who you are is the danger."

The stars were beginning to bloom in the sky. She thought they looked like tiny spirit fires in the dark.

"I want to remember," she whispered.

He placed his hand on her head. "You will. One day, you'll need to. And when that time comes, listen. You'll hear me in the wind."

She didn't know what he meant then. She hadn't known what loss really felt like. Not yet.

Years later, when the noise of her adult life drowned out everything sacred, she would try to return to that place inside herself. The place where his words lived. Where she could still remember the smell of pine and smoke and trust. It was harder to find now. The world had taken so much. But on nights when the wind scratched against the glass, she sometimes still heard him.

*Fear is not the enemy.*

Natalie needed that voice now more than ever. The dream of High Bear clung to her like a mist she couldn't shake. But when she opened her eyes again, she was not on the reservation. She was not ten years old. She was not wrapped in buffalo hide or seated near firelight or listening to her grandfather's voice tell her that the land remembers everything. She was shackled to a bed.

And the light, what little of it there was, skimmed her soaked skin in trembling waves. Candlelight. A dozen little flames dancing along the windowsill and the dresser and the bedside table, throwing strange shadows across the walls like specters mid-prayer. Her wrists ached where the restraints bit into her skin, raw and angry, and her head throbbed with a pressure that made her teeth hurt.

She couldn't tell how long she had been out. Minutes? Hours? A day? The vomit was still there. Cooling against her side. Her own body's betrayal, now dried and bitter. A sour film clung to her lips, and she gagged again, dry and helpless. There was no escape from it, or a way to move far enough to avoid the yellow puddle seeping into the sheets. It was soaked into her thigh, a cold reminder that she was nothing more than flesh at the mercy of others now.

She turned her head slightly, straining to see. The camera

was still there, fixed in place. That evil red light blinked steadily back at her like a pulse. It hadn't stopped recording. It was still watching. Someone was still watching. Natalie whimpered and yanked her arms again, twisting hard. The metal dug into her wrists with a merciless bite. She felt skin tear. Warm blood slicked against her skin. She bit her lip to keep from screaming. But she couldn't stop the sob that escaped.

It echoed in the empty room, like it didn't belong to her. Was this real? Was this hell?

No one came. She screamed, finally. A wild animal noise that scraped up from somewhere deep, some long-dormant place inside her that didn't care how polite or quiet or obedient she'd been trained to be. She called Martin's name again, this time laced with fury. But only the wind answered. Whistling through the warped window frames, stirring the curtains like ghosts.

She thought of her children. Of Eve, small and solemn, with her quiet gaze and her careful words. And Thomas, aloof and hungry for his father's approval. Were they safe? Was Vivienne watching them, being kind?

And if something happened to her here, if she never made it out, would Martin just explain it away and let his mother take control? Would he mourn her absence with crocodile tears and have a new woman on his arm inside of a year? She had no illusions anymore. Not after the STI. Not after the camera. Not after the blank, staring silence from the man who used to touch her with such tenderness and call her his whole world. She wasn't his world anymore. She was a stooge. And this was a place for something monstrous to play out.

Natalie turned her head toward the ceiling and stared at the beams. They were old and splintering, familiar in a way that made her stomach churn. This room. This bed. They'd made love here, once. Or something that passed for it. Before he stopped kissing her. Before he started issuing instructions instead of invitations.

She'd believed it was her fault. For a long time. She'd thought – *I mustn't be interesting enough anymore. I've let myself go. I'm not as spontaneous or sexy or charming as I once was.*

The kind of lies women tell themselves to keep the peace. But peace was an illusion, wasn't it? She remembered once, shortly after Eve was born, sitting in the tub alone while Martin was downstairs watching a Phillies game. Her skin had still been stretched, soft and strange, a body she didn't recognize. She'd cried quietly into a towel. And she'd told herself she was tired. Just tired. Hormones. Nothing more. But it hadn't been nothing. It had been the start of a long undoing. Now, her whole world was unraveling.

Natalie yanked again at the restraints. Her breath came faster, panicked and shallow. She didn't know if it was the medication or whatever they'd drugged her with or just raw fear. Her limbs felt heavy, her fingers trembled uncontrollably. She needed to think. She needed to get out. She closed her eyes and tried to slow her breathing.

*What would High Bear say?*

He would not panic. He would close his eyes and listen. To the wind. To the earth. To the sounds of the enemy. But there was no red dirt or coyotes howling in the distance. Just a wooden prison on a Pennsylvania lake, shuttered in candlelight and crawling with something foul.

She forced herself to listen. Really listen. The creak of wood as something shifted. Not her. Not a tree. Footsteps? A door? No. Just the wind. Or her mind. It was so hard to tell anymore. She felt her body trembling again. Cold sweat ran down the back of her neck. If Martin came back... would he be smiling? Would he pretend none of this had happened? Would he blame her?

*You drank too much. You got confused.*

Would he gaslight her like he always had? Natalie blinked against the salt sting of sweat and tears. She would not give him the satisfaction of her silence this time. Not anymore. She thought of Eve's small hand in hers. The soft press of her lips at bedtime. The way she watched Natalie at dinner like she could read her mind. That child knew. She knew things without being told.

She thought of High Bear's stories. Of his belief that the spirits never abandoned you even when the world did. So, Natalie breathed. She held the breath like a prayer and let it out slow. One after another. Until the panic thinned and her thoughts could move again.

*Wait. Count. Feel.*

She twisted her wrist again. Gritted her teeth. Felt the searing pain. And kept going. She would survive this. She didn't know how yet. Or when. But she would. And when she did, Martin would see her clearly. For the first time. Not as his wife. Not as a body to bind or betray. But as a woman who remembered who she was. Natalie Beaumont, not Lane, she would never use that name again. She was a daughter of the plains. Granddaughter of High Bear. And she would not be forgotten.

# 17

The first thing Natalie became aware of was her own breath. Slow and ragged, like wind through cracked glass. Then came the pain. A dull, spreading ache that sat like a bruise beneath her skin, in her thighs, in her ribs, behind her eyes. Her mouth was dry and metallic. She tasted something bitter on the back of her tongue and instinctively turned her head to the side, half-expecting to be sick again.

The sheets beneath her were damp with sweat. The smell was cloying, candle wax and mildew, body odor and something she wouldn't name. She blinked, slow and heavy. The curtains were drawn, but the fabric had shifted during the night, and a thin sliver of light had sliced across the floorboards like a blade.

She didn't move. Not yet. Her body felt foreign. Stretched, wrong, as if someone else had used it and abandoned it in the night. As if she were the haunted shell of herself.

And then she remembered. The man. The camera. His voice, slick and oily. The way he circled her like prey. And worse, the implication, the words he had dropped carelessly, like breadcrumbs: *"You were meant to be asleep."*

Her stomach twisted. A hot shame bloomed beneath her

ribs and tightened her throat. No, she couldn't go there. Not now. She pushed the memory away like pushing a burning match from her skin. She focused instead on the bird outside. A shrill call. Blue jay, maybe. It hopped from branch to branch, unseen, oblivious. A normal sound. A sound that meant the world hadn't stopped.

But hers had. Natalie turned her head and surveyed the room. Most of the candles had burned down to nothing but stubby wax islands, puddled onto the wooden floor. The camera was gone. The chair where the man had stood was empty now. The air was stagnant but no longer electric with menace. For a second, she could almost pretend the night hadn't happened. Almost.

She lifted her arm. Her wrist stung. The metal shackle still held it in place, tight enough to have cut into the skin. There was dried blood there, a crusted half-ring, angry and raw. The sight of it sobered her further. The other wrist was similarly bruised, the skin red and purpling. She tried tugging. Once. Twice. But the iron wouldn't give. She pressed her lips together, stifling a cry of pain. Think.

She scanned the room for something, anything that had sharp edges, loose screws, a nail she could dislodge. But everything in the cabin was just out of reach. The side table, the dresser. A cruel arrangement, she realized. She'd been placed just far enough that escape was impossible. And that's when she heard the car. Tires crunching over gravel. A soft purr, growing fainter. Then silence. Her breath caught. What if the man was leaving? What if she had missed her only chance to scream?

She opened her mouth but just as quickly, she closed it. Footsteps. Not outside. Inside.

Floorboards moaned on the landing. Slow. Deliberate. Familiar. Her blood turned cold. The door creaked open. And there he was. Martin.

He stood in the doorway, silhouetted by hallway light. He was dressed in the same clothes he'd worn last night, jeans, a navy pullover, sneakers. His hair was still combed neatly. He held a mug of coffee like this was just any ordinary morning.

Natalie recoiled against the headboard, her entire body trembling. The metal bit at her wrists again. Martin's face didn't change. Calm. Blank.

"Sleep well?" he said, stepping inside.

She didn't answer.

"I'd offer you coffee," he added, almost casually, "but... well, I'm guessing you don't trust what I put in your drinks anymore."

Natalie's throat worked soundlessly. Her mouth was a desert.

Martin walked to the end of the bed and looked down at her, eyes calculating. "I have to admit," he said, "I'm surprised. The wine should've knocked you out completely. It always has before unless I've used other methods."

The words hit her like a slap. *Before. Methods.*

Her eyes widened. Her body tensed. Her stomach threatened to revolt again.

"I don't understand," she whispered. Her voice was hoarse, barely audible.

He tilted his head, almost amused. "No?" He let the silence stretch. "We've been here before, Natalie, for party nights. You just don't remember. You never woke up."

She stared at him, her breath shallow.

"It's a shame, really, that you came round and ruined everything," he went on. "You were always so... compliant. Unaware. That's what made it easy and much more fun. But this? You spoilt it all."

Her chest rose and fell in short, panicked gasps.

"I knew you were acting strange," he said, pacing now, slow and measured. "You poured the wine away, didn't you? Thought I wouldn't notice. Thought you were being a clever girl."

Natalie shook her head. "Why?" she managed. "Why would you do this?"

Martin stopped. He turned to her, and something shifted in his expression. Something dead behind the eyes.

"Because I could. You were never anything special" he hissed, his voice colder now. "You were convenient and gullible so fitted the brief, which was to provide me with an heir, a son, and then provide me with entertainment whenever I wished."

She didn't reply.

"This house," he gestured around them "was my father's gift and legacy to me, Leon and Thomas. Just like his father's before him. It's a family place. And in our family, we have certain... traditions."

Natalie's stomach clenched. "What kind of traditions?"

Martin smiled. "Ones that go back decades. Quiet ones. Private ones. Things the world doesn't understand. Things it doesn't need to."

He crouched beside her then, bringing his face close to hers.

"You always thought you were safe, didn't you?" he whispered. "In your bed. In your marriage. In your mind."

A tear slid down her cheek.

"I did try to protect you," he said. "I tried to keep you blind to it. But now... now you're awake and you know. And we can't have that."

Her voice broke. "What are you going to do?"

He stood up and crossed the room to the window. He pulled the curtain back an inch and looked out at the lake.

"Lots of things sink in that water," he said quietly. "Boats. Old engines. Memories. Secrets."

He let the curtain fall and turned back to her.

"It's good at keeping secrets, the lake."

The threat hung in the air like fog. Heavy. Unspoken, but clear. He walked to the door and paused.

"You ruined it all, Natalie, for yourself and for the children," he said. "There's nothing more to be done."

Then he was gone. The door clicked shut. Natalie stared at the ceiling, her heart pounding so hard it felt like it would break through her ribs. Her mouth was open, but no sound came out. Her mind was screaming. Her skin crawling. She was alone. Trapped. And now she knew the truth her mind and soul had feared. She'd been violated. Again. Again. Again.

And all this time, she had no idea. Until now. The silence after Martin's footsteps faded was like being submerged. Heavy. Absolute. Natalie lay in the dim room, her body trembling, heart drumming a staccato rhythm that hurt. The restraints dug into her wrists, cruel and unrelenting, but her mind had begun to spin again, fast, like it was trying to run without her legs.

She was awake. She was *aware*. And that, apparently, was enough to ruin everything. She didn't know how long had passed, minutes, an hour maybe, before she heard the door open again. This time, there were no footsteps in the hall. Just the quiet *click* of the doorknob and the sound of breath, deliberate, measured, calm.

Martin stepped into the room. He was barefoot now. He'd taken off his pullover. His shirt was undone at the collar. He had the expression of someone about to tend to a chore. No glee. No frenzy. Just cold, clinical resolve.

Natalie didn't speak. She couldn't. Her voice had abandoned her. She pulled instinctively against the shackles again, even knowing they'd hold.

Martin closed the door behind him and locked it with a soft *snick*. Then he turned and looked at her, not as a husband. Not even as a person. But as an object. A thing.

"You don't have to make this difficult," he said quietly, as though he were offering her something kind.

She stared at him. Her lips trembled. Her fingers flexed

against the restraints. There was something odd about him, his pallor was deathly gray, and she noticed a slick sheen or perspiration on his skin and her first thought as he neared, was that he had taken something.

"You never used to fight," he added, stepping toward the bed.

Natalie couldn't bear to look at his sickly face any longer so closed her eyes for a moment and searched deep inside herself. For anything left. Her mind clawed at memories, of her children, of the warmth of her grandfather's hands as he held hers by the riverbank back home in Lander, of the sound of wind through the aspen trees. Of strength.

She opened her eyes just as Martin pulled at the filthy sheet, dragging it from under her and tossing it to the floor before he climbed onto the mattress, the bed shifting under his weight.

"Don't," she whispered.

But he wasn't listening. The air thickened. Natalie's breath came fast. Her muscles coiled. The mattress dipped further as he crawled closer, positioning himself over her. And in that single moment, perhaps a final act of defiance, of survival, Natalie raised her knee with every ounce of force she had left and struck.

The sound he made was something animal. A raw, guttural yelp of pain. His body folded instantly, collapsing sideways off her with a thud. He hit the floor hard, curling into himself, both hands between his legs, gasping.

Natalie didn't stop shaking. She stared at the ceiling, waiting for him to rise in rage. To grab her. Strike her. Finish what he came for. But something else was happening. The noises he made changed. From pain to something deeper.

One hand clutched at his chest now. His face was even paler, damp with sweat. His breaths were shallow, rapid. Panic rippled through every muscle.

"Martin?" she said, her voice hoarse.

He didn't answer. He tried to sit up but slumped back against the side of the bed. His eyes were wide now, staring at nothing. His mouth opened and closed like a fish pulled from water. Desperate. Knowing. Working out what was happening to him.

She could see it, too. Something real. Something terrifying. He was having a heart attack.

For a fleeting second, she was frozen again. Paralyzed by the dissonance of it. The absurdity. The horror. The relief. Then she began to cry. Martin was dying, and she could do nothing. Didn't want to.

She watched, terrified and fascinated in the same moment, still unable to move as he reached for something, maybe the bed frame, maybe her hand, but his arm collapsed beneath him. He let out one last strangled noise, halfway between a curse and a plea. Then silence. His chest no longer rose. His eyes stayed open. The room held its breath.

Natalie didn't. She exhaled, long and broken. The tears came hard now. Hot. She cried not for him, not for what was lost, but for everything that had ever been taken. For every lie. Every night she couldn't remember. She cried because she was still chained to the bed. And now, the only person who might have freed her was lying dead on the floor beside her. The room pulsed with candlelight. Wax pooled like tiny lakes around her. Martin must have soiled himself, the stench reaching her nostrils. She gagged and turned her face away.

Martin's hand had fallen just inches from the bed. She stared at it. The fingers were curled, knuckles taut. She hoped it hurt, really, really hurt when his heart had spasmed and given in.

She imagined what would happen now. The house was isolated. The lake was silent. No one was due to visit. The nearest town was fifteen minutes by car. She had no phone. No voice loud enough to reach the woods beyond the road. The other men would probably have finished their breakfasts and driven away from the diner, their stomachs full of eggs and coffee, their heads rammed with perverted memories to feed on for a while.

She might die here. And no one would ever know. Her body would fade slowly. Like the candles. Her breath would grow thin, her strength depleted. And she would become one more secret buried in the house that had buried others. The Lane legacy.

Natalie turned her face to the wall and whispered a name. *High Bear.*

She remembered his voice, deep and low like the rivers of Wyoming. She remembered his stories of vision quests and spirit guides. How he told her the land remembers everything, even when people don't. That truth can hide beneath roots and water but can't be erased.

"Help me," she whispered.

Nothing stirred. The room stayed still. But she wasn't done. Not yet. She looked at her wrists. Bloody. Raw. Still hers. She could endure. She had to for her children. Exhaustion overwhelmed her and as she drifted into a pain and trauma induced sleep, the past called her name and maybe to soothe her, fend off nightmares, took her back to a place and time when her body didn't ache and her mind was free of shame.

# 18

*Lander, Wyoming – Fall 2015*

The chapel stood like a relic on the edge of the reservation, its white clapboard sides weathered but proud beneath the golden sky. Sunlight poured over the scrubland and distant cottonwoods, turning the land into a burnished memory. The scent of dry sagebrush clung to the breeze, and somewhere far off, a crow called once, long and low, like a reminder.

Inside, the chapel was dressed in simple, tasteful flowers. White blooms dotted the ends of pews wrapped in twine, and a string quartet, two guitars, a violin, and a cello, played softly near the altar. The ceiling was high and exposed, the wood beams dark with age and dust. It wasn't glamorous, but it was hers. Lander. Home.

Natalie stood behind the modest curtain of the vestry, peeking through a slit in the fabric. She saw Martin at the altar in a crisp dark suit, whispering something to Leon, who stood at his side, tall and broader than she remembered. Her soon-to-be brother-in-law smiled in that quiet way of his, gentle and unreadable, but Martin didn't return it. His mouth twisted into a grin meant only for effect. Natalie felt it in her stomach.

Joy was behind her, fussing over a crooked strand of Natalie's hair.

"Stop fidgeting," her sister whispered, half-laughing. "You look like you're about to bolt."

Natalie didn't answer. She had barely slept. Her mother had been weepy all morning, her father stoic, and High Bear silent as a stone except for the words he whispered to her as he fastened the bracelet on her wrist.

"You walk toward him like you'd walk into a storm," he'd said, his voice gravel-rough and slow. "If your soul ever feels the wind change, don't wait for the thunder. Leave, child."

At the time, she thought it was one of his mystical flourishes, one of many he'd given her over the years. The same way he spoke about coyotes being messengers and the wind carrying the voices of ancestors. She'd smiled, kissed his cheek, and let his words fall into the ether. But now, standing behind the curtain and watching Martin adjust his cuffs with that impatient twitch in his jaw.

She tried to shake it off. Told herself she was just nervous. Everyone was nervous before their wedding.

"Ready?" Joy asked, gently smoothing the veil over her shoulders.

No. Not really. But she nodded. The music shifted. The guests stood.

Martin's mother, Vivienne, had arrived last and made sure everyone noticed. She wore a tailored navy dress with pearls that glinted like frost, her hair pulled back in a tight chignon. She hadn't stopped commenting on the venue since she stepped off the plane from Philadelphia. "Charming," she'd called it, which, from her mouth, sounded like "cheap." She didn't even try to hide her grimace when she saw High Bear in full regalia – feathers, beads, and all, standing like a totem among the guests.

Natalie's father took her arm, and they walked together down the aisle. The chapel held maybe sixty people. Most of them were from her side. A few of Martin's colleagues had made the journey, all stiff in suits and uncomfortable in the Wyoming heat. Bobby, Martin's father, sat front and center. He barely looked at Natalie as she passed. His eyes, small and cold, followed Martin the entire time. Leon smiled, though. She held on to that. Leon had always been kind. Always... different from the others.

At the altar, Martin kissed her cheek perfunctorily. His hands were cold and dry.

"You're beautiful," he whispered.

It didn't sound like a compliment. It sounded like a line. Like he'd practiced it in the mirror that morning.

The pastor began. The ceremony blurred in her mind even as it happened. Words about love and commitment and God's presence. She stared out the chapel windows instead, watching clouds creep over the mountains in the distance, like shadows folding over the past. She caught sight of High Bear in the second row, still and watchful. His eyes never left her. There was something in them that wasn't peace.

When the pastor said, "You may kiss the bride," Martin turned her face toward his with a firm hand. His lips were warm, but his mouth felt like a closing door. There was applause. A reception followed the ceremony, held out back under a white canvas tent. Her mother cried again during the first dance. Her dad raised a solemn glass of bourbon. Joy laughed and twirled Eve, one of their little cousins, until the girl collapsed in a heap of tulle and giggles.

Martin gave a speech about how lucky he was. How he had found the one person who understood him. Natalie's stomach clenched again, not from nerves this time but something deeper. She hadn't written her vows. She'd read them off a notecard like a school recital and was thankful she wasn't required to give a speech.

Vivienne cornered her during the cake cutting, her smile brittle and tight.

"It's a lovely dress," she said, eyeing the modest lace sleeves. "Very... rural, sweet in its own way."

Natalie said thank you. That's all she could say because she was concentrating on ignoring the sting of Vivienne's words.

Later, as the sun dropped behind the pines and golden hour bathed everything in a soft sultry glow, High Bear asked for a moment alone with her. They walked beyond the tents to the edge of the field. The scent of grass and dust and firewood clung to the air.

He didn't say anything at first. Just looked at her. Then, finally:

"That man is all smooth rock and no roots," he said.

She looked at him, puzzled.

"There are men who wear faces like masks," he continued, his hand resting lightly on her shoulder. "You think you're seeing them, but you're only seeing what they want you to see. He is that kind. There is a shadow inside him and a storm buried deep. I don't know how long it has been there or when the clouds will break but I see them."

"Grandpa..." she started to say, brushing it off, trying to laugh.

"You laugh now. But one day you'll wish you'd listened to an old man."

"I love him."

He nodded. "That's what worries me."

They stood there for a while. Silent. Listening to the wind in the trees. Somewhere, a hawk cried out. When she returned to the tent, Martin was deep in conversation with his father. Bobby gave her a nod that felt more like a terse acknowledgment than a warm welcome to the family. She took Martin's arm, smiling the way a good wife is supposed to smile, and let him lead her into the dance.

Later that night, in the small suite at the lodge where they were staying, Martin took off her dress with a mix of reverence and possession. She remembered staring at the ceiling while he kissed her neck, thinking only of her grandfather's words.

A storm. A shadow. A man in a mask. She didn't understand it then. She did now. And as if the wings of an eagle were taking flight, sweeping her off towards her children, Natalie's dreams focused on them, her precious son and daughter and the woman who she'd trusted to care for them.

Vivienne sat in the armchair Martin always favored, high-backed and dark brown, like a throne. She'd brought her own cushion from home. Something embroidered and stiff-looking, likely from a country catalog. It was wedged behind her back aiding her posture.

Across the living room, Thomas yanked a clump of hair from Eve's head.

"Stop it!" Eve yelped, hands to her scalp.

Thomas laughed. A mean, empty sound that shouldn't belong to a boy his age. Vivienne didn't flinch. Her pale blue eyes flicked up from her knitting, a sweater, red, dense, and angry looking and she gave the barest smile. Not one of amusement, not one of disapproval. Just... satisfaction.

"She's just being dramatic," Thomas said, shrugging. "She cried yesterday when I hid her stupid bear in the freezer."

Vivienne didn't respond. She counted her stitches in a low

whisper, the needles clicking rhythmically like tiny bones knocking together.

Eve looked pleadingly at her grandmother. "He hurt me. And it was mean, what he did with my teddy."

"Oh, sweetheart," Vivienne murmured without looking up. "He's just playing. You mustn't be so sensitive. You need to toughen up."

Eve backed toward the hallway, her eyes wet. Thomas smirked, victorious. Then, the doorbell rang. Vivienne placed her knitting down with the ceremony of a queen laying aside her scepter and stood, smoothing her pressed beige slacks as she looked out the window.

"Looks like it's your uncle."

She opened the front door with an expression of measured surprise, as if she hadn't been expecting anyone at all.

"Leon," she said. "What a lovely treat."

Leon Beaumont stepped into the doorway, tall and wide-shouldered, his button-down shirt wrinkled as if he'd driven fast and long. There were lines at the corners of his kind eyes.

"Where is everyone?" he asked.

Vivienne tilted her head. "Good day to you, too."

Leon brushed past her into the hallway as the children ran to him like magnets.

"Uncle Leon!" Eve wrapped her arms around his middle. "You're here!"

Thomas wasn't far behind, like a dog seeing its owner after a long absence. Leon embraced him and Eve, his expression softening as he took them in.

"I missed you two," he said, voice low, eyes scanning the room behind them.

"Where's your mom and dad?" he asked Eve.

Eve looked up at her grandmother, unsure.

Vivienne interjected. "They've gone away for a few days. To the cabin. Your father wanted to mark the anniversary."

Leon froze. "The cabin?"

Vivienne smiled, almost fondly. "Yes, Martin thought it would be romantic."

"No one told me," Leon said, his voice tightening.

"Well," Vivienne said, turning back toward the sitting room. "You know now. So if you want to go charging up there like a jealous teenager not invited to the party, you're perfectly welcome to."

Leon stared after her, his hands still resting protectively on the children's backs.

"They left yesterday?"

Vivienne sank back into her chair. "Late afternoon. You've still got time to join in the fun if you're in such a hurry."

Leon took a long breath and moved away from the children, pacing toward the front door again. "Why didn't he tell me? Why didn't you?"

Vivienne's face twitched. "You were his best man so ought to remember without a prompt, and maybe they wanted time alone without a third wheel."

"Is that what you're calling me now?" he said sharply.

Vivienne didn't blink. "You're not a child anymore. You've had plenty of fun up there so quit with the jealousy and stop acting like you've been left out. But anyway, you still have a choice. You can head on up there and join in or stay here and keep us company."

Leon opened the door again. The breeze from outside stirred the drapes. "I'm going to find my brother."

He didn't say goodbye. He just left. The door clacked softly shut.

Vivienne stood still, hands resting on the back of the chair, knitting forgotten. Her expression was unreadable. Not smug.

Not shaken. Just... resigned. Like she'd just broke up a sibling fight and knew it would be one of many, just like all the squabbles that had gone before. She looked at the clock on the wall, then turned her head toward the children.

"Go wash up," she said with a tone that brokered no refusal. "It's nearly lunchtime."

Eve hesitated. "Will Uncle Leon come back soon?"

"Perhaps, but he's very busy," Vivienne said with a smile that didn't reach her eyes. "He's got grown-up things to do."

Thomas ran upstairs without a word, sulking, his feet pounding the floor overhead. Eve lingered, hugging the banister. She looked down at her grandmother as if trying to puzzle out something. About the way her grandmother hadn't flinched at her uncle's anger, and just like with naughty Thomas, hadn't scolded, either. Hadn't really said anything when her brother yanked her hair. Something... was just wrong with it all.

"Eve," Vivienne said, sharper now. "Go."

Eve turned slowly and walked up the stairs.

Vivienne sighed and collected her knitting, then moved toward the kitchen. She didn't worry about his mood, or the drive, or what would happen up at the cabin because Martin was there and he, as always, would have it all under control.

# 19

Natalie stirred, her face pressed against the faint indentation of the pillow. She blinked once, twice, until the world came into focus. Her head throbbed, her chest heaved, and her arms ached, the sweat-damp shackles biting into her tired wrists.

Sunlight met her eyes with unwelcome warmth. The candles had burned themselves into nothing and the air smelled stale, heavy, like rot and old sin. She lay silent, muscles trembling. Next to the bed lay Martin's body. His face was slack, eyes open and empty. Not watching her anymore. Not controlling. Not masking. Just... gone.

Natalie closed her eyes and pressed her forehead against the pillow. She refused to stay here. She refused to die, alone, a victim of her husband's sick game. Not for him. Not for anyone. She thought of her children. She pictured Eve's shoulder-length hair and Thomas's stubborn chin, already setting like rock. They needed her. She needed to live – for them.

A voice crept in, low and steady. It was her grandfather's voice again, ancient and sure. High Bear. The words he'd spoken ten years ago in Wyoming flooded her mind.

*"Fear is not the enemy. Forgetting who you are, that's the danger."*

Natalie had let who she was, go. She had let too much slip away to become someone who watched a vile man refuse the dinner she had prepared and smile at the compliments he hadn't earned. But this time, she wouldn't.

She inhaled sharply, her lungs cramping around the effort. She slid her hand toward the edge of the bed, searching. Her fingertips brushed a splinter in the headboard. She yanked backward, the bedpost creaking beneath her weight.

She tested the shackle on her right wrist. It didn't budge. But she tried anyway. She lifted the arm, braced it against the leg of the bed. Her teeth clenched, and she pushed with everything left inside her. A snap. A jolt of agony. Her wrist twinged with an electric shock, pain that went beyond muscle or bone. But when she wiggled, escape followed. The metal slipped away with a grating sigh.

Natalie was stunned silent, her ruined wrist slick with sweat and blood. She had dislocated it. Not broken it completely. It ached with urgent stiffness. But she was almost free. Freed from straps that held her body. Not her spirit.

She gasped and wheezed, drawing in the air like her lungs had never worked properly. The room swelled and contracted as the pain ping-ponged between ribs and muscles. She didn't focus on it. She focused on the cold. She hauled herself onto her side, ignoring the weight of the other limbs that were still trapped.

Martin's body lay near her feet, stiff and final. She stretched over, nauseated by the sight. She hesitated, stomach knotting, before she reached down. His hand lay open, fingers slightly curled. She gently turned it over and at his wrist, spotted the leather band that held two small keys. Her heart hammered, fear and relief in equal measure. She looked away, closing her eyes, trying to stop her pulse from jumping through her throat as she unhooked the clasp with shaking fingers, praying she wouldn't drop it, lifted it onto the bed.

Natalie reached for the second shackle on her left wrist, fumbling with the key thanks to her shaking fingers. She found the small hole, slid the metal in, and turned it with careful pressure. The cuff opened with a click. She pressed it gently and wandered her wrist free of the leather loop then with the other key, did the same with her feet restraints.

She sat there for a moment, naked, sore, broken and suddenly free. She looked at Martin's face once more. Something triggered in her chest that felt like pity. But it lasted only an instant.

Then Natalie stood. Her wrist throbbed and her legs wobbled. Every breath felt like little razors, but she stood. She pressed her palm to the cold mirror on the wall. Her face was hollowed, pale but her eyes were still hers. Still alive. And now she would scream for help. She would find her children. She would remember who she was.

With her non-dislocated wrist, she reached for the door handle and pushed it open but it groaned on old hinges and refused. She pulled hard and didn't stop, the force echoing through the room until it gave. She wobbled through the doorway, still barefoot, and made her way into the corridor.

The carpet felt rough beneath her toes as she moved toward the stairs, each step a spike of pain. But she climbed just the same, toward the uncertainty beyond. She had left an evil dead husband behind but she carried her faith and her soul intact. Now she would reclaim her life, no matter how ruined. High Bear's voice echoed in her mind once more:

*"Don't wait for the thunder."* She was waiting no longer.

Leon gripped the steering wheel of the pick-up truck as it thundered down the uneven back roads, its engine growling beneath him like it knew where it was going. Dust kicked up in furious clouds behind him, spiraling like ghosts in the rearview mirror.

He hadn't bothered with music. The only sound in the cab was his breath, ragged and too loud, and the muttered fragments of conversation that kept spilling from his mouth as though he were arguing with someone who wasn't there.

"Should've known," he muttered, jaw clenched. "Should've fuckin' known."

The heat was unbearable. Sweat pooled beneath his shirt and soaked into his jeans. It beaded along his brow and down his neck, dripping into the collar of the faded Philadelphia Eagles T-shirt he hadn't changed out of. His face was red, like a man who'd been running for miles or about to face the enemy.

The trees grew denser as he turned off the main road, a forgotten artery winding through the woods near Lake Wallenpaupack. He knew every bump, every bend of this stretch. They'd spent their childhood summers here. Martin always claimed the cabin was a sanctuary. But Leon had stopped thinking of it that way a long time ago.

He adjusted the rearview mirror but didn't like what he saw, the look in his own eyes. Haunted. Furious. His mouth curled into something that wasn't quite a snarl. "What the hell were you thinking, Martin?"

The words slipped out like bile. It wasn't just that Martin and Natalie had gone to the cabin without telling him. That alone would have been enough to set Leon on edge. No, it was the *way* Vivienne had said it, with that chilly smile curling under her lipstick like a serpent. She'd offered the information too easily, like a lure cast into dark water. If she was being helpful, something was wrong.

He hadn't told her this, but he'd driven out to the cabin once last year, alone. Some restless impulse had yanked him out of bed and steered him north. When he got there, the place had been locked tight but there were tracks in the dusty earth. Like someone had just left. Like the trees were watching. He'd sat on the porch for half an hour, smoking, trying to decide if he was just winding himself up. He hadn't been back since. Until now.

The truck bucked over a pothole. Leon swore under his breath, hands gripping tighter.

Natalie. She was the reason he was out here. She'd always been gentle, quiet, the sort of woman who tried too hard to make everyone comfortable, even when she was visibly unraveling. But last time he saw her at dinner with his mother chirping away, she hadn't looked right. Too thin. Eyes too bright, like she hadn't slept in a month. And that tight smile she gave him when he said goodbye? That had haunted him for days.

He thumped the wheel once with his palm, the slap of skin on leather loud in the cab. "Goddammit, Martin. You promised me."

He should have said something years ago. But what would he have said? That he didn't like the way Martin talked about her when she wasn't in the room. That he didn't like the way Vivienne pretended Natalie didn't exist except as a vessel for her grandchildren.

That he remembered things from their childhood, moments, whispers, strange noises in the cabin when they were supposed to be asleep? He couldn't prove anything. And he'd never had the guts to ask Martin outright. But now, his gut told him the time for silence was over.

Leon wiped a hand down his face. It came away slick with sweat. The truck's AC was busted, but he didn't bother opening the window. The air outside was hot, humid enough to make you hate summer.

What would he find when he got there? He didn't know. That was what terrified him most.

He replayed the conversation with Vivienne in his mind,

repeatedly like a record stuck on a warped groove. *They've gone up to the lake,* she'd said, folding a cloth napkin in her lap. *You know, just the two of them. Anniversary trip. Stop acting like you've been left out.* And then she'd smiled.

*Left out.* He wasn't just left out. He was kept out. She *wanted* him to go now. Which meant the thing she was hiding was already set in motion and it could only mean one thing.

And maybe she thought it was too late for him to stop it.

The truck crested the last hill, and he saw the turn-off ahead. A jagged wooden sign nearly swallowed by moss pointed toward the cabin road. He swung the truck into the drive, gravel crackling under his tires like bones snapping. The cabin was miles away through the trees, but his pulse was already banging against his ribs.

He kind of knew what he'd find when he got there and something in his gut, worse than fear, told him he was already too late. Still, he pressed the gas. Because no matter what waited at the end of that road, he needed to be a part of it. He needed to see what his brother had done without him. And he was going to be a part of what he'd been keeping quiet for all these years.

# 20

Natalie stood barefoot on the landing, trembling, her legs felt alien beneath her, barely keeping her upright, each breath a rasp in her raw throat. Her left wrist throbbed, angry and ballooned from the dislocation. She clutched her arm against her chest like a child hugging a broken toy. Behind her, Martin's corpse cooled on the floor. His eyes had ceased judging her but she could still feel them. Still see the contempt in their glassy blue sheen. She didn't look back. She couldn't.

Instead, she took a step forward. Then another. Her bare heel smeared through something gritty on the wood, a trail of blood, hers. Natalie was mostly numb, shock acting like a drug, dulling the sharpest edges. She made her way down the stairs, pausing only once when the floorboard beneath her let out a long groan, like it too was weary of secrets.

Downstairs, the open-plan living area was cast in murky light from the thin slit between the blinds. The cabin was still and quiet, save for the faint tick of the wall clock and the screech of some bird out by the lake.

Natalie crossed the room on shaking legs, heading for the

duffel she'd packed the day before. It sat untouched by the sliding glass doors, beside the armchair where Martin had insisted they drink a toast to "ten years of happiness." She knelt slowly, her knees groaning with the effort, and tugged the bag open with one hand. A flannel shirt, faded jeans, socks. She dressed quickly, fumbling each piece on, barely able to thread her swollen wrist through the sleeve. Her own body felt like violated and foreign.

On the table stood the wine glasses from last night. One still held a measure of red, dark as blood, faint lipstick smudging the rim. Natalie stared at them for a long moment, then turned her back. That's when she heard it.

A sound. Low. Inhuman. Not quite a word, not quite a cry. A noise that rippled through the silence and struck her in the chest. It came again, a moan. From the back of the cabin. The bedrooms. The children's bedrooms.

Her feet carried her before her brain caught up. Past the half-kitchen, past the bathroom, until she reached the narrow hallway that led to the two small bedrooms where Thomas and Eve usually slept when they visited. The air grew rank and a total contrast to her memories of clean sheets fresh from the laundry as Natalie remembered Eve's voice, asking for another bedtime story on their last summer trip here. That small hand in hers.

She gripped the iron poker from beside the fireplace with her good hand. The moan came again, louder now. A woman's voice. Heart thudding like a hammer in her ears, Natalie turned the knob and eased the bedroom door open. What she saw didn't register right away.

There, on the small bed against the far wall, Eve's bed, a woman lay sprawled, shackled at the wrists and both ankles to the iron bedframe. She was completely naked, her skin a dull, waxy sheen of sweat. Her limbs twitched with disjointed motion, a slow, syrupy spasm that came and went. Her lips moved, forming fragmented words in a language Natalie couldn't recognize.

A camera stood at the foot of the bed. Tripod-mounted, its light blinking red. Natalie's breath caught. She dropped the poker with a clatter and rushed to the bed. The woman's face was young, twenties maybe. Flushed. Pupils dilated. Her lips were chapped and dry, one eye swollen, as if someone had struck her.

"Oh God. Oh God," Natalie whispered, barely able to think through the panic. Her fingers shook as she tugged at the restraints, trying to locate how they locked. Each tug sent fire lancing through her injured wrist.

The girl moaned again. This time it sounded like "Mama."

"No, you're okay," Natalie said, her voice cracking. "You're safe now. I'm here."

She didn't know if that was true. She saw a keyring sitting on a table on the far side of room and grabbing it she wedged it into the crude padlock at the girl's ankle. A few shaky turns, a twist, and it gave. Then the other. Then the wrist.

The girl collapsed into a heap. Natalie wrapped a thin cotton blanket from the closet around her, trying not to recoil from the smell, chemicals, urine, fear. The girl was barely responsive, her head lolling as Natalie cradled her.

"Can you hear me? What's your name?"

The girl opened her mouth. Nothing came out. Then something that sounded like, "Sienna."

Natalie blinked back tears. "Okay, Sienna. We're gonna get out of here."

Sienna groaned, eyes fluttering.

Natalie looked at the camera again. Still blinking. Still

watching. She kicked it over. It toppled with a crash, glass cracking. Then footsteps. Not real ones. Phantom ones. In her head, her chest. Or outside? She didn't know anymore. She needed a plan. Needed a car. Martin's keys. Anything to get out.

She pulled Sienna up but she was a dead weight. The girl was dazed, uncoordinated, barely able to walk. From the bedroom window the lake glinted in the late sun, rippling like it didn't know or care what horrors had unfolded inside the cabin. But the world she knew had shifted. She had shifted and needed to act.

Natalie moved fast, her bare feet soundless against the wooden floor, heart pounding as she filled a chipped glass from the kitchen sink. The water ran cloudy for a second, then cleared. She let it pour until it ran cold, then shut it off and stood a moment, trying to catch her breath.

The woman in the downstairs bedroom, Sienna, hadn't stirred since Natalie unfastened the restraints from the bedframe. But her eyes had fluttered, her body shivering in that jerky, drugged way, and Natalie knew she wasn't gone. Not yet. She wouldn't let her be.

Natalie returned with the water, crouched beside the bed where the woman lay huddled beneath the scratchy flannel blanket Natalie had pulled from the linen closet. Her skin was slick with cold sweat, face pale and drawn, lips dry as dust. She looked young. Not much older than Natalie had been when she married Martin. Her brown hair clung to her forehead in sticky strands. There were faint bruises forming around her wrists.

"Hey," Natalie whispered gently. "You need to drink this. You're safe now."

The woman moaned something guttural, unintelligible and turned her head. Her eyelids cracked open, unfocused and panicked. When she saw Natalie, she flinched like a wounded animal.

"It's okay," Natalie said again, setting the glass gently against her lips. "Just sip. I promise, it's clean. I wouldn't hurt you, look, they did the same to me." She held up her wrist so Sienna could see the damage.

Finally, she drank. Greedily. So much so the glass shook in Natalie's hands. Water ran down her chin and neck, soaking the blanket. When the glass was empty, Sienna coughed softly and fell back onto the pillow, breathing more evenly now. Natalie tucked the blanket closer around her shoulders, then sat beside her on the edge of the mattress. Her limbs felt like gelatin, but her mind was sharp, churning with questions she wasn't sure she wanted answers to.

Natalie smiled, hoping to reassure. "Sienna. I'm Natalie."

Sienna blinked slowly. "Where am I?"

"You're in a cabin," Natalie said. "On Lake Wallenpaupack, in Pennsylvania."

"I don't..." Sienna shook her head, wincing. "I've never been here before. I don't remember coming here."

Natalie hesitated. "Do you remember anything before this?"

Sienna licked her cracked lips. "I was... at home. With my husband. He made pasta. I told him I was tired. He said I should go lie down, that he'd bring me tea." She paused, visibly trying to piece it together. "He brought it in a mug with a sunflower on it. My favorite. I remember drinking it. And then... nothing."

Natalie's stomach twisted. "Sienna... where's home?"

"Newburg," Sienna said faintly. "It's north of New York. We live in a brown clapboard house on Pine Grove Road. It backs onto the woods."

"I'm a Kindergarten teacher" she added, still not really acknowledging the gravity of their situation. Instead, she spoke softly, detached, as it they were talking over coffee. "For seven years. My kids call me Miss Sienna."

Natalie smiled, a pained, involuntary flicker. "Where's your husband? What's his name?"

"Scott."

Natalie flinched. "Can you describe him?"

Sienna looked confused but answered. "Tall. Dark hair. Wears glasses when he reads. He's got this deep voice. He's... charming. Everyone loves him. My mother thinks he's perfect." Her mouth twitched. "He can be moody though... intense. Sometimes quiet for days. But he's... he's a good man."

Natalie's blood froze in her veins. The man she was describing, was one of the men in the cabin. The one who stood behind the camera while Natalie lay chained to the bed upstairs. The one who circled her, mocking her, calling her disgusting names while zooming in on her naked body. The one who said he preferred it when she was asleep, Natalie was sure of it but maybe she was confused by the many face she remembered from a hideous dream. Sienna's "good man" had been there though, and was part of this sick group, of that Natalie was certain.

Natalie stood up abruptly and moved to the far side of the room, nausea rising like bile. She pressed her palm to the wall to steady herself.

"He was here," she whispered. "Last night."

Sienna blinked. "What?"

"I saw him," Natalie said, her voice growing harder. "They drugged me too. He filmed me."

"No," Sienna said, barely audible.

"Yes." Natalie turned to face her. "I wish I was wrong. I wish I was dreaming. But I'm not. Something horrific has been happening in this house. And we were part of it last night."

Sienna stared at her, silent. Tears began slipping down her cheeks. She pulled the blanket tighter, shrinking into herself.

"No," she repeated. "He wouldn't."

"He did," Natalie said flatly. "I know what I saw. And I know where I woke up."

Sienna let out a choked sob. Her hands trembled as she pulled the blanket to her mouth, biting it to muffle the noise. Her whole body shook.

Natalie moved toward her, crouching again. "Listen to me. I don't know how long they've been doing this. But we're not the first. And we won't be the last if we don't leave. Do you understand me?"

Sienna nodded, her expression blank and stunned.

"We're getting out," Natalie said, more to herself than to Sienna. "I don't know how much time we have because one of them said they'd gone to the diner so they could come back at any minute but my husband's car is here. We can take that."

Sienna wiped her eyes. "But I don't even know where we are. I don't have shoes. Or clothes. Or..."

"I'll find us something," Natalie said. "We just have to move fast."

She stood and scanned the room. The closet. She moved to it and opened the creaky door. Inside: old winter coats, worn slippers, a stack of plastic bins. She dug until she found a pair of Martin's sweatpants, oversized but clean, and a hoodie from a college he never attended. She tossed them onto the bed.

"Put these on. They'll be big, but they're warm. We'll figure out the rest when we're out of this place."

Sienna obeyed, her hands shaking as she pulled on the clothes. Her legs were wobbly but holding.

"Thank you," she whispered.

Natalie looked at her, this woman who just yesterday was probably making finger-painting plans and packing juice boxes. Now she was here, in her daughter's bed, wearing the clothes belonging to her abuser.

"We're going to get out," Natalie said again.

Sienna didn't reply. She only nodded.

The two women stood in the doorway of the bedroom, peering out at the hall. Natalie bent and picked up the poker and tightened her grip, her heart knocking against her ribs. Outside, somewhere in the woods or on the winding gravel road, someone might be coming. But they weren't going to wait anymore.

## 21

Sienna clung to Natalie like a child would cling to its mother in the middle of a storm. Her body shook beneath the blanket, the cheap synthetic fibers clutched in her fists like a life raft. Her lips trembled, but her voice had mostly disappeared. When she tried to speak, it came out in a rasp, dry as broken leaves.

Natalie didn't know how she was still standing. Her own body was failing her, her wrist a grotesque twist of purple and bone beneath the skin, her legs weak, her vision swimming in and out of focus but her mind had locked into a tunnel. Get out. Get Sienna out. Survive.

She had tried every door. The back. The front. Even the tiny cellar entrance. Sealed like a tomb. Natalie had never felt time move like this. Slow, syrupy dread winding through her bones. She needed to think. But the only thing her mind could conjure was the camera. The red light. The sound of breathing that hadn't belonged to her.

"Stay here," she said to Sienna. Her voice surprised her, hoarse but clear, like someone else was speaking through her.

Sienna's eyes went wide. She reached for Natalie's good hand, but Natalie pulled away gently. "It's ok," Natalie said, crouching low, face level with Sienna. "Call out if you hear anything. A car. Footsteps. Anything."

Sienna gave the smallest nod, but her eyes stayed locked on Natalie, full of a fear that went deeper than words. Natalie forced herself to smile, even if it felt like her face might crack from the effort. She left the bedroom quietly, every step a jab of fire up her dislocated wrist and every breath sharpened with panic. The stairs creaked, each groan a betrayal. When she reached the landing, she paused, staring at the door to the master bedroom. Her legs refused to move for a moment.

Martin was still in there. His body. She pushed the door open. The smell hit her first. Not decay, not yet, but something warm and wrong. He lay face-up on the floor, his eyes staring toward the ceiling like he was waiting for something divine to pull him out of the mess he'd made. His mouth was slightly open. His hand, the one with the scar on the ring finger, curled upward as if in a final plea.

Natalie walked past him without looking again. The camera stood like a sentry in the corner. She crossed the room and crouched, her broken wrist screaming in protest. It took her a moment to work out the buttons. She didn't trust her fingers, not anymore. They felt foreign, like they belonged to someone else.

The playback blinked on. She saw herself first. Bare. Shackled. Still. She reached for the fast-forward button, her breath stalling in her throat. The footage moved and another man entered the frame. Not Martin. The other one. The one who'd brought the water. He knelt beside her unconscious body. His hand moved where it never should have. His mouth twisted into a smile that didn't belong to any decent human. Natalie stopped the video. She gagged, curling forward. The bile in her throat was acidic, but she swallowed it down.

She checked the file and saw that there were many albums, so she opened one randomly.

Another video. Another woman. Blonde. Limp. Then another. And another. Some of the dates were from years ago. Her hands started shaking. She bent and rested her hands on her knees. Her vision went white around the edges.

This wasn't just a moment of madness. It was a sordid archive. And without looking she knew that she'd been part of it. Multiple times. She had memories and haunted fractured dreams, bruises she'd never been able to explain, mornings at the lake house when she felt foggy, detached, sore. Martin had called it her depression. Her sleepwalking. Her *episodes*.

She went back to her file and watched herself be carried like a rag doll. Drugged. Displayed. Passed around like... She stopped the footage. No more.

Her wrist throbbed with renewed agony. The skin had split in places, smeared with dried blood and dirt. She couldn't stay in this room. She couldn't be near him. She limped out of the room, down the stairs, clutching the camera's memory card in her good hand then slid it deep inside the front pocket of her jeans.

Sienna looked up from the floor when Natalie returned. "What is it?" she asked, her voice thin.

Natalie didn't answer. She knelt beside her and placed both hands on her shoulders.

"We need to find a way out," she said.

Sienna blinked, and for the first time, some small flicker of strength returned to her face as she tried to smother the reason why she was there in the first place, the man she loved, and trusted. Memories flooded back. Of the day they left. The day her husband betrayed her.

The little second-floor apartment nestled on the quieter end of Newburg's Main Street. Sienna stirred beneath a thin cotton sheet, her bare shoulder warmed by the gentle light. It was the kind of summer morning she loved most, slow, soft, expectant.

Scott was already up, seated at the small kitchen table with his laptop. He hunched over it, shirtless, a faint glow from the screen reflecting off his wire-rimmed glasses. His fingers moved with a kind of twitchy energy, not quite typing – clicking, scrolling, tapping. His expression was tight with concentration, and he didn't look up when she padded in, barefoot, yawning.

"I see you've been up for a while," she murmured, voice thick with sleep.

"Couldn't nod back off," he said quickly, closing the screen halfway. "Got sucked into something."

He offered her a smile and Sienna nodded, not pressing. Scott often went down little rabbit holes he found in online groups that shared conspiracy videos, obscure investment forums, chess clubs, most of which she half-listened to and then forgot. It wasn't unusual for him to lose hours on the computer. But there was something different about him this morning. A jittery kind of eagerness, like he was waiting to tell her something.

She turned toward the kitchen to start breakfast. It was a Saturday ritual. Pancakes with syrup and frozen berries. He liked his extra sweet. She liked hers with Greek yogurt and they'd eat together looking out over the street, people watching Their apartment was small, cozy, walls lined with books and knickknacks from her kindergarten students – little clay animals, pipe-cleaner crafts. There was a warmth to their home, a domestic comfort that sometimes made her feel guilty for how bored she could feel inside it.

Still, she loved Scott. He'd been stable, reliable, nothing like the wild boys she'd dated in college who'd vanished without warning or drank too much and texted her at 3 a.m. Scott had a steady job in IT support and never yelled. He remembered her birthday, made her peppermint tea when she was sick, left notes with terrible puns tucked in her lunchbox.

But he wasn't spontaneous. So, when he suddenly stood, nearly knocking his chair back, and announced, "I have a surprise," she blinked, confused.

"What kind of surprise?"

"A good one," he said, that smile spreading again. "We're getting away for the weekend. Just you and me."

"Wait, what?" Sienna laughed, wiping flour from her fingers. "Where?"

"A cabin. By a lake. Romantic, private." His voice was excited now, as if he'd waited a long time to reveal this. "I found it online. It's a few hours' drive. I already packed the car with snacks and wine. You just need to grab clothes."

"You've never done anything like this before," she said, eyes narrowing in playful suspicion.

"Well, maybe I've turned over a new leaf." He came forward, wrapping his arms around her waist, burying his face in her neck. "You said we needed more romance. More surprises."

She laughed again, half thrilled, half baffled. "What's the occasion?"

"Does there have to be one?" he whispered. "Let's just... get away. No work. No phones. Just us."

Sienna felt a strange little flutter in her stomach. The idea of being somewhere secluded, with him, away from the classroom and spreadsheets and the same old dinners and TV shows, it was alluring. Maybe they'd reconnect. Maybe she'd feel excited again. Maybe this weekend would be the one where she finally fell pregnant. She kissed him back and darted down the hall to pack.

In their bedroom, she tugged open drawers, folding a sweatshirt, then her favorite red swimsuit. As she moved through her things, she found herself singing a Taylor Swift song. Her mind buzzed with possibilities. They'd been trying for nearly a year. No fertility issues, just poor timing. That's what her OB had said. But lately, Sienna had felt ready. Her body, her heart. Scott, she suspected, was slower to embrace the idea. So the fact that he'd planned this trip himself, private and romantic, made something flicker in her. Hope, maybe.

She glanced at the mirror as she dressed. Toned legs, thanks to her morning runs. Long dark hair pulled into a high ponytail. She looked younger than thirty, people always told her that. Her students loved her. She had a good life. Still, something in her gut fluttered again, but this time with less excitement. Unease? No. Nerves, probably. She always got this way when she traveled.

Scott stood in the doorway holding a small red cooler. "You'll love this place," he said. "It's... really private."

He hesitated before saying the last words. Sienna looked up. "Is there even Wi-Fi?"

He laughed. "No. That's the point."

It was around 10 a.m. when they left. She remembered because she'd glanced at the stove clock while pouring herself a final glass of water. The day was already warming up, the sky a clear, brilliant blue. She had no idea where they were going. He plugged the address into his phone and refused to show her.

"Just relax," he said. "Let yourself be surprised and pampered for once."

And she did. She let herself be surprised. She sat beside him in the car, the windows down, the wind lifting strands of her hair as they drove north. He played an old playlist from their early dating days, The Lumineers, Bon Iver, some silly romantic tracks they'd once danced to in their socks.

For a while, everything felt good. She remembered leaning her head on the window and thinking: *Maybe this is it. Maybe everything is about to change.* And she was right. It did. Just not the way she thought.

# 22

The floorboards creaked as Natalie searched for the door keys, every step pressing a bolt of pain through her dislocated wrist. She cradled it carefully, her other hand gripping the banister. The sun had dropped behind the trees, casting the inside of the cabin in heavy amber light that made everything seem slow and unreal, like moving through a dream. Her heart thrummed with each cautious step, eyes darting to corners, behind doorways, always expecting a sound, a cough, a creak, a voice. But the cabin remained quiet, unnaturally so.

Sienna sat on the couch, still wrapped in the fleece blanket Natalie had found in the linen closet. She hadn't moved much. Her eyes, hollow and dazed, were fixed on something invisible just past the far wall. Her fingers clutched the blanket like a lifeline, her entire frame folded into itself. The only sound was the ticking of an ancient wall clock.

"Nothing upstairs," Natalie said gently, as if the woman might shatter if she raised her voice. "All the windows are sealed. And the back door... it's locked with a padlock and bolt. We're not getting out that way."

Sienna turned her head slowly, her lips dry, eyes rimmed with red. "Are they... definitely gone?"

Natalie nodded once, slowly. "I think so. At least for now. No other vehicles outside apart from ours. No footsteps. No voices."

Sienna exhaled in a jagged breath and leaned back into the couch. Natalie walked carefully across the room, her body still sore, head pounding with every heartbeat. In her pocket, the memory stick from the video camera sat like a stone. Heavy, damning. She hadn't told Sienna. How could she? What good would it do? It would break her. What Sienna needed right now was calm, not truth. Not yet.

"I'm going to have to smash the door down so I need to find some tools, an axe, otherwise we can smash a window and climb out," Natalie said, softly. "There must be something here."

Sienna nodded, barely. Her lips trembled, and her eyes dropped to the floor. For a moment she looked like a child who'd been yelled at, lost in shame and confusion.

Natalie crouched in front of her, her voice like silk. "Do you remember anything else? Anything before you got here?"

Sienna blinked slowly. Then, after a moment, she spoke in a near whisper. "Scott said it was a surprise trip. Romantic getaway. We've never really done anything like that."

Natalie held her breath.

"I made pancakes," Sienna said. Her voice broke a little. "With berries. I usually went for a run but he said we were going to a lake house for the weekend. He seemed... excited. Weirdly excited. But I didn't think anything of it."

Natalie nodded slowly, her throat tightening.

"I got in the car. We drove for a while. He'd packed a picnic and drinks and after we'd eaten I started to feel... sleepy. Not just tired. Like... Like my brain was floating away. And then... nothing."

Sienna 's fingers dug into the blanket. She pulled it tighter around her.

"Next thing I know, I'm waking up to your voice. Here."

Natalie touched her shoulder lightly. "That's enough for now. Just breathe. You're not alone."

Sienna nodded but didn't speak again. She rocked a little on the couch, that slow back-and-forth motion of someone trying to stay grounded. Trying to stay sane. Natalie stood, every muscle in her body protesting. Her wrist throbbed with a fresh wave of agony, but she ignored it. She scanned the room for anything that might help them break out then her eyes moved toward the small storage area beneath the stairs.

The door creaked open to reveal boxes and cleaning supplies. She crouched, rifled through the nearest bin. Nothing of use.

Natalie returned and knelt beside her. "Do you think your husband will come back?" Natalie asked.

Sienna flinched. "I don't know. I don't know who he is anymore. He can't just leave me here, can he? When I don't show up for work my colleagues will raise the alarm so yes, I think he will come back for me at some point. Perhaps he thinks I'm still drugged or, oh God, what if they're going to do it all again tonight then get rid of the evidence, me, you, us."

Natalie stood again. She looked around the room, her mind panicking because what Sienna said was a possibility. She couldn't keep thinking like a victim. She had to plan. They couldn't stay another night here. The risk was too great. But until she could find a way out, she had to keep Sienna safe. They both needed food. Water. Warmth. And answers. More than anything, they needed answers.

She turned back toward Sienna. Her skin was blotchy, bruised in places. Natalie turned away as her own stomach twisted.

What had they done? What had been done to her? To Sienna? To the others? She touched the pocket where the memory stick sat. One day, soon, she'd show it to someone. Maybe the police. Maybe a journalist. Maybe whoever would take it and burn the whole damn Lane legacy to the ground.

But first, she had to survive. That's when she heard it: the crunch of gravel outside. A car.

Her stomach clenched. She raced back into the living room, heart pounding like a drum in her chest. Sienna was perched on the edge of the sofa, knees drawn to her chest. Her eyes flicked up in alarm.

"Someone's here," Natalie whispered, her voice sharp and urgent. "Go. Hide. Now."

Sienna stared at her for a beat too long, then scrambled to her feet and disappeared down the hallway. Natalie heard her duck into the room with the twin beds and hoped she'd hidden beneath one of the beds.

Natalie turned and grabbed the fire poker from beside the cold hearth, her grip slippery with sweat. Her body moved on instinct. She ran back upstairs and pressed herself into the shadows behind the wardrobe in the hallway, invisible from the stairs but with a clear line of sight.

Her breathing was ragged, shallow. The poker trembled slightly in her grip. She heard the sound of a key in the lock then the door creaked open.

"Martin?" a deep voice called out. "Natalie. You here?"

Natalie froze. The voice was unmistakable. Leon.

She blinked. Relief surged, and then faltered. Something in his tone... His boots thudded against the wooden floor. Natalie could see the outline of him now, tall, broad-shouldered, his face flushed from the heat outside. He wore jeans and a navy jacket. He turned in a slow circle, taking in the downstairs room.

Natalie was about to lower the poker, to reveal herself but

her breath hitched. Her arm stayed raised. Something was stopping her from lowering her guard. Leon walked deeper into the room, toward the dining table. His eyes paused briefly on the two wine glasses still sitting there, the lip of one stained pink. He sighed and pinched the bridge of his nose.

"Jesus, Martin, I knew this would happen," he said softly.

Natalie couldn't move. Her body was a statue of disbelief. Her mind splintered.

He knew something. Did Leon know what had happened here? Maybe not every detail. But maybe he knew enough.

She stepped out from the shadows, poker still clenched tightly in her hand.

Leon looked up, startled.

"Natalie," he said, his voice sharp with shock. "You're okay."

"No, I'm not okay," she hissed. Her voice was hoarse and raw. "Thanks to your sick brother and his perverted friends."

Leon was making his way up the stairs slowly and at the top, took a step toward her. "Natalie, please let me explain. I didn't..."

"Didn't what? Didn't know what your brother was doing to me? To the other women? Didn't know the unspeakable acts that happened in this place?"

His mouth opened and closed it again lowering his eyelids. "I knew something wasn't right. I didn't know..."

Natalie laughed. It came out high-pitched and wild. "You knew enough. You knew enough to keep your mouth shut."

He looked down at her wrist, at the grotesque angle of it, the mottled purple bruising. His face crumpled. " Natalie, I swear to God I never thought he'd do it to you."

She stepped forward. "Don't swear on anything. You're a monster, too."

For a long moment, silence fell between them.

Then Leon said, quietly, "Where's Martin?"

Natalie didn't blink or respond. Behind them, a door creaked.

"Natalie?" Sienna's voice wavered through the hallway.

Leon's head snapped toward the sound. Natalie held the poker tighter.

"She's one of them," Natalie said. "One of the others."

Leon's face went pale as Sienna appeared in the doorway, wrapped in the blanket like a ghost, her eyes wide and terrified.

Leon took a step back, lifting his hands. "I'm not here to hurt anyone."

"Forgive me if I don't believe a word you say," Natalie said. "You and your brother are a disease."

He swallowed hard.

Natalie shook her head, bitter fury curdling in her chest. "You let it happen. How could you."

Leon said nothing. He turned his eyes away then asked again, "Martin, where is he?"

"Never mind him, you need to help us get out of here," Natalie said finally. Her voice was flat now, scraped of emotion. "You want to prove you're not like him? Get us out."

Leon nodded slowly. "My truck. I can take you somewhere safe."

Sienna stepped closer to Natalie, still trembling. Leon hesitated a moment longer, then turned and walked toward the door. Both women had lowered their defenses and began to follow. They had very few other options available.

# 23

Natalie could hear Sienna breathing beside her. Fast, high, ragged, as if her lungs couldn't catch on anything solid. The poker in Natalie's hand felt like a lifeline. Leon stood in the doorway, backlit by the dim orange wash of cabin light. His eyes flicked over them like headlights catching deer.

"Okay, Nat," he said with a voice slick as oil. "Let's get you both out of here.We can talk about Martin later if that's what you want."

His tone held the kind of politeness that came just before something awful and Natalie barely had time to tense before it happened. Before the civility split clean open. Leon moved fast for someone his size. His hand snapped forward and his fist cracked against Sienna's jaw with a sickening thud. She collapsed like a stack of cards, hitting the floorboards with a dull, final sound.

Natalie screamed, turned, raised the poker, too late. Leon barreled into her, a slab of solid muscle and pure fury. The poker clattered to the floor and rolled down the stairs, clanging against each step. He slammed her against the wooden panel wall. Her skull knocked back. White light burst behind her eyes.

His hand pressed against her collarbone, pinning her like a dead butterfly. Her limbs were loose, her head fuzzy from the drugs still in her bloodstream, slow and treacherous.

"Sshhh," he hissed, like they were lovers caught mid-lie. "Don't fight me. You'll only make it worse."

Natalie twisted, kicked, clawed. Her nails found his cheek. He grunted and reeled back, just an inch, but enough. She dropped to her knees, scrambling for anything that might help her. Her body folded as he grabbed her by the arm, wrenching her up again, slamming her into the cabin wall so hard the picture frame beside her cracked and fell. The nail scratched her temple as it dropped. Blood bloomed warm and wet into her hairline.

"You don't get to fight," he growled, breath hot. "Martin screwed me over for the last time and now I'm gonna take what's mine."

She sobbed, "Why, what? Leon, please stop."

"No, you stop. Don't say my name like you don't know the truth, the thing you've ignored and pretended wasn't there for all these years." He grabbed her chin. Squeezed. "I *know* you know."

His fingers pressed deep, and his eyes scanned her face, not with concern. With hunger. Study. Like he was examining a thing.

His voice softened into something worse. "God, you're still beautiful. Even now. No wonder he kept you to himself for so long. I was surprised he shared you with me now and then but that's the deal, we Lanes have a blood-bond, and we like to share."

Natalie's heart slammed against her ribs.

"What, what are you talking about?" she whispered.

Leon's face twisted. "Martin. My big brother. Always such a greedy bastard with the ladies but Dad made him keep the faith and share you. Just like I'd have to share my wife if I had one but hey, maybe I'm not as dumb as Martin and Dad think I am."

He let go of her chin and took a slow step back. His smile was sour and crooked.

He gestured around. "This cabin has been in our family for years. Generations. But it was Dad that started his little club and when we were old enough we got to join for free and others, well, they pay for the privilege. We make a lot of money out of this place."

Natalie blinked, blood still trickling past her ear. "You're part of it, too."

His smile turned into a sneer. "Course I am. You think Martin came up with this shit on his own? No, no, sweetheart. This is our inheritance. Legacy. Just like Dad wanted but we tweaked it."

He smirked and then winked, and stepped closer again, lowering his voice like a man leaning in for a secret. "You know, Mom and Dad think I'm the soft one. Too slow. Always crying over girls but that's just a con. Martin, however, he's the one determined to keep the tradition going and I showed him how to make use of the internet and this idyllic getaway."

He scanned her body now, slow, invasive, pausing at the bruises on her arms, the cut on her lip, the barely buttoned shirt.

Then his voice dropped into something low and gleeful. "But now, seeing as I'm here and you're available I don't think Martin would mind if I took my turn, do you?"

Natalie's whole body turned to ice.

Leon leaned down until his mouth hovered near her cheek. "Come on, don't be shy."

"No," she croaked. "Please Leon, don't."

He grabbed her again, this time by the wrist and yanked her hard. She stumbled, feet sliding on the floor, her balance gone.

Behind them, Sienna lay still, blood trickling from the side of her mouth.

Leon's grip was iron. Natalie's knees screamed as she was dragged, the cabin floor biting her like broken teeth.

"Where is he? Has he gone to town with the other guys?" Leon snapped.

Natalie didn't answer.

He shoved her toward the stairs. "WHERE IS HE?"

"I don't know," she gasped, still dizzy, still stoned.

Wrong answer. He hit her. Open-palmed. The slap echoed like a gunshot in the small room. Natalie reeled, her lip split open.

Leon's rage twisted into something cooler. More calculated.

He bent down beside her, tugged her chin up again. Blood smeared her mouth.

"Have you worked it out yet, Nat?" he whispered. "That even when Martin comes back he won't save you, he might even watch like he did before, remember that night by the lake when you fell asleep?"

He let go. She crumpled.

He stood and wiped his hands on his jeans like she was dirt. "He didn't even care about Eve, that she's clearly mine and you... you never even joined the dots, that's how stupid you are."

Natalie couldn't speak, not while she was trying to compute what he was saying, joing the dots at last. Eve's eyes and hair. How could she have been so naive not to have realized.

But time for thinking was ober when Leon said, in a colder tone: "Now you know, about all this I suppose me and my bro are going to have to find a solution to the mess you've made but first..."

Natalie whimpered as he dragged her towards the bedroom, tasted blood, felt the floor lurch beneath her. She knew what waited inside. Martin's body. Cold. Lifeless. The bed still stained with what they'd done to her.

She tried to anchor herself. *Think. Survive.*

Leon grabbed her by the waist now, dragging her backwards towards the bedroom.

"I haven't got time to wait for an audience so looks like it's just you and me going to party."

Natalie went limp, forcing her body into dead weight, making every step harder. But he was too strong. Her limbs flopped uselessly. Her vision blurred.

Behind them, Sienna didn't move.

Her last thought as she was hauled backwards was *I have to live.* Even if it means becoming a monster. Leon's grip was a noose, his fingers clamped around her like he owned her. He used his boot to kick open the bedroom door, the old hinges shrieking like they wanted no part of what came next. Natalie's feet scraped uselessly across the floorboards as he dragged her into the room.

Then he saw the body. Leon stopped cold. For a moment, there was silence. Utter silence.

Then something broke loose inside him. A howl erupted from Leon's throat, not human, not animal, just pure, wounded rage. It tore out of him like a centuries-old curse. He shoved Natalie backwards with one hand, his fingers releasing her wrist only to wrap around her throat. Her breath cut out. She choked, vision pinwheeling.

"YOU KILLED HIM!" he roared, eyes blazing. "You filthy little..."

He flung her down onto the mattress. The bed groaned under her weight. Natalie coughed, air rushing back into her lungs like glass. Her vision swam, but she forced herself to stay conscious, to focus. Leon was already moving. He grabbed the shackles from the nightstand, the same rusted pair Martin had used before, and latched them to her wrists with sickening familiarity. The cold metal bit into her bones. She flailed weakly, tried to twist away, but he slammed her wrists down and clicked the lock closed with one final snap. Her arms went limp. The weight of the metal made them feel like anchors.

Leon turned his attention to the body now. He dropped to his knees beside Martin like a grieving lover.

He touched Martin's cheek. "Jesus, Marty... what did she do?"

His voice cracked, trembling for the first time. Then it changed, slithered back into something poisonous.

"You shouldn't have brought her here, we agreed, and you broke my trust but maybe... maybe you had a plan and wanted to keep me out of it, have an alibi while you got rid of the trash."

He turned then and looked straight at Natalie, making his point, then leaned down, pressed his mouth close to Martin's ear.

"You fucked up," he whispered. "But don't worry, I'll fix it."

Then, with a grunt, he grabbed Martin's ankles. His shoes scraped across the floor, catching on a snag in the rug, leaving behind a trail of scuffed blood and sweat. Leon didn't flinch. He hauled him across the floor like a sack of meat, Martin's head thumping once, twice against the doorframe before vanishing into the hallway.

Natalie tried to scream. The sound came out as a wet rasp. Leon came back. Calm now. Focused. He stood there, breathing like he'd just finished a workout.

The room reeked of sweat, rot, and fear. Hers. Natalie lay chained to the bed, limbs trembling, skin clammy. Every nerve in her body was screaming for action, but there was nowhere to go. She looked up at him, her face split with repulsion and hate.

Leon smiled. "That's better," he said. "You're quiet now."

"You're sick," she rasped. "You're a fucking disgusting pervert and I hate you."

"Oh, I know what I am," he interrupted. "And so do you now. You've been giving me the gooey eye for years, haven't you? I was that itch under your skin that you wanted to scratch but couldn't because you're a good wifey. Well, I didn't need your permission back then and I don't need it now."

He stepped closer. The floor creaked beneath his boots. Natalie flinched as he perched on the edge of the bed, hands resting on his knees. His face hovered inches from hers.

"I'm going to tell you a story," he said, like he was tucking a child in. "A family story. One that never made it into the photo albums."

She turned her face away.

He grabbed her chin and yanked it back. "Listen. Because it's yours now too."

His eyes gleamed. "It started with Bobby. My father. Martin's hero. He believed a man should take what he wants. That women are vessels. That pain is love's echo. He didn't hide it. He didn't *have* to. But Mom, Vivienne, she was tough and smart and worked out what was going on and how to swerve her turn up here at the cabin. She survived it. You think she was a victim?"

He let out a dry chuckle. "She was the architect. Once she'd given him his heirs, she allowed Dad free rein to have his fun if he left her alone."

Natalie blinked, her stomach turning.

"Oh yes. She trained us," Leon whispered. "Me and Martin. From the moment we could walk. Taught us that silence was strength. That control is devotion. That women *want* it, deep down. All of them. Even the screamers. Especially the screamers."

"You're lying, a woman would never do that to another woman, it's too sick," Natalie said. But the words barely had air.

Leon leaned closer. "She picked the girls. Martin's first was fourteen. Mine was twelve. Vivienne said they were 'practice.' She said it with wine in her hand and pearls at her throat."

Natalie began to cry. Not sobs, just silent tears leaking sideways into the mattress.

"You think you're special?" Leon asked, tracing a finger along the edge of her jaw. "You're not. Martin might've played house, but he never stopped being who we are."

He stood then, suddenly furious again, pacing the room.

"You could never tame him," he said, voice rising. "Or make him forget what he was. Soften him. Make him weak. I watched him train you like a dog on a leash. All those nice family dinners. The school meetings. You were always expendable and as soon as you started to unravel, oh yes, he told me all about your nightmares, it was just a matter of time until you were history. I get it now, why he brought you here. It makes sense."

He spun on her, eyes wide. "And now he's dead, Eve and Thomas will be mine and Mom's to train and do with as we wish, once I've cleaned up Martin's mess."

Natalie swallowed bile. Leon stepped toward the bed again, fists clenching. "It's my turn to lead, now."

He stopped at the foot of the bed, breathing hard. His gaze roamed over her body like a butcher picking cuts. Her stomach turned. Her mouth opened. But before he could climb onto the bed, she whispered, "You'll die here, too."

He paused. "What?"

"You're not him," she said, eyes burning now. "You're not smart enough. You're not as clever as you think. You're just his dumb shadow."

Leon's face twitched.

She smiled through her pain and fear. "That's why he never let you take over. And your mom treats you like the spare child."

For a moment, the fury drained out of him, she saw it,

replaced by something else. Something deeper. Maybe a wound he'd spent his whole life pretending didn't exist.

He moved again, this time slower, methodical. "You want to break me with words?" he said quietly. "You think you can do that, well you're wrong because Mama taught me all I know about sticks and stones?"

He crawled onto the bed. Natalie stared at the ceiling, feeling the mattress shift beneath his weight. But she wasn't broken. Not yet. And not for him, even though she could see it in his eyes. His lust and his legacy. The sickness that flowed through his blood and the evil ingrained deep within.

# 24

*Thirty Years Earlier – The Cabin by Lake Wallenpaupack*

The lake licked the edge of the dock with a lazy, slapping sound, like a dog working marrow from a bone. The sun hovered low and wide above the treetops, setting the water ablaze with ripples of copper and bruised orange. The fishing rods leaned against a tackle box like tired soldiers, and the cooler, half full of warm beer and two blood-specked trout sat open beside the wooden bench.

Bobby Beaumont squatted at the edge of the dock, a hand-rolled cigarette clamped in his teeth, squinting into the wind. His eyes were slits beneath the bill of his cap, jaw rigid with the easy dominance of a man who had never been told no. His shadow stretched long behind him.

Martin stood a few feet away, mimicking his father's stance. Thirteen years old and all bone and quiet intensity, the boy held his rod with the same practiced grip, lips pressed together in silent concentration. Every so often he'd glance sideways at Bobby, waiting for approval. Not needing words. Just a nod.

Leon, by contrast, was a clutter of limbs and sweat, hunched on a milk crate further down the dock. At eleven, he already had the awkward heaviness of a boy who'd grown too fast. His glasses kept slipping down the bridge of his nose. His rod bobbed unevenly in the water, and the line was a tangled mess of weeds and knots.

"You're strangling it, Leon," Bobby snapped without turning. "Hold it like it's a tool, not your damn dick."

Leon flushed, adjusting his grip. His fingers were damp, the cork handle slick beneath his palms. "Sorry," he muttered.

Bobby flicked the ash from his cigarette and reeled in his line with fluid ease. "Fishing's about patience. Control. Stillness. You move like you're on fire."

Martin smirked, just a twitch at the corner of his mouth. Leon saw it and looked away.

"Don't apologize," Bobby added. "Fix it."

The three of them fished in silence for another hour, broken only by the buzz of gnats and the occasional plop of a fish breaking the surface. When the sun finally kissed the trees and the wind turned colder, Bobby stood.

"That's enough," he said. "Reel it in. We're losing light."

Leon struggled with his line again, fingers fumbling at the reel. Martin had already packed up his gear with swift, neat movements. Bobby cracked open another beer and drained it in three gulps, the foam dripping down his chin.

They walked back to the cabin with the cooler between them, Bobby's pace steady and unhurried. The trees creaked above, their trunks blackening as night folded in. A crow screamed somewhere deep in the woods.

The cabin looked like a buried thought, two stories of warped timber and dull windows, crouched low against the brush. It looked like it had grown out of the earth. Leon always hated the way the place seemed to watch you. Martin loved it. Bobby pushed open the door, letting the smell hit them first: woodsmoke, sweat, dust and soon, the stench of gutted fish.

Inside, the lamps glowed dim yellow. At first, Leon thought they were alone. Then he saw the man on the sofa.

He was sitting back, legs wide, hands on his thighs like a king in repose. Mid-forties maybe, with a paunch beneath his shirt and a smirk on his flushed face. He looked up as they entered and raised a beer.

"Bobby."

"Rick," Bobby replied.

Martin froze behind his father, his eyes snagging on what lay beside the man. A woman. Curled up. Unconscious. Her head lolled against the cushions, mouth slightly open, a bruise already blooming along her jaw. Her dress, navy blue with white buttons, was hiked up around her thighs. She was barefoot. One leg twitched faintly, like a dying thing.

Leon stopped walking.

Bobby noticed. "Close the door," he said without turning.

Leon hesitated. Then obeyed. The cabin door slammed shut.

"Who's she?" Martin asked. His voice was too steady for his age.

Bobby set down the cooler, lit another cigarette. "A special treat."

Rick stood now, straightening his belt with slow, casual movements. "She's ours for the night," he said, chuckling. "Lucky us, huh?"

Martin's brow furrowed. "She doesn't look too good"

"She's fine," Bobby said sharply. "Just took something to help her relax. It's the rules."

Leon looked nauseous. "She looks hurt."

"She's not," Bobby said. "Men get rough sometimes when they have fun, that's all"

He turned to face his sons, the cigarette glowing like a tiny, furious eye between his fingers.

"Boys," he said. "This is what growing up and being a man means."

Leon flinched. Martin didn't blink.

"There are women," Bobby continued, "and there are *wives*. A wife is a contract. A vessel. She belongs to her man. And sometimes, if he feels like it, if it pleases him, that man offers her as a gift. To friends. To brothers. To the Circle. It's our choice."

"The Circle?" Martin asked.

Rick laughed. "That's what we call it. A private group. Been going a long time."

Bobby nodded. "Only the initiated can enter."

Leon's stomach turned.

Martin looked at the woman again. "She's very pretty."

"She sure is," Bobby said. "That's what makes her eligible."

"But she's not awake."

"She doesn't need to be," Bobby said flatly. "That's not her role tonight."

Leon took a step back, his throat tight. "Mom wouldn't like this."

Bobby turned slowly. His eyes were iron. "Your mother *knows*. She's known since before you were born. You think I kept secrets in my own house?"

Leon shook his head, backing toward the door. "Has Mom done this?"

Bobby advanced. "No. I chose not to share and she knows to be grateful for that, but she also understands what men like us need. That's what makes her strong. That's what makes her worthy. She wanted sons with iron in their blood. And I gave her that."

Martin said nothing. His gaze hadn't left the woman. He was studying her like a painting.

"Martin gets it, I can see," Bobby said. "He understands the weight of legacy. He's got the temperament."

He grabbed Leon by the shoulder. "And you'll learn. You're just slower. But you'll learn, son, and you'll enjoy it. I promise you that."

Leon felt tears prick his eyes. He shoved Bobby's hand off and ran into his bedroom. Behind him, he heard the man's laughter.

And Bobby's voice: "Close the damn door, Martin."

And with a smile on his face, he did as his daddy told him.

Now, many years after his first lesson, amidst the thick scent of sweat and candlewax, Leon turned his attention back to Natalie. He had lit new candles, moving from shelf to dresser to windowsill with the slow reverence of a man preparing for ritual. Natalie lay shackled to the bed, her wrists raw, her mouth dry. She didn't speak. She just watched him as he stood back, admiring the glow like he'd just set a scene for a romantic dinner. His chest rose and fell with deliberate slowness, but his nostrils flared. Sweat glistened along his collarbone, darkening the neckline of his shirt.

"Better," he said. "It's important to do things like this right.."

He moved to the foot of the bed and leaned down, hands on either side of her legs, breathing heavily. She could smell him – something feral. His face hovered over hers, not close enough to touch, but close enough to feel.

"Martin was always so excited to come up here," he murmured. "Impulsive. Couldn't see past his own hunger. He liked the rush. The mess. He didn't understand the patience it takes to make something *beautiful* but safe and now, he knows I was right all along."

Natalie turned her face to the side, bile rising in her throat.

Leon tsked. "Don't do that. Look at me."

She didn't. He placed a hand on her thigh. Her entire body went rigid.

"You know, they all thought he was the clever one," he said, his voice soft, almost sad. "Martin the doctor. Martin the golden boy. But they were wrong. He was weak and his thirst made him predictable."

He leaned closer, breath fanning across her cheek. "I've always been the careful one. The one who waited. Watched. Calculated."

His pupils were wide now, devouring the color in his eyes.

Natalie clenched her teeth. "Is that what this is? Cleaning up? Your last hurrah before you go running home to mommy to tell her what a big brave hero you are."

His smile split slow and proud. "This is my legacy now, and then Thomas's."

His hand drifted higher. She stiffened, heart hammering against her ribs. But she saw it then, just a flash. A sliver of movement in her periphery. The door had opened a crack. And behind it, Sienna.

She stood barefoot in the dark hallway, her face pale as bone in the candlelight. One eye swollen, her jaw streaked with blood. But her grip was firm. In her right hand, she held a kitchen knife. Big. Silver. Sharp.

Natalie swallowed hard and blinked slowly. Her mind went still. A plan took shape in the void left by terror. She turned back to Leon. And she changed. Her breath hitched but not from fear, but feigned understanding. Her last gambit and chance of survival. She shifted slightly beneath him, arching her back just enough for her chains to clink.

Leon paused.

Her voice was soft now. Coated in false sweetness. "You're right."

His eyebrows lifted.

"You're not like him," she whispered. "You're... smarter. More in control. That's why I was always drawn to you, but I could never say or act on it, but I wanted you, always."

Leon's breathing picked up. His chest rose faster. He licked his lips.

"I knew it the moment I first saw you, but it was too late," she said, each word slow and deliberate. "Martin... I think he was always scared of your inner strength. You did have power over him and that's why he shared me with you, to keep you onside."

Leon's eyes glittered. "He *was* scared when he was a kid and used to piss himself when Dad got angry. Then he kind of learned to hide it and Mom taught him other ways to be powerful but me, I had raw strength, and he knew it."

Natalie gave a soft laugh, as if they were sharing a secret. Behind him, the door creaked open a little more. Sienna stepped into the room.

Leon leaned in, elated. "You should have told me. Should've shown me what you really wanted, and I could've fixed it."

Natalie nodded, watching him, not breaking eye contact. "I'm sorry I didn't, I truly am and if I'd have known about Eve then it could have been so different. Is there still a chance, though, even after what happened to Martin? How can I make it right?"

"You can show me, right now, how much you want me." His voice was thick now. "I liked it when you were asleep but maybe it'll be even better when you give it freely, and I don't have to take." He lowered himself more. His knee pressed into the mattress.

Sienna crept closer.

Natalie whispered, "Tell me what you want, and I'll do it."

That was the moment. Leon shifted his weight forward, eyes wild, and in one fluid, beautiful movement – Sienna drove the knife into his back.

It sank with a sickening *crunch* between his shoulder blades, deep and violent. Leon let out a scream, half roar, half gasp and jerked upright. The bed shuddered with the force of his movement. His eyes flew wide, his mouth fell open in shock.

Sienna didn't stop. She pushed the blade in deeper with both hands, face twisted with fury. "You disgusting bastard," she hissed. "You're not a man. You're filth."

Leon stumbled backward, arms flailing, the knife still buried in his back.

He turned, tried to lunge at her, but he was already failing, his body betraying him, legs buckling.

# 25

Leon was slumped across one half of the bed, his body an unnatural angle of limbs and slack muscle, legs twisted beneath him like a broken doll. The knife still jutted out of his back, a grotesque exclamation point, its handle gleaming slick with blood in the candlelight. His breaths came in wet, animal rattles, labored, shallow. Each inhale whistled like a tire leaking air. But he was alive.

Natalie didn't flinch. She sat propped against the headboard, wrists raw and burning from the cuffs. Her pulse thundered beneath her bruises, but her mind had gone cold. Surgical. As though the terror had cauterized something inside her.

Sienna hovered by the edge of the bed, her face pale and smudged, eyes locked on Leon like he might still lunge, might still do damage. Her hands trembled.

Then Natalie said, very calmly, "The key, it's in the front pocket of my trousers."

Sienna turned sharply. "What?"

"The key," Natalie repeated, slower this time. "My right pocket. I think it's still there."

Sienna hesitated, then crossed the floor in two shaky steps.

She knelt beside Natalie, her hands fumbling at the waistband of the trousers Natalie had worn all night, drenched now in sweat and blood. Her fingers slipped once, then found the metal lump.

She pulled the key free and exhaled with a noise halfway between a sob and a laugh.

"Got it."

"Do it," Natalie said.

Sienna unlocked the cuffs, the mechanisms stiff with dried blood. The metal groaned as it opened, the click of each release echoing like a gunshot in the silence. As soon as the second cuff dropped, Natalie sat up straight. Her wrists ached, scored with red, but she didn't pause.

She crawled toward Leon.

Sienna watched, confused. "What are you doing?"

Natalie didn't answer. She shoved Leon onto his back with a grunt, dragging his torso to the center of the bed. He moaned in pain, the knife shifting inside him. Blood pooled beneath him now, seeping into the quilt. His face twisted in agony.

"Stop," he croaked. "Please, Natalie, help me..."

But she was already reaching for the cuffs. The same ones that had held her. She snapped the first around his wrist, locking it to the metal rung of the headboard. He groaned, thrashed weakly. The second one went on harder. Leon cried out as the cuff clamped shut around his bone. Natalie stood over him, chest heaving.

Leon blinked up at her, sweat running in rivulets down his temples. "You don't understand," he rasped. "You think this is revenge. But you... *you* won't win, not with Mom."

Natalie didn't speak. She didn't need to.

He coughed, the sound wet and thick, then leaned his head back and said, almost conversationally, "You know now I'm Eve's father so how will you look her in the eye after this?"

The words were a grenade. Natalie froze. The breath caught in her throat.

Behind her, Sienna's head snapped toward Leon.

"I won't tell her, ever, Natalie said, voice low, flat.

Leon grinned. Blood foamed on his teeth. "You'll let her think she's Martin's? But one day she'll work out who her daddy is. The little brown-eyed girl in a house full of blue. And if she doesn't, Mom will enjoy telling her."

Natalie shook her head. "Shut up."

"You know it," he wheezed. "But then again, she could be anyone's, couldn't she? Anyone at the cabin. Poor little Eve."

Sienna lunged. "You bastard."

Leon chuckled, then coughed again. Sienna spit in his face.

A long, deliberate gesture. It landed in his mouth, mixing with the blood.

"You're going to die alone next to the filth you call a brother," she said.

Natalie turned away. The candles were still lit. She walked to the one nearest the window and picked it up. The flame danced, unaware of its role in the scene.

Sienna watched, a breath caught in her throat. Natalie stared at the bed, at the man shackled there. He was panting now, barely conscious, but still whispering, nonsense or names, she didn't know. She didn't care. She looked at the curtain. Then, with careful precision, she tipped the candle. It hit the fabric. The flame hesitated... then took. It spread fast. The gauzy material went up like paper, the fire climbing greedily toward the beam above. Heat pulsed through the room. Smoke rose instantly.

Leon started screaming. "No... *no, no!* Natalie, wait. DON'T."

But she didn't look at him. She stepped back, watching as the flames spread across the curtain rod, crackling up toward the ceiling.

He was shrieking now, screaming curses and begging in the same breath. "You can't do this. UNSHACKLE ME. Jesus Christ, PLEASE. I'm sorry, they made me do it, they made me, can't you see that?"

Natalie turned to the door. Sienna opened it for her. Before stepping out, Natalie glanced over her shoulder one final time. Leon's face was red, twisted, wet with tears and blood and spit. He thrashed in vain, the chains rattling, screaming her name like a curse, like a prayer.

She didn't say a word. She just shut the door. The latch clicked into place and the screams went on behind it.

The first step away from the bedroom was like walking out of a nightmare, except the nightmare was still alive on the other side of the door.

Leon's voice echoed down the stairs, raw and fractured. "NATALIE. NATALIEEE! You bitch. PLEASE!"

His screams clawed at the air, a mix of agony and rage, bouncing off the walls of the cabin as the fire began to swallow it. A rattle was threaded through every shout, the sound of a punctured lung burning itself down.

Sienna flinched at every syllable. Natalie didn't. She kept moving. Down the stairs, barefoot, shaking, her legs threatening to give out with every step but she moved like a woman who had decided. Not someone who hoped to survive. Someone who had *decided* to.

Behind her, Sienna's footsteps dragged. The further they descended, the more muffled Leon's screams became. Softer. Distant. The heat from above pressed downward, and the air began to shift, smokier, carrying with it the charred scent of the past combusting.

Natalie turned at the bottom of the stairs. "We don't have long."

Sienna looked up, eyes wide and rimmed with black. "It's spreading fast."

"Yes. Come with me."

There was a coat rack near the door, a drawer in the sideboard with backup clothes Bobby must've kept for his "guests." She ripped it open, found another flannel shirt.

"Here," she said, tossing it toward Sienna. "This will keep you warm."

She didn't argue

Natalie nodded. "Good. Let's go."

She shoved open the front door. Outside, the cold was brutal, like a slap to the face after the cloying warmth of the cabin. The trees loomed, black silhouettes against the night, and the wind whistled through them like a warning.

Sienna hesitated on the threshold. "What if he gets out?"

Natalie turned. Her face was carved from stone.

"He won't." She stepped through the door and didn't look back.

The two women crossed the porch, the boards groaning beneath their weight. Somewhere behind them, a faint scream, short, guttural, rose and then cut off sharply.

Inside, two men remained: one dead, one about to burn.

Natalie didn't say a word. She just kept walking, boots crunching over old pine needles, eyes locked ahead.

Sienna stumbled after her. "Where are we going?"

"There's a road," Natalie said. "I remember seeing it when we first came here. If we follow the tree line east, we'll find it."

Sienna's breathing was ragged. "I don't know if I can."

"You can," Natalie snapped. Not cruelly. Urgently. "Just stay with me. No stopping and watch for headlights in case it's one of them coming back. We can't risk being stopped by one of them."

They plunged into the woods. Branches snagged at their skin, thorns tearing at bare ankles and the exposed flesh of their arms. Leaves rustled above like voices whispering in the dark. The ground was uneven, packed with old roots and loose stones. Sienna tripped more than once, but Natalie grabbed her, yanked her upright, and kept moving. Her own legs felt like jelly. Her stomach twisted with hunger. Every step sent fire through her calves. But she didn't stop.

They were running on fumes, days of no food, no real sleep, the drugs still buzzing in their bloodstream like static. Natalie's vision blurred sometimes, her ears ringing with the blood pounding inside them. But she kept pushing forward.

Sienna whimpered behind her, stumbling. "Everything hurts..."

Natalie didn't break stride. "That means we're still alive."

Branches slashed across her cheek. She didn't flinch. The woods seemed endless. The darkness thickened. Every step was a battle against collapse. But Natalie didn't let it take her.

She had spent years dissolving, shrinking to fit the corners of a life built by someone else. But not now. Now, she widened. Took up space. Owned every ragged breath. And she would get them to safety. She would see her kids again.

They walked for what felt like hours but couldn't have been more than five minutes. The cabin faded behind them, swallowed by the trees. All they could hear was the wind. And their breathing, the raw sound of their survival.

Eventually, the forest began to alter. The ground leveled. The trees spread further apart. The sound of distant tires met Natalie's ears. A road.

She grabbed Sienna's arm. "Come on. We're close."

They broke through the last of the brush and stumbled out onto a strip of black asphalt cutting through the wilderness like a blade. The stars above blinked indifferent. No streetlights. No signs. But the road was real.

Natalie turned toward the distant glow of headlights far

down the stretch. Then she stepped into the middle of the road. They had to take a chance, pray whoever it was would be a friend, not foe. Sienna followed. They stood there, two battered women, blood-streaked, barefoot, their hair tangled and wild, their clothes hanging off them in ruin. Natalie raised both hands and waved. Then screamed.

"HEY! HELP! PLEASE!"

The vehicle kept coming. A truck, maybe. A van, the logo on the front told her he was a mechanic. It slowed slightly.

Sienna joined her, waving both arms like a human flare. "Stop! Please! STOP!"

The headlights grew brighter, closer, then the engine groaned, and the tires screeched slightly as the vehicle came to a halt only feet from where they stood.

## 26

The road was a black ribbon winding through nowhere. It had no markings, no streetlights, no signs. Just cracked asphalt and the hush of trees pressing in on both sides like watchers. The only light came from the stars overhead, pinpricks of cold white fire and the dim yellow glow of headlights blinding them. Natalie stood in the middle of the road, barefoot, bleeding, and unmovable.

Behind her, Sienna stood on the verge, also barefoot, exhausted, barely upright. Her arms hung limp at her sides. She didn't speak. She didn't move. She just watched Natalie with the glassy stare of someone who had already been hollowed out and stitched shut.

The vehicle, an enormous gas-guzzling beast of a thing, some kind of Dodge SUV, silver with dented panels had skidded to a violent stop only feet from Natalie, the front end dipping hard as it rocked on its shocks. Steam rose from the hood. The engine ticked loudly in protest. Natalie didn't flinch. She didn't wait.

She ran forward, straight to the driver's side, and started pounding on the window with both fists.

"PLEASE! HELP US! PLEASE!"

The driver, a man in his late fifties, maybe early sixties, wearing a flannel shirt and a look of pure terror jerked back in his seat like she'd jumped from the underworld. He fumbled for something at his hip, his phone? A weapon?

Natalie didn't stop screaming and made the sign of prayer with her hands. "PLEASE! Let us in! She's hurt, we're hurt, we need help, we *need* to call the police."

The man slowly lowered the window a few inches, his face slack with confusion. "What the hell is... Jesus..."

He saw her up close now. The blood in her hair, the gash on her cheek, the dried handcuff bruises ringing her wrists. Her eyes, hollow and blazing at the same time. Maybe the smell of whatever clung to her skin hit him, too. Then he looked past her and saw Sienna. She was standing half in the trees, wearing someone else's flannel, eyes too wide in her face. Her skin was sallow, her lips cracked. She looked like a ghost in the headlights.

The man opened his door slowly, like he wasn't sure whether he was dreaming or about to get mugged. He stepped out, one hand raised instinctively, palm-out.

"Okay... okay," he said, voice uneven. "Take it easy. You two... were you in an accident?"

Natalie stepped back. "No, not an accident but we need help. Please. Just take us anywhere. A hospital. The police station. Just somewhere safe."

He blinked at her. "You been out here long?"

She nodded, her whole body shaking now that the adrenaline had somewhere to land. "Yes, we escaped from a cabin and ran through the woods but I don't know when or for how long."

He exhaled, nodded. "Okay. Get in. Both of you."

He looked at Sienna. "Miss? You okay to walk?"

Sienna didn't speak, but she moved forward, slow and stiff like a marionette on broken strings. The man opened the back passenger door of the cab and helped her inside. She sank into the seat like she was folding in on herself. Her head lolled against the window, eyes still open but unfocused.

Natalie climbed into the front passenger seat and slammed the door behind her.

The heat inside the car was a punch of comfort. It smelled of old leather and there were fast food wrappers on the floor and a bottle of orange Gatorade in the cup holder.

The man buckled in and turned toward her.

"I'm Joe," he said, still blinking too much. "You wanna tell me what happened?"

Natalie shook her head. "Not right now but thank you, for stopping."

"Fair enough."

He put the car in drive and eased forward. As they pulled away, the forest swallowed the road behind them.

Joe glanced at Natalie again. "You sure you don't need an ambulance?"

"I just need to be around people we can trust, then we can explain what happened to us."

Her voice cracked. She rubbed at her face and came away with blood, sweat, soot.

Joe kept his eyes on the road. "You got names?"

Natalie stared out the windshield. "Natalie. The girl in the back is Sienna."

He nodded. "Where were you coming from?"

Natalie's jaw locked. She didn't answer.

Joe didn't press. They drove in silence for a minute. The churn of tires against old road. The occasional pop of gravel. In the back seat, Sienna's breathing had evened out, though she still hadn't closed her eyes. She stared out the window like she was trying to prove to herself the world was still there.

"You're both hurt," Joe said gently. "And no shoes. In the middle of nowhere. I can tell something real bad happened to you."

Natalie turned toward him slowly. Her voice was flat. "We were held in a cabin. By men. Our husband's and other men were all part of it. We were drugged and unconscious and I think they were going to kill us both and dump us in the lake. Does that answer your question?"

Joe's hands twitched on the wheel.

"I see," he said after a long pause.

"They did things and filmed us," she said. "Horrible things. I can't explain them. Not yet."

Joe swallowed hard. "Okay. I'm gonna take you to a gas station up ahead. They've got a phone and it's lit. We'll call the cops from there, yeah? The signal is so bad here nobody can use their cell."

Natalie nodded. "Thank you."

"You're welcome, and I'm sorry, about what's happened to you." he said quietly.

They drove on, the car filled with silence. Natalie let her head fall back against the seat.

She didn't cry. She was too tired for that. The truck purred along the empty road, a warm bubble of light and engine purr gliding through the deep hush of nowhere. For a while, no one spoke.

Natalie stared straight ahead, her shoulders heaving less violently now, the frenzy in her chest slowly subsiding. She could still feel the phantom weight of the cabin pressing on her lungs, but the fresh air, the wheels in motion, Sienna's continued breathing in the back seat, they were all proof she hadn't imagined their escape, and this wasn't part of a drug induced fantasy. But it was that word, as it pinged into her head that triggered a thought. What if nobody believed them? What if Leon was still alive, or one of the others came back, Sienna's husband came to finish her off? And what if Vivienne somehow heard about the fire, what happened there. Eve and Thomas might be in danger. She had to get to them – quickly.

"I need you to drive where I say," Natalie said finally, her voice firm. "Please don't ask questions. Just listen to me."

Joe's eyes widened slightly, but he nodded. "Okay. You got it."

"Take the next left. Then keep following that road. There'll be a gravel turnoff about a mile in."

He nodded again. Hands tight on the wheel, eyes darting to the rearview mirror like he expected to see something evil on his tail.

Sienna sat curled in the back seat, knees hugged to her chest, trembling. Her skin was pale, almost translucent, and her eyes stared out the window but saw nothing. Natalie glanced back at her once and saw her lips moving silently, maybe praying, maybe just counting her own breaths.

Outside the car, the woods blurred past, thick with shadow. But above the treetops, the sky had started to glow. A soft, pulsing orange. It wasn't sunrise or sunset.

Joe noticed it, too. "That, uh… is that a fire?"

Natalie didn't answer.

He squinted toward the horizon. "Looks like it's getting bigger."

Natalie let her hand rest on the door handle. Her fingers, bruised and bloody, tapped once. Then stopped.

"Please keep driving until I tell you to stop."

"Okay." Joe's voice came out shaky. "Sure. Sure thing."

The car rolled forward, every turn of the wheels moving them closer to the inferno they'd barely escaped. The heat wasn't visible yet, but Natalie could feel it in her bones. A memory, burning behind her eyes. She saw Leon's face every time she blinked, the rattle in his throat, the gleam of candles, the soft hiss of curtains catching flame. No one deserved what he'd done. But he deserved what he got.

The road narrowed. Gravel replaced asphalt. Trees leaned in close. The orange light grew stronger.

Joe gripped the steering wheel tighter. "Ma'am, I'm not trying to be difficult here, but are you sure this is the right way?"

"Yes, I'm sure," Natalie said.

He nodded but looked nervous. A turn appeared. A broken post marked the road. Natalie pointed.

"There. Pull over."

Joe braked gently, bringing the truck to a crawl, then stopped just before the bend. Natalie turned in her seat to face him fully. Her expression was different now, steel-eyed, jaw locked, her whole body vibrating with control. The wild edge was gone, replaced by something colder and more determined than ever.

She looked like someone who had survived too much and wasn't about to start explaining herself to anyone.

"I have to do something and I need to be able to trust you to look after my friend, and after what we've been through I hope you understand how hard it is for me to do that," she said, nodding toward Sienna. "Will you take her to a hospital and make sure she's safe?"

Joe blinked. "What?"

"She's been drugged and she's dehydrated. Tell them how you found us by the side of the road."

He shifted in his seat, confused. "What about you?"

"I'll be okay but I have to get to my children... we panicked when we left but now I can see things more clearly and I have to go and check something ... also, call the fire department and tell them a cabin by the lake is burning."

Joe opened his mouth. Closed it.

"I don't understand."

Natalie leaned closer. "You don't need to understand, Joe. Just do what I said, please, and promise me you'll take care of her."

He stared at her, then he nodded. "I promise."

Natalie turned around, reached over the back seat, and touched Sienna's knee gently. The woman flinched, then looked up.

"You're safe now, and Joe is a good man who will take care of you, he's promised," Natalie whispered.

Sienna's lip quivered. Her eyes welled, but no tears fell.

"Don't leave me alone. I'm scared," she pleaded.

"There's something I have to do but you need to go to the hospital." Natalie removed the memory card from her pocket and handed it to Sienna. "And I need you to take this. I'm trusting you with it. Give it to the police. It explains everything, just in case..." the words melted away.

Sienna looked down at the card in her hand and nodded once.

Natalie opened the passenger door. The cold hit her like a slap, but she didn't flinch. She stepped out, bare feet crunching on gravel, and closed the door behind her.

Then she smiled weakly, the best she could do and said, "Joe, I'm trusting you but please, go, now. Thank you for saving us."

Joe didn't hesitate. He hit the gas. The tires spun briefly, then caught, and the truck lurched forward into the night.

Natalie stood there alone, watching the glow on the horizon grow brighter. Her breath turned to mist in the air. The grind of the engine faded. Silence returned. But inside her, something had changed. She wasn't a victim anymore.

# 27

The flames were a living thing now. The top floor of the cabin was fully engulfed, a howling furnace of fire that turned the black night into a hellish sunrise. Orange and gold ribbons whipped skyward, sparks flying like embers from a dragon's mouth. The wood cracked and groaned, breaking apart in loud, splintering collapses. Smoke clawed at the treetops, thick and greasy and alive.

Natalie stood still, twenty meters from the blaze. Her bare feet rooted into the cold dirt, her arms hanging limp at her sides. Her body was covered in soot, blood, and bruises but none of that registered now. Her mind was elsewhere. Inside the cabin was everything that had tried to destroy her. Martin. Leon. The legacy. The circle. All of it, burning.

She saw Martin laughing in the early days when they lived in that apartment above the florist and he used to make her breakfast every Sunday. Eggs, overcooked. Toast with a smiley face drawn in jam. Back when she thought she'd won the lottery marrying a doctor.

She saw him at the hospital, holding Thomas for the first time. His voice cracking as he promised he'd always protect him.

The way his hand trembled when he touched his downy cheek. She saw Thomas's first steps. Martin filming it. The way they both cheered and laughed and cried like idiots.

Then she saw the shift. The way his eyes hardened when they landed on Eve. Grew colder after his father's funeral. The day he snapped at her for wearing a skirt that showed "too much thigh." The night he told her she was embarrassing in front of his colleagues. The time he called her hysterical for suggesting they needed therapy. The way Vivienne always arrived with her critique, her disapproval, her sly, icy contempt.

And the cabin. It was all going up in smoke – the secrets, the rituals, the blood. She'd salted the earth. Nothing would grow there again. It would soon be erased and yes, Bobby's sick legacy would become a shameful legend when the locals found out what happened there.

But now she knew they were dead because nothing could survive the flames, the brothers and their perverted ways extinguished for good, she could leave. Keys. She needed the keys for Martin's car that he always hung on the hook by the front door. She should've taken them when they left but she was too freaked, panic overriding logic. She had to get them now, but it would mean going inside a burning house, risking her life. Then she saw the faces of her children, and then another, of the evil woman caring for them and Natalie knew she had no choice. Covering her mouth and nose with her arm, she ran towards the cabin.

Thick black smoke billowed from the open front door, stinging her eyes which she closed and used the sense of touch to navigate her way. The hook was to the right of the door, all she had to do was feel for it, and as her fingers traced the wall, raging heat burned her face and she imagined her skin peeling from the bones and was about to give up when she made contact. The fob dangled from the hook and with a mixture of elation and renewed panic, the sound of crumbling beams and the crackle of fire impossible to ignore, she yanked the key, palmed it tight, and ran.

Martin's car sat at the edge of the dirt track like a forgotten soldier, battered and dust covered. The same silver Audi that had brought her here like a prisoner in plain sight, a lamb for slaughter. She raced toward it. Every step was a vow. She reached the driver's side and pushed the button on the fob. Click. She got in. Her blood dripping from a re-opened wound on her wrist smeared onto the steering wheel as she gripped it with both hands. She inserted the key into the ignition. Turned it. The engine coughed once, then roared to life. Her hands trembled. But her mind was razor sharp.

She had been reacting before. Surviving. Escaping. Saving Sienna. Running. But now –

Now she was planning. She was thinking clearly. Dangerously. And she knew exactly where she was going. Back to Haverford Township. Back to the red brick house. Back to Vivienne. Because her children were there. And no one, *no one*, was going to keep them from her now.

Not that evil woman. Not the police. Not anyone.

She shifted the car into gear. The cabin burned in the rearview mirror as Natalie drove toward the dark and home. The road unspooled in long, empty stretches under the thin beam of the headlights. The Audi tore down the highway like it had somewhere to be, and Natalie gripped the steering wheel with fingers stiff from rage and resolve. The engine purred beneath her like a beast finally set loose.

The world outside the windows was a blur of trees and signs she didn't read. No cars. No life. Just the relentless thrum of tires on tarmac and the heat pulsing through her body. She was running on something wilder than caffeine. More potent than fear. Adrenaline and fury.

She should have been dead hours ago. Or catatonic. Or sedated in some ER bed while a nurse whispered about shock and trauma and resilience. But she wasn't. She was here. She was coming. And Vivienne had no idea.

The dashboard clock blinked 12:47 AM. In her mind, Vivienne's voice rose, sharp and syrupy.

"I do hope you're not planning on breastfeeding *again*, Natalie. At your age, it's frankly embarrassing."

Natalie clenched her jaw.

"You always look tired, dear. I'd kill for a nap in the afternoon, but I suppose that's what happens when you let your children run wild."

Barbs dressed as advice. Condescension camouflaged in silk. Years of it, slid under her skin like needles dipped in sugar. She used to bite her tongue. Smile. Nod. Because Vivienne was the matriarch. Because Martin needed her to be polite. Because she wanted to believe she was being paranoid. But now she saw it. The disdain had always been real. The contempt.

Not just for her as a mother, but as a woman. As someone who had dared to exist in their house without pedigree or power.

She saw the way Vivienne used to watch her with the baby, lips pursed, eyebrows arched. The comments about Eve's weight. About Thomas's "discipline." She remembered the morning Vivienne let herself in, again, and found Natalie crying in the kitchen. She hadn't slept. Martin had yelled the night before. Thomas had wet the bed. Eve wouldn't latch and Natalie had cracked.

And Vivienne's response? "Oh darling. If you can't cope, perhaps Martin should consider full-time childcare."

Not: Are you okay? Not: Can I help? Just: Get out of the way. Admit you are weak.

Natalie's knuckles tensed on the steering wheel. She pressed harder on the gas when signs for Haverford Township began to appear in the mist.

Vivienne had known. Not just about Martin's violence. About his secrets. About the cabin.

She *knew*. And she chose silence. Leon was brazen about that, he'd confirmed it. Worse, Vivienne had *enabled* it. She had sat at her pristine kitchen table with her silver sugar bowl and her cruel smile and known. Because she had found a way to swerve it. Because Bobby had been played, thinking he was molding and shaping her when she was the one who really took control, for her own good. Then she trained her sons to be obedient and monstrous.

Natalie's stomach turned. Some might see Vivienne as a woman who'd done what she had to survive, but there were other ways, like tell the police for a start. Instead, she'd encouraged the sickness that flowed through their veins so in Natalie's eyes, she too was guilty of the most hideous sins.

Natalie had been hurt, violated, manipulated, and she would go to her grave making sure it was never passed it on. She wouldn't turn her children into currency. Wouldn't become an accomplice to evil.

Vivienne had made a choice. And now Natalie would too. She would take back what mattered. Her children. Her voice. Her power. The radio crackled briefly. A voice from a late-night station announced a low-pressure front and a fire warning in the western forests.

Natalie let out a bitter laugh. Too late for warnings.

She pictured Bobby's face, red and smug, always smiling like he knew something others didn't. She remembered the way Martin used to watch him. Like a god. A blueprint. And she pictured Vivienne's eyes. Cold. Icy. Blue steel wrapped in Chanel. Vivienne hadn't just watched the legacy unfold. She *protected* it. With silence. With calculated looks and quiet nods.

And Natalie had been too blind, too afraid, too desperate to believe anything other than the version of the family she was fed. But now she saw. She saw everything. With each mile the truth grew brighter, crisp and clear, until it became a beacon showing her the way. She wasn't just going back for her children. She was going back for *justice*.

# 28

The tires whispered against the stone drive as Natalie eased the Audi to a halt. The glow of the porch light reached across the gravel like a silent spotlight, and for a moment, the car's engine idled in time with her heartbeat, steady, unrelenting. Then she turned the key and killed it. Silence.

She sat there for a beat, her palms still on the wheel, her eyes scanning the front of the house. The bay window. The manicured lawn. The box hedges Martin insisted be trimmed every Thursday. It looked so normal. So detached from the blaze and the blood and the secrets that had just burned to ash in the woods.

Natalie reached for the handle and stepped out of the car. Her boots crunched against the gravel. Her hair was dirty, hanging in uneven clumps around her face. She looked like a woman unrecognizable from any photograph on the walls inside. But her gait was calm.

Measured. Like she was arriving home after a long shift.

She reached up and swept the tangled strands behind her ears, smoothing her shirt, tugging her jacket sleeves down as if she could iron away the night. Then she walked around the side of the house and slipped her hand under the topiary pot by the fence and pulled out a key. The emergency spare.

She returned to the front of the house and looked at the key, the metal glinted under the porch light, yellowed, catching the glow like a warning. She stared at it and gripped it tightly, walked to the door, and slid the key into the lock. The mechanism clicked like the trigger of a gun. She stepped inside.

Warm air and the odor of whatever they'd had for dinner greeted her. The hallway lights were dimmed, just as Martin and by proxy, his mother, liked them, casting ethereal shards of silver across the parquet flooring.

Natalie stood in the threshold, her breath caught in her throat. The walls were lined with photographs – snapshots from a life that had always looked perfect from the outside.

There she was in a red dress at Martin's fundraiser. There they were with the kids at the beach, all coordinated swimsuits and sunburnt smiles. Thomas's third birthday. Eve's christening. Frozen moments in time, perfectly curated, carefully chosen. A story told in frames. A big fat lie.

She stepped forward slowly, her legs suddenly uncertain beneath her. The essence of the house unnerving her. Her stomach twisted. *They're upstairs.* The thought hit her like a punch.

Her children. Sleeping. Unaware. Innocent.

She could almost hear their breathing. The rustle of sheets. The creak of the hallway floor outside their bedrooms. Her knees buckled slightly, and she grabbed the edge of the sideboard for balance. Pain stabbed through her wrist, but she didn't wince. She barely felt it. The adrenaline was still carrying her, dulling everything that didn't matter. The framed photos on the sideboard blurred for a second before coming into sharp focus again. She picked one up. Her and the children on the hill behind the house, the sun setting behind them. Thomas with his toothy grin, arms flung around her neck. Eve, smaller then, with a shy smile and a squint into the sun.

Thomas looked like Martin. There was no denying it. The same chin. The same mouth.

But Eve. Natalie narrowed her eyes. There was something about her daughter's expression. The angle of her eyes. The shape of her face. Leon's words crawled back into her mind, and she banished them, knowing now the truth of every syllable. Eve was his. Fact.

Her stomach turned. She wanted to shake it off, to silence the echo. But it lingered like an unwanted guest. She set the photo back down, gently, like it might crack under her fingertips. Then she felt it. Another presence. She looked up.

Vivienne stood at the top of the staircase, draped in a white cotton nightdress, her face pale but composed. Like a soldier surveying a battlefield. Not shocked. Not scared. Prepared.

Her hands rested on the banister, perfectly manicured fingers curled over the wood.

Natalie met her eyes. Neither woman spoke. The air between them tensed. And somewhere upstairs, just out of sight, Thomas and Eve slept on. Natalie didn't speak. She didn't have to. She watched Vivienne watching her, and for the first time since they'd shared oxygen, Vivienne looked uncertain. Her icy veneer had cracked just enough.

The fact Natalie was there at all would signal something had gone wrong. She didn't know what Natalie had seen. Didn't know what Natalie had survived. She only knew that Natalie was alone and that something had changed.

Still, the performance continued. Vivienne descended the stairs with slow, deliberate grace. Her cotton nightdress whispered around her ankles. A touch of pale pink lip stain still clung to her mouth, and her hair was swept into a low twist like she'd stepped out of a 1950s movie set.

"Natalie, this is a surprise," she said, voice light, as if greeting a stray cat on the porch. "You're home early, dear."

Natalie didn't reply.

Vivienne's smile didn't falter, though her eyes landed on her surprise arrival, perhaps to gauge just how wild Natalie looked. How filthy. How changed.

"I wasn't expecting you until tomorrow."

Natalie stood still, hands at her sides, breathing slow and deep.

"I thought you'd be with Martin. Where is he? Unpacking the car I expect." Vivienne tilted her head.

Natalie's eyes narrowed.

"Let's go into the kitchen," she said calmly. "I don't want to wake the children."

Vivienne gave a hollow smile. "And neither do I."

She walked past her, the scent of rosewater and talcum powder wafting in her wake. Natalie followed.

The kitchen was pristine. Spotless. Magazine-worthy. The marble countertops gleamed. The overhead lights glowed soft and golden. A single orchid sat blooming on the windowsill.

Vivienne moved like she owned every inch of it even if she didn't.

"Would you like some cocoa?" she asked breezily. "It might help you sleep. You look dreadful, darling."

Natalie didn't sit. She leaned against the doorframe, arms crossed. Vivienne bustled around the stove like a benevolent matriarch, pulling out a small saucepan, humming something classical under her breath. The normality of it was obscene.

Natalie's eyes followed every movement.

She said quietly, "You asked where Martin is."

Vivienne didn't turn.

"Oh, darling." She sighed as though exhausted by Natalie's eternal drama. "It's obvious he's not with you and you've had some kind of tiff but that is between the two of you, isn't it? I try not to involve myself in marital business. It's so... distasteful."

Natalie stared at her. The clink of the spoon against the side of the pan sounded thunderous. Vivienne turned then, gliding to the kitchen island where she set down two mugs, white china with gold rims.

"It was more than a tiff, I can assure you. It was more like a revelation, discovering the type of man and family I'd married into." Natalie watched and waited.

Vivienne smiled again, this time more tightly. "Ah, I see. The thing is, darling, some men, when they truly admire a woman, they want to share her, you know. It's not... wrong. It's a compliment, really. It's about pride and desire."

Natalie's heart went still.

Vivienne's eyes gleamed. "You were lucky, Natalie. You were *chosen*. By Martin and then, approved by me."

It was as she went to pick up the spoon for the cocoa that her right hand trembled just slightly, and Natalie noticed immediately.

"I was so glad to have been chosen by my Bobby," Vivienne said gently as she stirred their drinks. "It was a privilege. An honor to become a Lane. One that isn't extended to just anyone."

She moved back toward the dishwasher, slowly. Natalie didn't break eye contact as Vivienne took the spoon from the side and reached inside the open door. Her hand slipped into the silverware rack. When she turned again, her right hand was behind her back.

"Cocoa's ready."

She stepped forward, steam swirling from the rims of the cups. Natalie still didn't move.

"Won't you sit, dear?" Vivienne asked sweetly. "Let's talk like grown women. It's been so long since we had a proper, honest conversation."

Natalie's lip twitched. "We've never had one and I'll pass on the cocoa. Never know what you might have put in there."

Vivienne's smile didn't falter. Natalie glanced once toward the ceiling, where Thomas and Eve lay asleep, untouched by the rot that had festered in their family for years. She couldn't risk waking them.

Vivienne moved to place the cups on the island, the carving fork that Natalie had seen her take still hidden behind the drape of her nightdress, waiting to be revealed.

# 29

The second the cups touched the island's surface, Vivienne dropped the act. Her face slackened. The saccharine smile melted into a sneer. Her spine straightened, her chin lifted. No more grandmother. No more giver of advice. Now she was the woman Natalie had always known. A monster wrapped in white cotton.

"You're an ungrateful little bitch," she said coolly, the carving fork still tucked behind her back.

Natalie didn't flinch. Vivienne shook her head, slow and disdainful, as though disappointed in a pet that had pissed on the rug.

"You never appreciated what you were given. What we *offered* you. A place. A family. Respectability."

The kitchen felt suddenly colder, like the temperature had dropped ten degrees. A buzz filled Natalie's ears. Her jaw tightened, but she said nothing yet. Let the woman talk. Let her hang herself with her own words.

Natalie took a step forward. Her voice was ice. "Is that what you call it?"

Vivienne clicked her tongue. "You think the world gives a

damn about you, Natalie? About some poor, damaged girl from Wyoming or wherever you crawled out from? You think anyone cares about whatever tales you think you can tell?"

She stepped around the island, the fork now visible in her hand. She looked like a normal grandmother in a movie if you ignored the weapon and the contempt burning in her eyes. The overhead light cast shadows across Vivienne's face that made her look skeletal, ghoulish.

"You had everything," Vivienne spat. "You were *chosen*. Do you understand how rare that is? You were allowed to serve your husband. To *strengthen* him. You gave him children. You gave him *power*. That's what we do. That's what women are for."

Natalie's fists clenched at her sides. Her nails dug into her palms until crescent moons of pain bloomed there, steady anchors to keep her rage from boiling over too soon.

Vivienne kept talking, the words spilling like poison from a cracked chalice. "Bobby taught me well. He was brilliant. He understood that obedience breeds resilience. That submission creates legacy."

She waved the fork as if conducting a symphony. "And Martin, well... he was always going to follow in his daddy's footsteps because he had promise. Until *you* started to ruin his life with your frailties which is why you had to go."

The floor tiles were cold underneath Natalie's feet as she shifted. Outside, the wind picked up, brushing dry branches against the kitchen window like skeletal fingers. Natalie's breath caught at Vivienne's words. *Had to go.*

Vivienne saw it and spat out more hatred. "Oh yes. Your disobedience. Your coldness. Your refusal to accept your place it *weakened* him because a man needs a loyal woman. A servant."

"I am *not* anyone's servant," Natalie growled.

Vivienne's face twisted with something between amusement and rage. "No. You're a wreck. And now? Now you've ruined everything and when Martin gets here, you are going to be sorry."

Natalie stepped closer.

"Martin is dead," she said evenly.

Vivienne froze. Natalie watched her eyes panic, widen and express fear.

Then the calm returned. The cruelty calcified.

"I don't believe you so if you think you can bluff your way out of here with the children then think again. They belong to me now."

"He's dead. And Leon too."

Vivienne's lips parted, just slightly. But she didn't ask how. She didn't ask why.

She only said: "Then if that's true you've destroyed my family and it means I will have to do the same to you."

Natalie shook her head. "No. No you won't and I'm not responsible for what happened up there. You did that. You trained them. You fed into their sickness. You watched it fester. You *knew* what they did to women, girls, innocents."

Vivienne's grip on the fork tightened. "I *endured*. Just like you could have. But you were weak. Selfish. Pathetic."

Natalie's voice broke. "I am not pathetic, you are. I *fought*. I survived. And I came back for my children."

The air between them pulsed with unspoken violence. Every tick of the kitchen clock seemed to hammer louder. The house held its breath.

Vivienne moved closer. "You don't deserve them."

Natalie didn't move. She could hear her own heartbeat pounding behind her ribs, like a drum of war.

Vivienne lifted the fork just slightly, as if testing. Measuring.

And Natalie smiled. It was slow. Cold. Final. "Try me."

Natalie's entire body was trembling, but not from fear. From fury. Rage radiated off her in waves, coiling through her spine, setting her nerves alight like copper wire.

Vivienne didn't blink. With the carving fork raised, she tilted her head, a portrait of haughty control. "You think you've done something noble, Natalie? Something brave?"

Natalie's jaw tensed. Her fingernails dug deeper into her palms.

Vivienne's voice dropped to something slower, measured, almost confessional. "I know what they did to you. I know what Bobby did to others, because I saw, I watched."

Natalie flinched, caught off guard.

"I wasn't always this," Vivienne said. "I was like you once. Sweet. Quiet. Hopeful. I had dreams. I used to read novels under the covers and fantasize about romantic trips to Paris." She chuckled darkly. "And then I married Bobby."

Natalie's lip curled.

"I fought back, in my own way once I knew the truth and what was in store for me once I'd had my first son. Of course I did. And I knew how Bobby's father had ways of breaking a woman down. Bobby told me all about it." Her eyes narrowed. "The belt. The closet. The pills. She was taught what obedience meant. And when I was pregnant with Martin, I taught Bobby what loyalty looked like and a new and more powerful way to be and that with me on side, he could do whatever he wanted with whoever he wanted, and I would help him."

She took a step toward Natalie, barefoot, slow. "I learned. I adapted. I realised there were only two types of women in this world. The used, and the users."

Natalie said nothing. Her hands were shaking at her sides. Vivienne continued, her tone softening but Natalie knew she was like a serpent sliding closer.

"I didn't stop him, no. I offered him alternatives. I kept myself useful. I *let* him take others. Girls like you. And you know what that did? It made me powerful. I was no longer a victim. I was part of something bigger."

"You became an extension of him," Natalie whispered.

Vivienne smiled, lips thin and mean. "No, darling. I became *better* than him."

Natalie shook her head slowly. "You're worse, that's true. Sicker, more warped, a disgrace."

She took a single step forward and held up a hand, not to plead, but to silence.

"So don't say another word. I've listened to enough of your deluded poison for a lifetime."

Vivienne blinked, startled. She wasn't used to being interrupted. Not like that.

"You stood by and watched your husband break women, and you helped him. You raised your sons to carry on the disease. And you call that survival?"

Vivienne's smile didn't falter, but her eyes narrowed to slits.

"You're not just complicit. You're the warped architect."

Vivienne studied her like she didn't recognize the woman standing before her. The same daughter-in-law she'd dismissed for years had morphed into something unyielding.

And then Natalie spoke, calm and flat: "Martin is dead. Leon is dead. They both died in agony. I watched Martin writhe in pain and then heard Leon scream as a knife tore through his insides and then, heard him beg as he burned to death."

The air shifted. A silence expanded between them, weighted with the finality of truth.

Vivienne's bravado drained, like someone had punctured her lungs. Her mouth opened, but no sound came.

"I don't need to embellish further," Natalie added. "Just know that their deaths were earned."

Vivienne's hand twitched. And then she lunged.

The carving fork turned into a steel serpent strike, a blur of silver and intent. Vivienne's eyes were wild, her mouth twisted in fury. Natalie gasped and stumbled back, her hand slamming into the counter for balance.

They collided, Vivienne's momentum slamming them both into the wall near the pantry. The fork sliced Natalie's upper arm, a searing line of fire. Blood bloomed through her shirt.

Upstairs, there was a sound. A soft thud. Natalie's thoughts shot to Thomas. To Eve. Vivienne raised the fork again, screeching like something feral but Natalie caught her wrist mid-air. The two women grappled, strength against rage. Age against fury.

The fork wavered inches from Natalie's throat. She could see her reflection in the polished lampshade above the counter, wide-eyed, blood streaked, furious.

"I should've killed you when you got here," Vivienne hissed.

"And I should've left this house years ago," Natalie panted, "but here we are."

Natalie twisted, slammed Vivienne's hand against the cupboard handle. The fork clattered to the floor. Both women stumbled. Natalie kicked the weapon away. Vivienne staggered back, breathless, her nightdress now smeared with blood and sweat. Natalie stood panting, heart hammering in her ears, her wounded arm hanging limp at her side.

From upstairs, the floor creaked again. Natalie turned to the ceiling. "Not here," she murmured. "Not where they can see."

Vivienne wiped her mouth with the back of her hand. "You think you've won?" she snarled. "They'll never believe you. I'll tell them you killed my sons then you came here to kill us."

"You don't get it, do you," Natalie said. "There's a witness and evidence, videos of martin and Leon brutalizing women like me. He told me all about your involvement and the witness, she heard it all, every single word and by now, the police will have what they need, and they'll come for you."

Vivienne's chest heaved. Natalie took a single step forward.

"Go ahead," she said. "If you still want to kill me, try again. Nothing can be worse than what your sons did to me, or what I saw on those videos, but I promise you this, I will fight you till my last breath to protect my children."

Vivienne looked at her and for the first time, Natalie saw something unfamiliar in those cold blue eyes. Fear.

# 30

In a moment, less than a heartbeat, the kitchen became a battleground. Vivienne twisted and grabbed a knife from the block and lunged again, steel flashing under the overhead lights like a silver fang. Natalie twisted just in time, pain lancing through her dislocated wrist as she shoved the older woman backward. Her entire arm screamed, but she pushed through it. She had no choice.

Vivienne recovered with terrifying speed. Her white cotton nightdress clung to her in sweaty patches, the hem flaring with each crazed movement. She shrieked something unintelligible, raising the fork for another strike.

Natalie dodged, her shoulder crashing into the fridge. A cascade of magnets and a child's drawing fluttered to the floor. She kicked out, catching Vivienne in the shin, sending her reeling into the island. The knife scraped across the counter. The kitchen lights were too bright, too revealing. Every shadow, every breathless movement, every drop of sweat and smear of blood was laid bare in brutal clarity. This was no shadowy nightmare. This was real. And deadly.

Vivienne was no longer composed. Her mask had shattered.

Now she was simply unhinged, a snarling, feral matriarch fighting for her legacy and freedom.

"You ruined everything!" she screamed.

Natalie's foot caught on a broken mug and she slipped, catching herself on the edge of the countertop. Her wrist gave out. She howled in agony but kept upright. Vivienne closed the gap, slashing wildly. The knife sliced the air an inch from Natalie's face. The gleam of it felt electric.

Natalie grabbed a cast iron skillet from the stovetop with her good hand and swung. The heavy metal collided with Vivienne's forearm, and she yelped, dropping the knife. The two women slammed into each other once more.

Groceries from earlier in the week, an apple, a bruised banana, a jar of peanut butter tumbled from the counter and burst on the floor. It was chaos. Shards of glass sparkled underfoot. A chair toppled. Natalie's chest heaved with exhaustion, but she kept going.

Vivienne shrieked again and tackled her around the waist, sending them crashing into the table. For a second, the whole world was upside down. And then Natalie flipped her. She wrestled her to the table and pinned her down. Somehow, she had the upper hand now. Her wrist throbbed. Blood oozed from a gash along her shoulder. But she didn't stop.

Vivienne writhed beneath her, bucking and spitting like a cornered animal. Natalie looked down at her, panting, strands of damp hair plastered to her cheeks. She wanted to scream. To cry. To make sense of any of it.

But then –

A small voice. "Momma?"

Natalie froze. She turned her head slowly, heart pounding, blood rushing in her ears. Eve stood in the kitchen doorway, rubbing her eyes with one fist, a stuffed rabbit dangling from the other.

"Gran-gran?" she said again, voice small and confused.

Natalie's heart cracked clean down the middle. The sight of her daughter so innocent, so trusting, cut through the rage like a scalpel.

Vivienne went still too. Her eyes flicked to Eve, then back to Natalie. Something smug flickered behind the madness. As if even now, she could weaponize the child.

Natalie looked into Eve's wide, sleepy eyes. She saw the question there. The confusion. The fear starting to bloom.

"Run," Natalie whispered. "Get away, go get help."

Vivienne snarled beneath her. "It's too late. I'm going to kill you then make sure she never utters another word of this. I'll say you did it, that you're a murderous psycho bitch."

Natalie snapped. With a guttural scream, she wrenched the knife from the floor with her good hand and plunged it into Vivienne. Once. Twice. Again.

Vivienne gasped, choked, writhed. Her blood smeared across the floor, dark and wet.

Natalie stopped and took it all in. The face of evil. This woman had raised monsters. Had smiled and stirred cocoa while orchestrating torture. Had stood by while Natalie was broken, again and again. Had almost taken Eve.

The kitchen was silent but for the shallow, rhythmic breaths of a small girl watching from the doorway. Natalie turned slowly. Eve still stood there. Not screaming. Not crying. Just watching.

Natalie dropped the knife. It clattered against the table leg as blood dripped onto the floor.

"Baby…" she whispered. Her voice cracked like brittle ice.

Eve blinked, then padded forward. She placed one small hand on her mother's leg and looked up at her.

"Are you hurt, Momma?" she asked.

Natalie knelt, hugging her close with her good arm. "A little bit, baby. Not too bad, though."

She pressed her face to Eve's hair, breathing her in. The smell of childhood. Of soap and sleep.

The nightmare was over. Or was it just beginning? The kitchen had become a slaughterhouse. Vivienne lay sprawled, her white nightdress soaked in deep crimson, her limbs slack and twisted. Blood dripped slowly, steadily, onto the once-pristine tiled floor each drop a ticking metronome in the hush that followed the violence.

Eve was stiff and silent. Natalie's heart squeezed. She cradled her tightly, tucking Eve's head beneath her chin, her mouth trembling against her daughter's hair.

"It's okay. It's okay now," she said. "You're safe. I did it for you. I did it all for you."

Eve whispered, "I know Momma. Gran-gran was gonna do bad things to us. I heard what she said."

Natalie scrunched her eyes, knowing that coming back from this was a mountain they had to climb together so said it again, and again. Each time, the words frayed further, their comfort unraveling at the edges.

"You're safe now. I'll keep you safe. It's over. She can't hurt us now."

But Eve's eyes remained fixed on the body. On the sag of flesh, the stillness. She blinked slowly, mechanically, like her brain couldn't quite catch up. She didn't cry. But they stayed like that for what felt like a lifetime. Curled up together on the blood-slicked tiles while morning slowly crept through the windows. Natalie didn't move until the sound of soft footsteps broke the silence.

Thomas. He stood at the threshold, hair messy from sleep, wearing flannel pajamas with cartoon tigers. He rubbed one eye and frowned.

"Mom?"

Natalie looked up.

"My boy," she said, voice barely more than a breath. "My boy."

She got up on shaking legs, gathered him into her embrace. Her body ached, her muscles screamed, but she didn't care. She held him close. Buried her face in his hair.

"My boy. My boy."

The phrase rang in the air like an echo of something old and bitter, Vivienne's voice, long ago, crooning it over Martin's head. Natalie froze and vowed to never say those words again. Then slowly, she pulled back and looked into Thomas's eyes. No. She was not her. She would *never* be her. And he would never be his father, she would make sure.

She wrapped both her children into her arms, anchoring them to her chest. "Go back upstairs," she whispered. "Go to your rooms. I'll come soon, I promise."

Thomas blinked. "Is Gran-gran okay?"

Natalie's throat closed. "Don't worry about her."

Eve didn't speak. She walked away quietly, following her brother who for once did as he was told, her rabbit dragging behind her. When they were gone, Natalie straightened. She was soaked in blood, Vivienne's, her own, hard to tell anymore. Her dislocated wrist hung limp and swollen. Scratches and bruises marred every inch of her exposed skin. But she was standing.

She crossed to the kitchen counter, where the cordless phone rested in its cradle. She picked it up, her fingers trembling as she dialed.

9… 1… 1.

It rang once. Twice.

"911, what's your emergency?"

Natalie inhaled. Her voice cracked. "I need the police. And an ambulance."

"Ma'am, can you tell me your name and address?"

She did. Mechanically. Like she was reading from a card.

"There's been a death," she added. "An attack. I was attacked."

She didn't say who. Not yet.

"Are you safe now?" the dispatcher asked.

Natalie looked toward the stairs.

"Yes," she said. "My children are safe now. That's all that matters."

She ended the call and let the phone slip from her injured hand. She raised it to inspect it. It hurt so bad and she winced. And then she remembered. The memory card. She'd given it to Sienna. A small sliver of proof. And the one in Martin's study which she sensed would contain more of the same sick footage. Some hope of justice.

Natalie slumped into a kitchen chair. Her limbs trembled. Her face was a ruin of fatigue and pain. But she was alive. She had survived. Outside, sirens began to wail in the distance.

And the sun rose on what remained of the nightmare.

# 31

The apartment was in a state. Toys littered every available surface, piles of laundry waited to be folded on the sagging couch, and a teetering stack of moving boxes towered in one corner like an unstable monument to chaos. Somewhere beneath it all, Misty's once-pristine order had drowned.

Natalie sat at the cramped breakfast bar, elbows on the Formica counter, watching her children dart in and out of the narrow living room. Thomas was on his tablet that blared racing car noises while Eve sat cross-legged beside a pile of coloring books, her expression faraway as she shaded a cartoon deer.

"Careful with those pens," Misty muttered, side-eyeing the chaos from behind her tablet. She was on the sofa, perched on the last cushion that wasn't overtaken by dinosaurs or laundry. Her tone wasn't cross, just exhausted from the never-ending chaos as she swiped through social media half-heartedly, pausing on a headline before scrolling on. Then scrolling back.

Cabin Lake Murders: Public Still Demands Answers Four Months On.

She didn't click it. She couldn't. Her thumb trembled a little as she scrolled past it and minimized the app altogether. Natalie hadn't seen the article. Thank God.

It still rattled Natalie whenever Sienna got in touch with updates about her recovery and the case against Scott. The horrors of the 'club' and their sordid financial arrangements were filtering through with each suspect tracked down and arrested, some of them confessing and implicating others, the rest pleading the fifth.

What almost finished Sienna and Natalie had been the revelation that large sums of money swapped hands and was shared by Leon and Martin, and when Scott left his wife at the cabin for the weekend, for men to do with her as they wished, he'd been paid handsomely. He expected her to be so drugged and incoherent when he went to collect her that she'd believe she'd been sick with a fever. What he found when he arrived was a burnt-out cabin and the emergency services in attendance. He was arrested on the spot.

Natalie's voice snapped Misty back into the present, and regardless of the chaos it was a place she much preferred, rather than the swamp of the past and what happened at that cabin.

"I'll clear all this up later, I swear," Natalie offered quietly, gesturing at the mess.

Misty snorted. "It's fine. Who needs living space?"

There was understanding beneath the sarcasm, but not the kind that cracked and exploded. This was the kind that friends share and accept, knowing that one day they would laugh about it all.

"Hey, Miss Dreamy. You sure about Wyoming?" Misty asked finally.

Natalie snapped out of her daze and exhaled. "Yeah. I think so. I know so."

Misty raised an eyebrow, unconvinced.

"It's quiet. Remote. And the schools are good. They'll need anonymity and structure."

"Yep, I agree. They also need therapy," Misty said, not unkindly. "Plus, they need roots and you need sleep."

Natalie rubbed her temple. "I know. And so do you."

Thomas whooshed past, nearly knocking Eve's coloring pile over.

"Thomas!" Natalie called, too late.

"I'm bored! I wanna go outside," he yelled, zooming around again.

Misty gave a dry chuckle. "Kid ain't got no concept of space. Or boundaries."

"I think for now boundaries are exactly what he needs," Natalie murmured, almost to herself.

Eve looked up but didn't laugh or even smile. She hadn't done much of either lately.

"Look," Misty said, setting down her tablet. "I'm not trying to push you out and you can stay here as long as you need. You *know* that so please don't jump into a decision."

Natalie nodded. "I know, but it's not fair on you and this place is too small for us all."

"It's not about space or about the past catching up, or anonymity" Misty hesitated. "It's about what happens if you get it wrong and then all of it just... stays with you. Forever."

Natalie looked down at the half-empty coffee mug in front of her. Her knuckles were still raw, the scabs fresh. "I don't want them to grow up in the shadow of what happened and if we stay they will. Nobody will forget. So, I will have to go it alone and anyway, my folks have promised to help. Kids make friends quickly and seeing as I'd rather keep myself to myself, it'll be fine."

Misty didn't reply, but her silence said everything. Natalie was right about the folks in town but the media wouldn't let go, either. The public was obsessed. Reddit threads and YouTube videos dissected everything from the police reports to old family photos. A cult. A legacy. A mother who killed her mother-in-law in front of her daughter. Misty knew Natalie had stopped reading the headlines a long time ago, but she hadn't.

"I want them to be kids," she whispered.

"You sure Eve's okay?"

Natalie's eyes flicked to her daughter. Eve was coloring quietly, but there was a discord to her movements. Mechanical. Detached.

"I do think she's getting through it in her own way. She doesn't cry. She doesn't scream. Not even in her sleep," Natalie said.

"That's not necessarily better. Just because she doesn't have bad dreams doesn't mean she won't have bad thoughts and memories."

Natalie nodded then silence stretched between them.

Misty reached for the last doughnut in the box and sighed. "You're really brave, you know."

"No. I'm just... what's left of who I was before and what I've salvaged for their sakes."

Misty didn't correct her.

"Are you looking forward to the move, to going home, just a little bit?" Misty ran her eye over the growing pile of packing boxes in her hallway.

"Yes, I am because I never should have left Wyoming in the first place. That's what he wanted, and it was a mistake." Natalie said quietly.

In the other room, Thomas cursed because his tablet had run out of battery and was searching for his charger amongst the mess. Eve didn't even look up. And outside the window, the city went on as if nothing had happened.

. . .

The moving truck belched smoke and exhaustion as it pulled away from the curb, leaving behind the people who were at the beginning of a new life. Natalie stood in the driveway of the modest ranch house, her hands on her hips, the wind tugging at the hem of her cotton shirt. The sky above was a crisp Wyoming blue, so wide it made her feel both infinite and invisible.

Thomas scrambled up the ramp and dragged another box toward the porch, grunting as he heaved it along. Eve trailed behind him with a smaller box marked "Books," her gaze darting every few seconds toward the unfamiliar street.

Natalie followed, steadying the wobbly load in her arms as she stepped inside. The house was quiet and bare, but echoing with possibility. White walls, scuffed hardwood floors, no furniture yet, just a shell waiting to be filled. The new stuff would be delivered the next day and Natalie kept repeating that it would signal a fresh start. They'd sit on a sofa and sleep in beds that didn't hold tainted memories from a house that lacked joy. They'd eat from a table where dinner times would be fun and filled with laughter. That's all Natalie wanted. To see her kids smile.

"This one's the living room," Natalie said, more to herself than anyone else, setting the box down and straightening her back.

Outside, a curtain twitched. Then another. Small-town hospitality with a side of suspicion. She didn't blame them. A single mother, two kids, no husband in sight. She'd grown up here. She knew how people whispered. But she wasn't afraid of whispers anymore.

The sun was warm on her face as she stepped back onto the porch. She closed her eyes for a second and listened to the wind moving through the grass, the rustle of dry leaves scraping along the curb. And then on the breeze came something familiar, dust and sagebrush. And something else. Smoke?

Her head jerked. The scent was fleeting, gone almost as soon as it arrived. But it stirred something deep in her chest, a tiny a flutter of dread, the hint of panic. Then she heard it. A voice, thin and distant, barely carried on the thermals.

"Natalie."

She froze. Her skin chilled despite the sun. Her grandfather's voice. High Bear. Was it a warning or a welcome? The rest of the words were too soft, the message lost in the wind so she blinked it away, shook her head as if to clear it and blamed her imagination.

She grabbed another box and turned back toward the house. As she did, she spotted Thomas kneeling at the edge of the lawn.

"Thomas?"

He didn't answer. She set the box down and walked toward him, her boots crunching on gravel. He was hunched at the curb, poking at something on the ground with a stick. A crow. Dead. Its wings spread wide, black feathers fanned like a warning flag.

"Thomas, don't touch that."

He looked up slowly. His smile was strange. Crooked. A glint of something not quite right in his eyes. For a heartbeat, just one, Natalie saw Martin's face staring back at her. That same smile. That same tilt of the head. Her heart gave a sharp, traitorous jolt.

But then it was gone. It was Thomas again. Just her boy. A little too quiet these days, a little too intense, but still him.

Natalie nodded, forcing calm into her expression. "Come help me with the boxes, okay? Then we can head over to the motel and get dinner. We've got a big day tomorrow when the carpenter comes to fix up your beds and all our new stuff arrives. Won't that be fun."

He nodded and wiped his hands on his jeans before trotting

back toward the house. Natalie stood by the crow a moment longer. Its eye was open. Glassy. Watching.

She walked away and stepped inside, the house that was full of the sounds of new beginnings: the pull of tape from cardboard, the distant laughter of a child, the creak of floorboards beneath unfamiliar feet. Natalie took a deep breath and smiled. A real smile. She was in control again. But behind her, at the edge of the lawn, the crow remained. And on the wind, her grandfather's voice whispered once more.

*"You are strong. You have shown who you are. Remember, Natalie, that fear is not the enemy. Forgetting who you are is the danger. Hold on to who you are, my child. You have made me proud and now, you are where you belong, you are home. And I am by your side. If you ever need me, ask, listen. You'll hear my voice in the wind."*

# EPILOGUE

*Lander Public Library – Eight Months Later*

Fold-out chairs lined the space beneath the arched beams, filled with women of all ages –some in loose sweaters, others in business attire, many somewhere in between.

At the front, beside a lectern with a chipped edge and a poster for "Voices of Survival: A Day of Sharing & Strength," sat Natalie.

Her back was straight. Her dark hair, now cropped into a blunt, chin-length bob, framed a face that was older yet softer than it had been a year ago. Her arms were folded loosely in her lap. She wore a charcoal grey blouse tucked into black jeans, neat, restrained, unremarkable. Exactly how she liked it since she had become a symbol. Not willingly. Not happily. Eventually accepting.

The press called her "The Mother Who Fought Back." Online forums labeled her everything from a hero to a harbinger of the apocalypse. She was referenced in half a dozen true-crime podcasts and one particularly lurid Netflix documentary still in production.

People recognized her on the street. They whispered in queues. They called her brave.

Some called her unstable and a fantasist. And she was still here.

She smiled politely as a round of applause broke out for the last speaker, a woman named Denise who had spoken, with shaking hands and a tight voice, about surviving her abusive ex-husband. As Denise stepped down, the moderator, a sandy-haired woman in her sixties, nodded at Natalie.

"Our final speaker today is someone who... probably doesn't need much of an introduction," the moderator said gently, "but let me just say this: we're honored to have her with us, and her story, painful though it is, has lit a fire in so many. Please welcome, Natalie Beaumont."

A second round of applause. Natalie rose, smoothed her palms down her thighs, and stepped to the lectern. She hated this part. Not the speaking. She'd learned how to do that again. Not the content. She knew her story better than anyone. But the role, that was what she loathed.

Survivor. Spokeswoman. Symbol.

"Thank you," she said, voice steady. "Thanks for letting me be here."

She took a sip of water. She didn't need notes. She knew what they wanted.

"I'm not going to tell you everything that happened," she began. "Because some of it, I still don't understand. And some of it... I don't want to give any more power to."

A murmur of agreement moved through the room.

"But I will tell you this. I was married for nearly a decade to a man who wore a mask. Not a literal one, but one that was just as effective. He was charming. Intelligent. Controlled. And I learned, too late, what was under that mask. I learned what had shaped him. What kind of legacy he came from."

She paused. Looked at the floor for a beat. Then lifted her eyes again.

"I learned that monsters don't always roar. Sometimes they smile. Sometimes they kiss your cheek goodnight."

A flicker of movement in the crowd caught her eye. A woman near the back, small-framed, auburn hair pulled tight, leaned forward slightly. Something about her posture snagged Natalie's attention.

"I escaped," she went on. "Barely. Not just the cabin, but the life that came before it. And in doing that, I became something I didn't expect. I became someone people wanted to talk about and to."

Her voice faltered but she recovered.

"They wrote about my strength. My bravery. My revenge. But what they don't write about is the way I flinch when someone slams a door. The way I sleep with the windows locked even when it's ninety degrees outside."

More nods. More quiet murmurs. She was saying what they all knew, but few could say out loud.

"I don't feel like a hero," she said. "Most days, I feel like a woman who lost everything she thought was real and had to build a life from scratch. And if any of you in this room are in aa situation like mine, please believe this. If I can do it, so can you."

She stepped back from the mic. "That's all I wanted to say. You know the rest and I wish you all well."

The applause this time was slow. Earnest. It built, wave by wave, into something that filled the library with warmth. Natalie gave a small nod and returned to her chair. Misty wasn't there. She'd offered, but Natalie had declined. Some things still needed to be done alone.

The session ended with tea and biscuits in the reading

corner. A few of the women came to thank her. A couple asked for hugs. Natalie gave them all, quietly, graciously. But she didn't linger. She was gathering her coat when the woman with auburn hair approached.

She was older than Natalie had thought. Late fifties, maybe early sixties. Her eyes were pale, almost translucent.

She didn't introduce herself. She just leaned in, so close that Natalie smelled rosewater and stale breath, as the woman whispered –

"There are more of them. Organized groups who share what they think they own. The same way they shared you. You need to use your voice, your platform to push for change, dig deeper, expose those in circles who wield unbelievable power and allow this to go on. You mustn't give up because this is just the start and we need you."

Natalie's spine went rigid. The woman pulled back and smiled politely, like she'd just commented on the weather. Then she turned and walked away, her shoes soft on the carpet.

Natalie stood there, breath caught in her throat. She didn't chase after the woman. She didn't ask questions. She just breathed. Deep. Slow. And then, as if someone had flicked a switch inside her, she straightened her back and walked out of the library into the Wyoming morning, feeling as she did so much lately, High Bear's presence, quietly walking by her side.

She had many things to do, children to raise, a life to rebuild, a future to navigate. And she wasn't done fighting for justice and women like her. While she had breath in her body, belief and truth on her side, she would never stop.

Printed in Dunstable, United Kingdom

68574306R00143